HOME FRONT

Sever Squad

Book 4

A.R. KNIGHT

Homecoming

AURORA HAD MISSED A BUTTON, again. The man standing across from her in the passenger assembly, a broad empty space normally reserved for cargo on freighters like these, laughed at the sour expression Aurora had never figured out how to hide. She took criticism like most people took gut punches, and getting caught out by the same guy three times over a two week journey . . . Aurora wanted to hit something, but the freighter didn't even have simulators.

"Don't worry," Deepak said, throwing an anger-dousing grin her way. "I'm sure you'll take it out on me when we get to the real action."

"I will," Aurora said, fixing the rogue button. "Thanks for pointing it out."

They, and the other hundred recruits onboard the freighter, were due to dock with their new flagship, their home with DefenseCorp, the galaxy's largest mercenary contractor and, really, the biggest military force around. Aurora had found that out the hard way when her security gig on a space station had been supplanted by DC troops, but when she'd gone to protest at the new offices, the manager there had signed her up and shipped her out instead.

Deepak came from a tighter background, a full schooling regime that had him set up to play a more administrative role on the *Nautilus*. Jumping right to an officer's rank, which meant, as soon as they set foot onboard the flagship, Aurora would have to watch her insults.

"You excited?" Deepak said as the displays around the passenger bay shifted to show the docking process, a countdown till the bay's big doors opened and their new lives began. Some official DC talking head gave some speech about their new lives that nobody seemed to be listening to. "I'm, at least, ready for better food."

"I'm ready to get out and do something," Aurora replied. "I've never spent this much time stuck on a starship before."

"Guess we'll have to get used to it," Deepak said. "The way I understand it, this ship will be our new home."

"For you." Aurora pointed to the rank on Deepak's chest. "If I'm on this ship too long, then I'm not getting what I'm here for."

"Which is?"

"Cash, Deepak," Aurora said, and the man laughed. "You think I'm doing this for my health?"

"I suppose, then, that we can hope getting one doesn't mean losing the other."

The countdown hit zero, the bay doors marking the occasion by hissing their way open. The crowd shifted towards the exits, and the first shouts from squad leaders calling to their recruits echoed overhead. Aurora heard her name, held up a hand in goodbye towards Deepak, who replied with a nod of his own, and Sever Squad's newest rookie vanished into the adventure.

· · ·

Homecoming

AURORA HAD MISSED A BUTTON, again. The man standing across from her in the passenger assembly, a broad empty space normally reserved for cargo on freighters like these, laughed at the sour expression Aurora had never figured out how to hide. She took criticism like most people took gut punches, and getting caught out by the same guy three times over a two week journey . . . Aurora wanted to hit something, but the freighter didn't even have simulators.

"Don't worry," Deepak said, throwing an anger-dousing grin her way. "I'm sure you'll take it out on me when we get to the real action."

"I will," Aurora said, fixing the rogue button. "Thanks for pointing it out."

They, and the other hundred recruits onboard the freighter, were due to dock with their new flagship, their home with DefenseCorp, the galaxy's largest mercenary contractor and, really, the biggest military force around. Aurora had found that out the hard way when her security gig on a space station had been supplanted by DC troops, but when she'd gone to protest at the new offices, the manager there had signed her up and shipped her out instead.

Deepak came from a tighter background, a full schooling regime that had him set up to play a more administrative role on the *Nautilus*. Jumping right to an officer's rank, which meant, as soon as they set foot onboard the flagship, Aurora would have to watch her insults.

"You excited?" Deepak said as the displays around the passenger bay shifted to show the docking process, a countdown till the bay's big doors opened and their new lives began. Some official DC talking head gave some speech about their new lives that nobody seemed to be listening to. "I'm, at least, ready for better food."

"I'm ready to get out and do something," Aurora replied. "I've never spent this much time stuck on a starship before."

"Guess we'll have to get used to it," Deepak said. "The way I understand it, this ship will be our new home."

"For you." Aurora pointed to the rank on Deepak's chest. "If I'm on this ship too long, then I'm not getting what I'm here for."

"Which is?"

"Cash, Deepak," Aurora said, and the man laughed. "You think I'm doing this for my health?"

"I suppose, then, that we can hope getting one doesn't mean losing the other."

The countdown hit zero, the bay doors marking the occasion by hissing their way open. The crowd shifted towards the exits, and the first shouts from squad leaders calling to their recruits echoed overhead. Aurora heard her name, held up a hand in goodbye towards Deepak, who replied with a nod of his own, and Sever Squad's newest rookie vanished into the adventure.

. . .

AURORA WALKED down the ramp into the *Nautilus* for what could've been the hundreth, the thousandth time. The polished, gleaming floors occasionally marred with the asteroid making up much of the *Nautilus*'s frame looked as they always had. The too-bright lights made her wince as they always did.

The guns in her face? Those were new.

A full squad, sporting power armor in various colors and configurations, packing hard heat, waited for Aurora to descend the ramp. Sever's other four squaddies followed, spreading out behind Aurora as she hit the floor and suffering through, as she did, an up close inspection to pull out any hidden weapons.

The troopers didn't find any, because Aurora had made sure her squad wasn't going to try anything stupid.

The conversation hadn't been a fun one. As Eponi guided their newly stolen ship, the *Prisa*, away from the blackrock planet Wexer and towards the *Nautilus*, everyone figured they ought to be ready for a fight. Sai wanted to bring his katana, Gregor his hammer, and Rovo whatever-the-hell his scythe thing was. Eponi just wanted to stay on the *Prisa*, where she could turn its lasers on anyone that gave her an ugly look.

That they were going into a bad situation was obvious for them all, but the alternative was worse. DefenseCorp, Deepak and the *Nautilus* made it clear they would pursue Sever as far as Sever ran, and while Aurora had no desire to get back into the giant company's fold, she didn't want to spend her days getting hounded by heavily armed fighters.

"We take this deal," Aurora had said with the *Prisa* on approach, "we play by the rules this one last time, and we're free. Think you all can do that?"

"Doubt it," Gregor rumbled a reply, "but I can try."

Assenting nods all around after that, and the grudging go-along had the five standing inside their old headquarters, disarmed and at the mercy of an organization that, less than a day ago, had burned down part of a city to find Sever.

"I'm glad you made the right decision," Deepak said, coming into the bay once his inspecting squad gave the all-clear. "Clearly, we didn't part on the best terms, but in my view, Sever Squad still deserves respect for all you've done for DefenseCorp."

The *Nautilus* admiral didn't look all that different from when Aurora first met him on that freighter. Continuous missions had added scars to Aurora, both mental and physical, while Deepak's time showed in the gray lines strewn throughout his dark hair, the sagging bags beneath his eyes and a striking, deep wrinkle along his left cheek.

The man's uniform, in DefenseCorp's crimson, had every button perfectly placed.

"All that respect didn't get us much," Aurora replied, very aware that she and Sever stood in a jumbled civilian clothing mix ransacked from the *Prisa*'s prior owners.

"It will, if I can do anything about it," Deepak said, then he spread a look beyond Aurora to the others. "Aurora and I are going to work out the terms of the deal. While we do so, the rest of you are free to head to the mess, or to the Quartermaster to retrieve your things. Should our conversation proceed as we both expect, you'll be back on your craft before too long."

Separating the captain from her crew. Aurora wasn't all that surprised, but if Deepak had bad intentions, splitting Sever apart would be a good first step. Then again, if Deepak wanted them dead, the *Nautilus* could've roasted the *Prisa* once Eponi brought the ship close.

Slow down, Aurora. Not every move needs to have an ambush at its end.

Aurora glanced back at her squad, "You heard the admiral. Take a breather. Get some food. Once we get off this boat, it might be awhile before we have a chance to stretch our legs."

"You sure you want to go alone?" Sai offered, hands loose, eyes watching for Aurora to sign back a better clue.

Except, there wasn't anything to sign. Aurora had to trust Deepak here, trust that working with DefenseCorp to find Kaia would keep Sever alive and safe.

"I'll be fine," Aurora said. "Deepak's too scared to threaten me."

"All too true," Deepak agreed.

At Deepak's gesture, Aurora formed up beside him as they left the bay. The *Nautilus* built itself like a cube inside a sphere, with three main levels, each with three length-spanning concourses connected by numerous smaller hallways, larger rooms, and vertical lifts. Crew members, active troops, and bots crawled all over the ship, tending to maintenance, mission prep, and the general chaos onboard a big cruiser like this one.

After days spent on Wexer, breathing in dust and feeling its constant cool breeze, Aurora didn't mind the recycled air, purified to almost nothing. The hum and churn of the big ship, a vibration that lingered in her nerves, felt more like home than the still earth they'd been sleeping on. Even the overhead announcements calling this and that person, squad, or specialty to this location or that area felt like buttery background noise, comfort sounds for the soul.

Breaking from the bay into one of the main corridors, Aurora and Deepak broke left, heading towards the *Nautilus* bow and, presumably, its bridge. Deepak would have rooms there they could use for a private discussion. Sever's other members split right, disappearing into the crowd.

"That went rather well, I think," Deepak said as they walked. "Nobody started any fights. Almost better than your normal post-mission returns."

"We're tough, Deepak, but we're not suicidal," Aurora replied.

"And yet, you deserted. An act tantamount to suicide."

"You and I both know DefenseCorp doesn't give a damn about deserters. Not enough to chase them with a ship like the *Nautilus*, anyway."

"Most deserters don't get themselves involved in dangerous webs before they run away."

Aurora looked over Deepak as the man spoke. The admiral kept his eyes ahead, a straight face, but frustration lingered in the words as they floated through the air. Deepak had sent Sever on the mission to Dynas, the one that started all this, without any information about what really lay on the swampy planet, about the hidden city and its less-than-legal experiments.

And without any notice that DefenseCorp itself had an interest in keeping Dynas secret.

"You didn't know," Aurora repeated what Deepak had told her before the *Prisa* docked. "You said you didn't know, and you sent us to Dynas, and now you're angry about what we found?"

"I'm not angry at you, Aurora," Deepak replied. "Never was. You know me. I'm always on the side of my soldiers. When the call came in, the buyer and the request, I should've cleared it. Would have, too, except the grade was minor. A single person extraction? On an empty planet?"

"It sounded like someone had stranded themselves."

They reached the *Nautilus*'s bow lift bank and snagged one of the dozen-person containers to send them up. Deepak went inside first, Aurora followed, and several others poured in behind them. A couple squaddies, chatting about their soon-to-start shift, and two more, wearing maroon-and-black rank-less uniforms with their eyes buried in their wristlets.

"I received a message from up the chain not long after you landed on the planet," Deepak said. "At first, the order was simple. I had to call for you to withdraw. When I explained that you couldn't do that—"

"Because you only gave us a drop shuttle."

"A normal thing for Sever! Your missions actually have *better* outcomes when I don't give you a real ship to defend." Deepak held up a hand, as if to calm himself. "When I explained I couldn't get you off world, couldn't even reach you, that's when things got difficult."

"For you."

Aurora didn't try to keep the sarcasm away: Deepak had been dealing with some spicy messages while Sever had been fighting for its life on a mission that'd gone way beyond any expected scope. Tough to square those two.

"Right, I don't expect any sympathy," Deepak said.

"Good."

Deepak laughed, a bitter bark that took Aurora back a step. The admiral had always been a happier one, confident. Not one to let things get to him, but the person Aurora saw before her now didn't have that same carefree glow.

"I'm glad to see all your running hasn't changed you," Deepak said. "Because it's changed me, Aurora. For the first time I feel like I'm being watched. This whole deal? What I'm offering you? All I can say is that you should take it."

"It's not just me," Aurora replied as the lift settled into the top level, doors opening. "Sever has to decide together. We made that call when we split from you."

The chatting soldiers went off first, dipping into the concourse without a second's thought. The other two, eyes still on their wristlets in silent browsing mode, didn't move. Deepak put a hand on Aurora's shoulder, gave a slight push to get them going outside. Aurora shrugged off the gesture as Deepak nodded across the way, to a locked section dedicated to high priority personnel.

"Then you'll want to get them to say yes," Deepak said. "I know threats don't mean much for you, but this isn't just about you anymore. Not just about Sever either."

"Can't wait to hear who it is about, then," Aurora said as they wove across the crowd to the other side.

Deepak set his badge against the lock, which flashed blue and opened. Beyond a tighter hallway showcased rooms on either side, and again Deepak used his hand to guide Aurora into the closest one on the right.

As rooms went, this one kept it basic: a long oval table with eight chairs set around it. The room's back wall doubled as a big screen, and a single long silver light overhead made sure Aurora could see everything just fine. Which meant she had a clear view of the room's only other occupant, a man in Deepak's crimson uniform, but one coated with more insignias than Aurora had ever seen. Insignias that she stopped caring about when he turned to look her way.

Aurora had seen that face before in one place, flickering in the gray halo reserved for long range video communications. That face had threatened their lives, had told them in no uncertain terms what waited for Sever if they didn't give DefenseCorp everything they knew about Dynas.

Except, unlike Deepak, the only reward for coming clean would be a swift death.

"Aurora," Deepak said as she stopped. "Sit down. Please."

Behind her, two more people filtered into the hallway, crowded the doorway. The wristlet watchers from the lift. Aurora had Deepak next to her, two goons behind her, and the salty, plastic face in front.

Not everything had to end in an ambush.

Right.

TWO

The Drive

ABOARD ANASKYA'S SHIP, after Dynas, Sai voted to say goodbye to the *Nautilus* forever. At the time, flush with their escape and riding the emotions that came with victory over a virus that should've turned him to sludge, Sai didn't think too hard about what he'd left behind. What was waiting for him at the Quartermaster's holdings.

After Sever's trio left the bay, they split up again at the next crossway. Gregor declared a need to fill his stomach, and Rovo echoed the sentiment, while Eponi stayed behind to make sure the *Prisa* was good to go for a longer journey. That left Sai heading towards the *Nautilus*'s aft and the section dedicated to the massive ship's supplies.

While you could walk your slow way through the *Nautilus*, moving walkways enhanced the speed for those willing to slide through idling personnel. Sai, feeling eyes all over him in the shabby clothes he'd taken from the *Prisa*'s former owners, took the opportunity to cement his unusual appearance by all-but running along the walkways.

The speed was both unnecessary and absolutely so:

back on Wexer and before, Sai had written off the chance of seeing his family, actually getting a video with his children's faces, his wife's patient smile. Such things didn't easily transfer across the cosmos, much less when the target kept moving. Sai had been able to send messages out to them, directed across galaxy-wide satellite networks, that would leverage physics tricks to get home before too long.

Any reply sent his way would reach nothing and nowhere, because Sai wasn't standing still.

The *Nautilus* had been Sai's last permanent station, and in the belongings now held by the Quartermaster, Sai's saved recordings would be waiting. He could pull up videos of birthdays, of school plays, friends, and holidays. All beamed to the *Nautilus*.

"Can I get them loaded onto a stim drive?" Sai asked when he reached the Quartermaster, a big section sitting over the engines.

With its name spread over the long entry in big red letters, the Quartermaster split its space between windowed slots where *Nautilus* personnel could request to give or take their own items, or requisition general supplies. Bots stood at attention at each slot, requiring the proper forms and permissions for any interaction.

DefenseCorp had long ago assumed any position that could be corrupted, cheated, or otherwise compromised should be handed over to mindless machines, though Sai had heard these spindly bots could be reprogrammed by anyone with enough time and effort.

This one, certainly, seemed slow. The giant camera lens in the bot's center, a stem-like piece blooming into those lanky arms at the top, blending down into a wheeled base at the bottom, flashed an angry red Sai's way after a long minute considering the ID number Sai had delivered.

"Sorry, those recordings are now classified," the bot

said. "You do not have clearance to access criminal belongings."

"Criminal belongings?"

"Correct," the bot said. "The ID number you provided belongs to an individual charged with deserting DefenseCorp. While this charge is pending, we cannot release any items to those without proper clearance."

Sai stared at the machine. Willed it to make a different choice. When that failed, and the bored trooper in line behind Sai asked whether he'd be moving along sometime this century, Sai stepped aside and tried to come up with a different strategy.

Deepak had deliberately said to go check the Quartermaster, but Sai, and presumably everyone else in Sever, was still labeled as a criminal. So either Deepak didn't know they were locked down, or he wanted to shove Sever's status into their faces.

"Hey," said a voice behind Sai, and he turned to see one of the Quartermaster's human supervisors, wearing DefenseCorp crimson with a bright white QM badge on the chest. She looked like she'd been on the *Nautilus* for a while and hadn't been sticking hard to the recommended exercise regimen. Not fat, but bendy, as if her bones couldn't quite hold up her body. "What're you doing here?"

Sai hadn't made many trips to the Quartermaster while he'd been on the *Nautilus*—Sever tended to get whatever they needed between missions delivered, due to their deadly-and-dangerous status—so he didn't recognize the woman, didn't understand her question.

"Trying to get my own videos back," Sai said. "Apparently the system thinks I'm a criminal."

The woman nodded, "Because you are."

Okay, jerk.

"Great, thanks for clearing that up," Sai said. "Did you come out here just to tell me that, or did you have a point?"

"Good to know you've got some spirit in you," the woman said, "You're going to need that, if Deepak's right." She sent a look over Sai's shoulder. "Don't turn now, but keep your eyes open and you're going to notice some new people on the *Nautilus*. Can't say much about it here, but I can give you this."

The woman reached out, and at first Sai thought she wanted a handshake, but then she pulled him into a tight hug, saying loudly that she'd thought he'd been lost on the last mission. Sai gradually took to the idea and returned the squeeze, feeling a small object find its way into his pants pocket as she pulled away.

"What was that?" Sai said, low.

The woman smiled in that sweet way customer service people have when they're done dealing with you, "I hope you have better luck clearing your name, Sai. Great to see you again."

Sai wanted to, could have reached out to grab the woman and hold her for some sterner questioning, but her words, her tone said that'd be a bad idea. Instead, forcing himself not to look behind him, Sai went back to walking, this time crossing the *Nautilus* and making for the barracks.

Sai's former room would be gone, but the *Nautilus* had guest quarters. He felt the device in his pocket, the small rectangle. Sharp ends. A storage drive. Now he just needed some way to play it, and every guest room on the *Nautilus* had a terminal.

But, and Sai had plenty of moving walkway time to ponder this, what the hell was that?

Deepak makes a subtle allusion to go get stuff from the Quartermaster and now Sai's walking around with a drive with who-knows-what on it? The woman made it sound like Deepak had planned all this, which begged the question. . . why? Wasn't this Deepak's ship?

Sai remembered the woman's comment about strangely dressed people onboard and dedicated his walking time to sweeping looks across the concourses. DefenseCorp's crimson uniforms felt universal, all tweaked ever-so-slightly to note a person's designated rank and assignment. Bundled in were folks dressed like Sai in civilian clothing, vendors and specialists on the ship for assignments.

Nobody screamed strange at first look. Nobody stood back to the wall, talking into a wristlet and watching Sai like a spy.

Sai tried to play the game: Even if Deepak wanted to pass along a secret message to Sai or whomever from Sever happened to visit the Quartermaster first, why turn to Sever in the first place? Deepak had a whole ship filled with loyal troops he could use.

If Sai, or any of Sever, actually had their own wristlets anymore, he would've called up Aurora or Gregor and asked what they thought. Without the devices, Sai had to keep the secret to himself while he made his way to the barracks.

And all he'd wanted was to see his wife and kids.

The barracks took their design cues from the asteroid making up the *Nautilus*, building into the rocky core with a mesh between mineral and metal. On the *Nautilus*'s mid level, near the main mess hall, the barracks had enough room for the fifty thousand soldiers stationed on the *Nautilus*, with triple that spreading around and below for guests and supporting staff.

Coming from the aft, Sai's entry listed out the nearest rooms accessible from the closest double doors sitting aside the central concourse. The big hallway functioned as the *Nautilus*'s artery, and what few concessions Deepak allowed for decor hung here: squad pictures highlighting members, mission and campaign posters and decals, the frequent words-on-a-background pumping out optimistic slogans.

From the outside, the overwhelming propaganda could feel almost laughable, as if DefenseCorp wanted to drive its people into a homogenous mass that thought only in terms of objectives accomplished and contracts completed. For Sai, all the spirit brought him back, pulled at the sense he'd been missing in the weeks since Sever broke away and ran.

He'd traded his real family for DefenseCorp's different, but very real in its way, version. Now, well, now Sai had Sever, and only Sever. Whether their fivesome would fit as well, Sai couldn't be sure.

The barracks required a scanned ID to enter, something Sai had forgotten about until he stood in front of the doors, checking for a wristlet he didn't have. Habit struck again.

"Need help?" said a younger man, coming up next to Sai. He wore a crimson uniform like the others, albeit one with some black stripes along the sides that Sai didn't recognize. "Everyone forgets their wristlets sometimes. I did it last week."

Forgot their wristlets? Sai never took his off. Literally never, even in the shower. But different people had different ideas.

"Yeah," Sai said. "I'm trying to get to a guest room. Just arrived and don't have things all sorted yet."

"Things are a mess right now," the man nodded, scanning his wristlet on the barracks doors, which shot open. "A lot of newcomers on the ship."

"Heard that," Sai said. "You know why?"

The man shook his head, "Guess DefenseCorp's changing things around again. You know where to go?"

"Yeah, I've been here before," Sai said. "Thanks for the help."

Sai started walking into the thinner, emptier barracks hallway, where lights interspersed with gray and brown rock to give the whole thing a more natural appeal. He stopped when the man came walking in with him.

"Going this way?" Sai asked.

"Yep, need to make a pit stop myself," the man said. "Like I was saying, I tend to forget things."

"Happens."

The two kept going for another few minutes, the man peppering Sai with questions about where he'd been, what he was doing on the *Nautilus*. Sai propped up excuses with the truth, talking about his former military experience, that he used to work for DefenseCorp on this very ship before leaving for more private contracts.

The turn to the guest quarters, a room bundle tied together towards the *Nautilus's* right side, came up and Sai made for it, only for the man to follow him again.

"Remembered that you'll need another scan to get inside one of the rooms," the man said, wearing that ever present light smile.

"Really?" Sai said. "Guess they've stepped up security. Never used to need one once you got past the barracks doors."

"Like I said, lots of change."

Except when they hit the guest quarters, Sai didn't see any locked scanners on the doors. The rooms displayed the names of whomever happened to be staying there—set via the terminal inside the rooms themselves—and could tie their locks to the guest's wristlet, but any room open was, well, open.

Sai stopped in front of a green-glaring scanner, ready to go inside, but the man had followed him this far. Stood close now, watching.

"So when are you going to make your move?" Sai said. "Because you're running out of time."

"Am I?" the man replied. "I'd hoped you'd go inside first. Keep things a little quieter."

Sai shrugged, tapped the green scanner that sent the door whooshing open.

"So who're you with?" Sai said, looking at the man. "Someone hunting deserters?"

"Doesn't matter," the man replied, keeping that sanguine look going. "You'll be too dead to care."

"Thought your bosses wanted us alive?"

"Only some of you." The man nodded to the guest room. "Shall we?"

THREE

Inspectors

FABRICATED FOOD FILLED Gregor's tray, all grown by spinning together proteins in the *Nautilus*'s food banks. After setting the tray down on the cool sheet-metal table, painted over in waving blues in a concession to the *Nautilus*'s inspiration, Gregor stared at his feast, watching as the solid, real meal before him obliterated the last weeks spent guzzling powdered calories.

The mess hall, too, bubbled with constant conversation. The big space, on the *Nautilus*'s lowest level, could seat thousands in its multi-tiered arrangement and offered up several creations at all times for those on the ship to indulge. The wide room, like the table, played up the watery vibe, with preferred walking paths painted out with strange fish and sections denoted by otherworldly coral drawings.

The way Gregor had heard it, the *Nautilus*'s lead chef at the ship's christening had declared he wouldn't serve in a mess so devoid of spirit. Needing something for the troops to do en route to their first contract, the DefenseCorp squads spent their time turning the mess into a place unlike any other on the ship, on any ship.

For all his gruffness, Gregor may have let his lips turn up when he saw the place.

"You going to eat that?" Rovo said, sitting across from him. "Or is the nice woman's generosity going to waste?"

"I'll eat it," Gregor said. "I appreciate my meals."

Before Gregor could take a bite, the nice woman Rovo referred to set her own tray down next to the big man, claiming a seat on the long bench nearly touching him. She'd been behind them in the line and offered to cover Gregor and Rovo when they realized that, without wristlets and their DefenseCorp accounts, they couldn't actually buy the food they'd picked up.

"Me too," the woman said, her build, her attitude, suggesting hard times spent for DefenseCorp. She wore the company's classic crimson too, through the black stripes up the sides marked a division Gregor didn't recognize. "You never know when your next might be coming, or what you might have to do to get it."

"Like ask for charity from a stranger," Rovo said. "Thanks again."

"We're all DefenseCorp here," the woman said, "Not a problem."

Gregor nodded and they all commenced with a bite or two or seven. The food was both as good and as solid as Gregor remembered, though the bites did have that flavorless tinge that came with lab spun protein. As if, with every chew, Gregor went a little further behind the curtain to see the nothingness at his food's heart.

"I'm not sure where you two come from," the woman said as the munching continued, "but I like to know who I'm sharing a table with. Name's Zaydi, and while it's been a long time, I'm from Poppyseed Nine."

Gregor's eyes sparked at that name. Not Zaydi, which he couldn't care less about, but Poppyseed Nine. The Poppyseeds and a few other similar-named sectors had earned a reputation for their perfection. Multiple planets in habitable ranges, life everywhere. Those with means, with DefenseCorp backing them up, had taken the sectors for their own. Anyone born on those planets had no business eating in a DefenseCorp mess.

"I'm Rovo," the rookie said, covering for Gregor's silence. "And, uh, I'm not really from anywhere important. Did you say Poppyseed Nine?"

Rovo, such a smooth talker.

Zaydi set a smile that said she'd answered this question a thousand times, "You're wondering why I'm not eating with the admiral and telling him how I'd like to buy his ship?"

"Frankly, yeah?"

"Because I didn't like it," Zaydi crossed her arms, leaned her elbows on the table. "Care to hear a secret?" That little grin widened. "The Poppyseeds are where the galaxy stashed all its awful people."

Zaydi, having opened the door, went on while Rovo and Gregor devoured their meals. Whipping up stories about this and that awful person, beats that sounded much like the corrupt worlds Gregor had parlayed into a Sever position. What a non-surprise to learn yet another sector suffered from human problems.

"So what're you two doing after this?" Zaydi asked in the relative silence after her last story. "Big plans for your first day on the *Nautilus*?"

"Waiting for our captain to decide whether we live or die, basically," Rovo said, and Gregor grunted an agreement.

"How's she going to do that?"

Gregor stopped, spoon halfway into his mouth. Rovo started answering Zaydi's question, and Gregor resumed eating, covering up the pause. Neither Gregor nor Rovo had mentioned their role with Sever, had mentioned Aurora, yet Zaydi hadn't seemed surprised at Rovo's words.

The big man took a closer look Zaydi's way as Rovo finished a blurred over description about why they were here, a potential mission to find someone that would be dangerous. Gregor had to give the rookie credit: the man could make up plenty on the fly, where Gregor would rather shake his head and say nothing.

"What's your outfit?" Gregor said, the black lines on Zaydi's uniform unwilling to be forgotten.

"My outfit?" Zaydi asked.

"Your squad."

"Oh," Zaydi looked at her own uniform, as if discovering it for the very first time. "I'm with an inspection team, running a tour on the *Nautilus* to make sure it's going right."

"Is it?" Rovo asked. "The *Nautilus*?"

Zaydi sighed, "Honestly? There's some problems." She looked between the two of them. "I can trust you both, right? No sharing?"

Gregor wanted to say that no, Zaydi had just met them. She shouldn't be trusting them with any secrets, small, large or in between.

"There's nobody for us to tell," Rovo said.

"Okay, well, apparently someone's been working in the armory here," Zaydi said. "They're putting together new suits that go against our policies." Zaydi tapped her lips, came to a discovery. "You use power armor, right? On your missions?"

"We do." Rovo looked like a lap dog, all in on Zaydi's question.

"Then maybe you can help me out," Zaydi said. "Nobody on my team works with heavy weapons, and we need to decide if the modifications are too dangerous. You said you're new here, right? So you'll be able to keep an open mind?"

"We don't work for Deepak," Rovo replied. "I'd love to help you."

Gregor felt the slightest tap on his ankle. On the front. Gregor shifted his elbow, knocked his knife off the table to the floor, where it bounced with a sharp clink. He bent down to grab it, gave a look Rovo's way as Zaydi gave more details about the armor question, and caught Rovo's right hand lingering below, offering up hand signals.

Rovo didn't quite have Sever's hand signs down to an art yet, but he managed the gist well enough. The rookie would lead, Gregor should follow.

Lead where, follow how? That remained a mystery.

At least it seemed like Rovo understood something about Zaydi wasn't right.

"You have time now?" Zaydi asked at the end of her description. "It shouldn't take long."

"Do we?" Rovo asked Gregor. "Don't think the captain wanted us back to the ship till late."

Gregor shrugged. Because the whole squad had lost their wristlets, Aurora had gone back to the stone age and set a post-dinner time for everyone to head back to the *Prisa*. The *Nautilus* had clocks on screens all over the place, so time tracking wasn't an issue, and right now they had hours yet to burn.

"There's your answer," Rovo said to Zaydi. "Lead on."

Zaydi took them from the mess hall towards the bow, eschewing the lifts to keep them on the *Nautilus*'s lowest level. Gregor hadn't spent all that much non-mess time down here, as the spaces were dedicated more to engineering, cargo storage, and analysis.

Few hammers, and fewer targets to smash than the other levels.

The mess hall bisected the lower level's central concourse, and leaving the hall put them back in what, up a level or two, would've been a packed section. The bowward hall should've been replete with bots and squaddies running this way and that. Messages should've been playing overhead.

Instead, leaving the mess hall through heavy double doors—Gregor noted these were blast shielded, unlike the mess hall's other exits—brought the trio to a quiet concourse. The sides here, rather than bearing motivational posters and DefenseCorp sayings, were plastered with safety guidelines, reminders about form requirements, and hard red warnings that the work could endanger the whole ship.

"Looks like a fun place," Rovo said as they walked along. No moving walkways speeding things up here, maybe due to crowds, maybe due to the hazard. "You ever come back here, Gregor?"

"Once," Gregor said. "A long time ago, to get my hammer."

"Hammer?" Zaydi asked, honest curiosity in the question.

"My favorite weapon," Gregor replied. "Most prefer rifles. I find them too easy."

"I . . . see," Zaydi said, clearly not seeing. Instead, she pointed at a yellow-clad door, one sporting an ID scanner. "Here's the lab we're using."

The label over the door marked what lay beyond as *Weapons Three*. Further down the concourse, then, would be

Weapons One and *Weapons Two*. The latter had been where Gregor earned his hammer, bought with most of the DefenseCorp cash in Gregor's account at the time, and very much worth it.

"Remember," Zaydi said. "Not a word of what you see in here."

The door whooshed to reveal . . . another doorway with a slight, featureless hallway in between. A control gap, meant to keep anyone peeking in from seeing inside. The trio bundled into the space, Zaydi tapped her ID on the second door, and with a chirp, their way back shut and their way forward opened.

Weapons 3 wasn't much larger than the *Prisa*'s central gathering space or the living room in the pod Gregor had lived in on the comet. Not that it needed to be: the ceiling crawled with mechanical arms and other devices, all slid into brackets that could be released by the massive control center opposite the door.

The room's middle held the star. While the outside floor mirrored the polished silver seen throughout the *Nautilus*, a hard yellow-painted steel circle claimed center stage. That yellow paint bore scratches and burns from trials long since over.

Though, given the huge power armor suit resting on that circle, perhaps ready to start again.

Gregor had worn his fair share of the suits, had destroyed enemies aplenty with their kinetically-charged arms and legs, their holsters for a hundred different weapons. The older suits, though, had been designed with movement in mind, with giving the body a shell that would move with its owner's demands.

This one looked more like a tank that would surround the user and render them a slow-moving death machine. Arms and legs stuck out from the dense crimson metal, but surrounding the limbs were numerous other, well, limbs. Most sat empty, attachments waiting for an enterprising owner to decide which deadly implements they wanted to take today. Some looked set up for *Weapons 3*, holding a tube-like rifle, a spiked ball plugged into a narrow launcher, and one bearing a big case with a white cross on the suit's back.

"Big one, isn't she?" Rovo said, and Gregor grunted an agreement.

"Right?" Zaydi said. "We were a little surprised to find it here. Your Deepak has a sense of adventure, certainly."

Not the words Gregor would use to describe a man who hid from the front lines and sent squads to do the work, but fine.

"What did you want us to do?" Gregor asked.

Zaydi went further into the room, all the way to the control panel and started tapping away, "See, you two said you use power armor. I haven't. So I'm not sure whether this is working or not."

Something Zaydi did had an effect, and the power armor lit up. Gaskets across its body released, causing the armor's front to swing out and away. Ready for its next user.

"You want us to get inside it?" Rovo said.

"One of you," Zaydi replied. "Unless you think you both can fit."

"Power armor is solo," Gregor said. "Rovo, this one would match me."

"Go right ahead." Rovo rubbed his own shoulders. "I'm fine staying outta power armor for a while. Bad memories."

"Oh?" Zaydi asked, crossing back to stand by Rovo as Gregor moved towards the suit.

"Building fell on him," Gregor rumbled. "Tough break."

Approaching the armor, Gregor positioned his face near the visor and stood still. The power armor picked up on his stance, and a slight blue light shot out from within the suit as it measured Gregor's size and shape. The big suits couldn't completely morph themselves, but by tightening and loosening various bolts and bands, they could hit as good a comfort as possible.

The light blinked green and Gregor stepped forward. As his feet closed into the boots, the armor's back swung into place, sealing Gregor into the suit. Hisses and clicks rattled around as the armor settled itself into Gregor's size.

The visor clicked on, flooding what had been a black nothing into a clear view of the control center. Flashing yellow words in the upper left indicated the armor was in trial mode. No weapons enabled, so Gregor couldn't go around destroying the ship because he'd had a bad day.

Rovo and Zaydi came into view, the latter going back to the control center. Rovo waved at Gregor's face, and Gregor waved back, the slow hand sluggish and heavy. Whomever was designing this suit would have to tweak those settings, because having to heave an arm just to wave would get tired fast.

"What's it like in there?" Rovo said. "Feel like the future?"

The future? Gregor started to say that it felt like a prototype when the blinking trial mode in his visor changed to a hard red *LOCKDOWN*. Not a mode Gregor had used before, but old training had told him its purpose: keep the suit from doing anything stupid while you made changes.

Through the visor, Gregor saw Zaydi stand away from the control center, her movement answering who could've put the armor in lockdown. The suspicion Gregor had felt in the mess hall flared into full-on danger.

Zaydi wasn't moving like a flouncy inspector anymore. She had a professional's sure stance, carrying out her mission.

"You hearing me, buddy?" Rovo said, leaning in towards Gregor and laughing. "I know you're in there!"

Gregor tried to move. Spoke the keywords that should've triggered an emergency release from the suit. Nothing worked. If the arms had been heavy while the suit was on, in lockdown mode and without any assist, they were immovable.

Rovo rapped a hand on the armor's visor. Behind him, Zaydi reached into her uniform, pulled on a set, hard face, and drew out a small pistol.

Gregor heard his shouts.

The rookie did not.

FOUR

Show and Tell

SEVER THOUGHT they'd returned home when the *Prisa* landed on the *Nautilus*, but Eponi understood the reality: the *Prisa* was the squad's true home now. Stolen, yes, but their home nonetheless.

And Eponi couldn't be happier about it.

Not since she'd raced karts had Eponi found herself piloting a ship this fast and sharp. A three-pronged body with its narrowing cockpit set in the center, the *Prisa* kept things svelte. Two turrets dotted both side prongs, controllable by whomever took the gunnery seats at those ends. A retractable laser cannon and hard missile launcher sat beneath the cockpit if Eponi herself wanted to get frisky.

Right now, though, Eponi stood in the *Prisa*'s aft, the wide back stretching across those prongs. The ship's crew quarters, tight for a half-dozen, sat above Eponi while her current locale, the engine banks, flared out beneath. The *Prisa* used cluster thrusters, nestling a hundred tiny jets in clumps along its back. What sounded like a nightmare, and was very expensive, gave the pilot precise control over where to aim, how fast to fly.

"I've never felt this way about a ship before," Eponi said, running a finger along the console outlining, in happy greens, the *Prisa*'s tip-top shape. "You and I, we're going to get along just fine."

At least, Eponi hoped so. Given that Sever was apparently wanted by the most powerful corporation in the galaxy, and they'd just landed on one of DefenseCorp's heavy cruisers, making it off with the *Prisa* still intact was far from a given.

A bright chime interrupted those thoughts, echoing through the *Prisa* and repeating every few seconds as Eponi clambered from the engines back to the cockpit. Maybe someone from Sever had come back early, finding the *Nautilus* not quite up to their memories.

Instead, Eponi saw a single person waiting below, holding up their wristlet to show they were the ones pinging the *Prisa*. The stocky man had on a formal DefenseCorp uniform, crimson with some new black stripes along the sides that gave the suit a racing vibe. Not a bad addition.

"Hello?" Eponi asked, settling into the cockpit chair.

By reflex, she eyed the *Prisa*'s energy counts. The shields, weapons weren't active, but could be flipped on in a heartbeat. The engines could boost the ship into space soon after. The *Nautilus,* as part of Aurora's negotiations—and at Eponi's insistence—had left the bay doors open. The ship's magnetic shielding would keep air, people, and everything else from getting sucked into vacuum anyway, and Eponi had no desire to get herself locked into a ship with people trying to kill her.

"Howdy howdy," the man chuckled, throwing up a disarming grin as he waved. "Hope you don't mind me saying so, but I've never seen a ship quite a beautiful as this one. Where'd you find her?"

Eponi sat back in the chair, looked at the man. She'd worked on the *Nautilus* long enough to know people didn't just wander into random docking bays and chat with pilots. DefenseCorp kept you busy, and this guy was in his uniform, so he certainly wasn't off-duty.

"We got lucky." Eponi decided to play it neutral. See what she could pull off the man. "Thanks for the compliment."

"Very lucky, I might say." The man leaned forward, as if scoping out the *Prisa*'s forward landing strut. "Are you giving tours?"

Hah, no way.

"Sorry, she's closed for visitors."

"That so?" The man gave the most exaggerated head shake, his whole body half-turning with the motion. Eponi had the impression he wasn't capable of standing still. "Too bad. Maybe you could talk me through, then? Or at least let me meet the pilot lucky enough to call this ship home?"

Eponi tapped on the *Prisa*'s communications program, flaring it up on a panel to her left before remembering that Sever didn't have any damn wristlets anymore. She wanted to ring up Aurora or Sai, let'em know there was a pest bugging their ship.

"Look, buddy," Eponi said, trying to think of a different tactic. "Appreciate the interest, but we just landed here. I'm busy taking care of my ship. Maybe come back later?"

The dude spilled into a frown, crossed his arms and looked down at the bay floor. Didn't walk away though. Eponi went back to her communications panel. Decided to give *Nautilus* central a try.

"Hey, *Nautilus*, this is the *Prisa*, in bay—" Eponi looked at the big black-painted number on the bay's back wall.

"Seven. I'm looking for Admiral Deepak, and really, someone he's with. My captain, Aurora? Mind helping me out?"

The comm crackled, "*Prisa*, Admiral Deepak's currently unavailable. We're not familiar with your captain. Anyone else we can reach?"

"Maybe?" Eponi looked back outside, but the man had disappeared. She focused on the bay's exit doors, closed and quiet. No way he'd left that fast. "Mind sending some security down here? I've got someone snooping around that I don't like."

The comm crackled again, "Of course, we'll send a couple along."

"Thanks," Eponi said, and cut the line.

Tapping away, Eponi swapped the panels from communications and systems status to the cameras wrapping around the *Prisa*. Standard issue for any ship nowadays to give a total visual outside. The view out the front showed the *Prisa*'s long nose skewering the frame's top, and nothing below. Both sides revealed pristine bay walls, empty aside from standard repair and charging equipment.

The back showed static. Eponi flipped the camera on and off. Still static.

Cameras could malfunction.

Sure.

Eponi turned to the last view, the one right beneath the ship's belly. The man stood there, holding what looked like a small pistol. He squinted up at the camera, aimed, and fired. Another black view.

"*Nautilus*," Eponi said, punching the comm again. "Where's that security force? This guy's shooting out my cameras, and I'm going to charge you for each and every one of them."

"Sorry, it looks like the team heading your way has

been re-routed," the comm officer replied, sounding like she didn't quite believe what she saw. "I'll, uh, get in touch."

"You do that."

Eponi cut the call, stood up and went to the storage cabinet behind the cockpit. Opening it showcased a rifle, pistol, and Rovo's strange scythe weapon that he'd won on Wexer and insisted on keeping nearby. As Eponi pulled the rifle out and checked the power pack so she wouldn't be left spewing fumes, the *Prisa* pinged a different sort of alarm.

"Now you notice," Eponi said, slinging the rifle over her shoulder and clipping on the pistol with its holster. "Next time, tell me when the guy zaps the first camera, why don't you?"

There were two ways off the *Prisa*, a long central ramp and a faster, cockpit-adjacent elevator meant, so Eponi assumed, to get the crew right where they needed to go in case a fast escape was necessary. Escape, though, wasn't the only option.

"Hey," Eponi said, back in the cockpit and broadcasting over the ship's loudspeaker. "I'm going to lower the ramp, and then we can chat, okay?"

She didn't wait for the bastard to reply. Eponi told the ramp to drop, then went to the elevator. She waited until the *Prisa* hummed as the ramp began its descent, counted to a quick three, then hit the drop button for the elevator. As the platform shot down, Eponi raised the rifle and squared it right on the man's crimson-uniformed back.

"Aww, didn't see two exits coming?" Eponi said as the platform settled to the bay's floor and the man, still facing the ramp, raised his now-empty hands. "Keep those up, and start talking. Who the hell are you and what're you doing to my ship? If you answer real quick, I'll tell Deepak to kill you quicker."

Again the man did that whole-body head shake, this time punctuating it with a rippling sigh.

"Shucks," the man said. "You weren't supposed to make this so difficult."

"Did I say be all cryptic?" Eponi countered. "No, I did not. Talk straight."

"You're traitors, and we can't have that."

"Wrong, bucko, we're deserters. Big difference. But who's this 'we' you're talking about? This a royal we situation?" Eponi had run into plenty of high-minded kart pilots who adopted haughty talk with their trophies. Nothing felt better than taking away glittering hardware from the pompous drivers. "Or do you have friends, hard as that is for me to believe?"

"Friends aplenty, I'm afraid. Bad news for you, little lady, no matter what you're planning on doing with that rifle there."

Eponi rolled her eyes, "Call me little lady one more time."

"Can do, little lady."

Fine. Guy wanted to get shot? Guy was gonna get shot. Eponi tilted her aim just outside the lethal zone, put her hand on the trigger, when, behind her, the docking bay's doors shot open. Holding the rifle with her right hand, its weight made easier by the *Nautilus*'s limited gravity, Eponi opened her stance, drawing the pistol with her left and pointing it towards the opened doors.

Some might call it paranoid to greet a sudden sound with a drawn weapon, but Eponi's shit-on-a-stick meter had hit maximum, and she wasn't playing around anymore.

Three people came through the door, carrying rifles

and the security vests common to the *Nautilus*'s personnel. Relief that should've iced Eponi's hot temper froze when she noticed, beneath those vests, the same crimson-black uniforms as the camera zapper. More than that, the damn vests weren't even on right, their straps hanging loose and the sizes all wrong.

As if they'd punched out a real security force and threw on their gear.

"Stay back," Eponi said, and the trio stopped, though they didn't drop their rifles. "I'm getting a real ugly vibe right now, but if one of you wants to explain what's going on, I might not act on that vibe and shoot you all."

"The reports all said you'd be violent," said the camera zapper. "Too bad, really. Would've liked to see this ship, you know."

Eponi flicked her eyes between both sides, knowing that she couldn't keep beads on both groups. The longer this standoff went on, someone would make a mistake, and Eponi couldn't afford that someone to be her.

"Can't argue with the reports," Eponi said, and pulled the triggers.

The rifle shot hit home, burning into the zapper and sending him howling to the bay floor. The pistol shot went wide as the trio scattered, bringing up their rifles and hunting for cover in the barren bay. Eponi didn't wait, hitting the lift's riser with the back of her hand.

The *Prisa* obeyed, sucking Eponi up before any return fire came her way. As soon as the lift clicked into place, Eponi took two long strides into the cockpit and slapped the button to raise the ramp. Heard its grinding as she flipped the *Prisa*'s panels to those cameras, cursing as a black void showcased where the zapper ought to be.

The ramp clicked up. Eponi turned around, raising the rifle and the pistol, and saw nothing, nobody out from the cockpit all the way into the ship's central space. She let out a long-held breath real slow, then snuck a look out the ship's front.

Two men dragged the zapper along the floor, leaving a bloody trail towards the bay doors.

Two men.

A metal clank rang through the *Prisa*, echoing through its quiet insides. Then another.

Footsteps.

FIVE

Bad Hit

THE POWER ARMOR'S visor didn't show much from the outside, but Rovo caught Gregor's eyes, and that was enough. The big man's orbs were narrowed, angry, and focused behind Rovo. Couple that with Zaydi's overall weirdness, and Rovo turned, crouching and moving aside at the same time.

Zaydi fired, the pistol shot grazing Rovo's side and sending a hissing burn through his nerves, one followed real quick by the charred smell from his now-ruined clothes. Zaydi didn't look finished by her miss, and tracked Rovo for shot number two.

So Rovo went for the tackle.

Weapons 3 didn't have much space for its experiments, and Gregor's giant suit currently claimed most of that space for itself. Zaydi had three meters between the room's control center and the armor, distance Rovo closed with a side-stepping lunge.

But Zaydi had enough time to get off a second blast, this one scoring Rovo in the chest. A hot wave added to the sting from the first laser, Rovo's lungs feeling like they were

36

about to melt. Lasers, though, don't do anything to stop momentum, and Rovo's carried him through, right into Zaydi.

They hit the floor in a wordless struggle, Rovo trying to get the pistol away while Zaydi tried to zero in a third shot. The woman had skill, but Rovo had desperation. Zaydi managed to curl her wrist even as Rovo held it, getting the pistol in line for a fatal shot to Rovo's head. Rovo, instead, used his head to deliver a sharp ram to Zaydi's own, cracking into her with a blow that left Rovo's vision blurred, and Zaydi's body limp.

"Okay, that sucked," Rovo hissed, his breath whistling down his throat and vanishing into fiery pain.

First things first: Rovo ripped the pistol from Zaydi's hands. He could've blasted her right there, and man did he want to, but Rovo had seen too many intelligence reports come across his old desk to ignore the value a hostage might have. Instead, he stood up, looking towards that control center.

As Rovo straightened, his vision warped again, this time going fuzzy. His arms and legs felt alien to him, as if he'd slept with rocks on all his limbs. A step towards the blurred console felt like tripping through another world, and Rovo vaguely realized this was what happened when a laser burned its way through your insides.

He'd never really been shot before. Not like this. Not without power armor or a vest or something to blunt the blow.

Turned out, getting hit by a laser was not a good thing.

A second shaking step sent Rovo into a stumbling fall forward towards the console, his hands dropping the pistol to catch himself on the console's edge as Rovo planted on its base. One hot breath later and Rovo pulled himself back up again, choosing to ignore the deep red stain where he'd hit the console.

Thankfully, DefenseCorp didn't make its systems all that complicated. *Weapons 3* offered up a simple options menu, and Rovo unlocked Gregor's suit with a single button press. Behind him, chirps and hisses sounded as the suit once more responded to Gregor's inputs.

Arms grabbed Rovo's shoulders and threw him back from the console and to the floor. Zaydi, now holding a small knife she must've pulled from elsewhere, went for a thrust towards Rovo's heart.

The rookie rolled, embracing the agony, using the adrenaline. Zaydi's stab, aiming to be the coup de grace on a dying man's day, went slow and missed, the knife glancing off the floor. Lifting his leg, Rovo kicked Zaydi back against the control console. She hit the boxy, metal thing, shook her head and swore.

"You're not supposed to be this hard to kill," Zaydi said, lunging back at Rovo, knife held in both hands.

"Sorry to disappoint," Rovo said, catching the diving attack with his hands wrapping around Zaydi's wrists.

Zaydi had weight, momentum, and Rovo's steadily sapping strength on her side. The knife came down, its point gunning for Rovo's throat. A target it would hit, and Rovo felt an odd panic as he realized there wasn't any damn thing he could do about it.

But he didn't have to. Two huge metal hands swooped in, crunching around Zaydi's shoulders and pulling her away from Rovo. She shouted, squirmed to try and get away, and failed as Gregor lifted the agent over his head and threw her right into the control console. The screens shattered, sparked as Zaydi crashed into and rolled away from the computer.

"Nice toss." Rovo laid his head back on the cool floor. "Good timing."

Behind him, the suit popped as Gregor came out, and the big man's mug filled Rovo's view for a single, concerned moment.

"Bad hit," Gregor said.

"Uh huh."

Rovo, using his arms, tried to sit up. Saw Zaydi lying on the floor, not moving. Gregor ran to the suit's other side. For a second, Rovo wondered whether the man had abandoned him. Then he remembered: the med kit, of course. Good old Gregor, caring for the rookie after all.

"Empty!" Gregor cursed, then came back around the power armor, looked at Rovo with as much concern as the rookie had ever seen in the man's eyes. "The med bay's not far. Can you walk?"

"Look at me," Rovo said, smiling despite himself. "What do you think?"

"Right," Gregor said. "Hold in your guts."

"What?"

Gregor squatted down, slipped his hands beneath Rovo's legs and back, then lifted the rookie up. Rovo managed to keep from shouting at the sudden pain, reducing the noise to a hissing gasp instead. Tears flooded his eyes without warning. Warmth pooled around his chest, cupped in Gregor's arms.

He didn't need to ask what it was.

Weapons 3, like most rooms on the *Nautilus*, required a badge to get in but didn't ask for it to leave. They went into the small room, Gregor turning to the side to fit with his cargo, then bustled into the concourse.

Rovo watched these events with a numbing detachment. He knew, objectively, that the reason why he didn't feel so much constant pain anymore was due to shock. His body was doing what it had to do in order to keep Rovo alive, or at least feeling that way. His mind? Oh, his mind turned.

The unconscious pulled at him, but Rovo pushed it away. Focused, instead, on Zaydi. On the woman's uniform, her seemingly random appearance in the mess hall line. She'd been so ready to pay for their meals, so ready to sit with them and have a conversation, as if she had no other friends eating lunch on the ship.

And the line about Aurora? Knowing their captain was a woman?

All that leading up to the assassination attempt.

Why kill Rovo and, presumably, Gregor? Back on Wexer, in their brief captivity session, the video message from whomever that officer was implied DefenseCorp wanted Sever alive for an interrogation. Apparently that stance had changed, and apparently the *Nautilus* wasn't the peace treaty Aurora thought.

More importantly . . .

"We have to tell the others," Rovo croaked, shoving himself back into full consciousness.

"Getting you help first," Gregor said between breaths as he ran down the concourse. "We're almost there."

Over Gregor's shoulder, Rovo picked out a white and red hovering form. A medical bot, scrambled when someone on the *Nautilus* noticed Gregor holding Rovo's wounded form. The bot, a meter-long oval, bristled with small compartments. Each one packed emergency supplies, the things that could keep Rovo, maybe, alive until better care arrived.

"The bot," Rovo said, trying to lift an arm to point and finding himself lacking the strength. As if the strings tying his brain to his muscles had frayed, leaving only a dull pressure. "Can't that help?"

"Too slow," Gregor replied. "Quiet, now."

The *Nautilus* med bay had enough room for a hundred patients. Rovo hadn't spent time here, but he gathered most of Sever had enjoyed its glossy confines in the aftermath of one of their missions. Laid out in descending rings, with more critical patients in more expansive rooms towards the middle, the whole med bay allowed human providers in its middle to track and operate the bots doing most of the actual care.

Dark with localized lighting to let patients sleep, the med bay resembled a neon nebula, the ramp Gregor descended glowing light purple. Rooms studded their levels with even-paced walls, each one emitting a soft outward aura for its patient's condition. The low population meant green and blue rooms shown in between empty black stretches.

In the air around and above them, medical bots like the one trailing Gregor glided from room to room. Food, meds, and diagnosis updates were delivered through the little things, and occasionally a doctor's voice could be heard coming through a bot's speakers, delivering a remote discharge. Only in the med bay's central, high intensity center, did any real action happen.

When Rovo stopped by on his first week's tour of the ship, he'd found the med bay a calm, sanitized place where mechanized competence put DefenseCorp's troops back in action before they had any right to be there.

Now, as Gregor clomped down the steps with Rovo in his arms, all that calm vanished. Bots and humans cleared out a room for Gregor to drop Rovo into a bed, the big man no sooner setting him down than mask-clad physicians pushed him away.

Bright lights clashed down at him while new pokes found their way past Rovo's shock-numbed nerves. Beeps sounded, long and sharp mixed with short and dull. Rovo tasted iron, smelled something sticky sweet.

"Rovo?" Gregor's voice cut over the medical chatter. "I'm going to warn the others. I'll be back."

Rovo tried to say he heard the big man, but then a doctor slapped an oxygen mask over his face and he couldn't utter another word. Couldn't imagine another one to say, either, as the drugs began to do their work.

The pain didn't so much vanish as recede into a tiny bubble, there on the absolute edge, while Rovo drifted. His eyes hazed again, but he picked out a bot hovering over him, its many little metal limbs stringing up an IV bag. Almost cute, the thing. Sever ought to have one on the *Prisa*, given how many times they were likely to get shot.

The *Prisa*. Eponi would give Rovo endless crap for this. She was always telling him to stay on edge, to keep a watch for someone doing something stupid. Here he'd known Zaydi had something weird going on, and he'd still turned his back on the woman.

Rookie mistake.

SIX

Reversal

EVEN WITH THE simulator's air conditioning, Aurora left the training room covered in sweat, her Sever uniform's black-and-white detailing damp, her hair plastered to her face along with a sharp smile. Her half-dozen had come out ahead in the skirmish with Sever's A team through a combination of smarts, quick orders, and Aurora's own life-saving double shot into some forgotten power packs near the enemy's base.

Nobody called her rookie after that.

"Have to say, I'm impressed," Deepak said as Aurora left the training room. Her squad headed off, a few glancing back Aurora's way, but she waved them on. She saw them every day, all day. "You're clever."

"You sound surprised?" Aurora said, folding her arms as they stood in the crowded concourse.

"I, uh—"

"Just messing with you." Aurora slapped on a grin, took in Deepak's always-crisp uniform. "Aren't you supposed to be doing something important?"

Rescued from his own words, Deepak flushed into

something approaching relaxation, though the man couldn't stop folding and unfolding his hands, "Break time. Saw your squad on the schedule, thought I'd stop by. You have any plans for lunch?"

"I'm real gross right now."

"Then I'd say, between the two of us, we're about right," Deepak countered.

Hard not to give into those bright eyes, spend the victory rush sharing a meal with someone fun. They laughed through that lunch, and the next, and the one after that, until the *Nautilus* reached its destination and the assignments started coming in.

WITH TWO GUARDS BEHIND HER, a liar in Deepak next to her, and a mysterious enemy pointing to a chair, Aurora played the only card she could: she sat.

With the tone called, the move to the chair came both fast and slow. Aurora drew in the room with different eyes than she'd first seen it, looking this time for weapons, for stances, for possible ways out or opportunities.

First, Deepak. He looked troubled, almost panicked. Not at all like someone who'd just pulled the prey into his trap. His uniform, crisp and perfect, lacked the slack or the holsters to carry weapons. Aurora didn't recall the admiral being much of a fighter himself, but his sweaty, nervous attitude suggested he might be as much a prisoner here as Aurora.

The guards behind her, caught in view as Aurora walked to her chair, pulled it out, and sat down, held a different sort of casualness. A bland confidence in their inevitable victory. That, at least, Aurora had seen time and again on the faces of her soon-to-be victims. Everyone believed they were a winner until they lost.

These two packed pistols, the weapons lingering on belts at their waists. They kept their eyes fixed on Aurora, but one let his trail to his wristlet while the other scratched at his nose. Hardly robots, then. Relaxed with their power.

Easy to surprise.

The officer across from her, his crimson uniform devoid of medals and ranks aside from black stripes running down its sides—just like the guards—plastered an accommodating smile across his wide, smoothed face. He kept his hands clasped, but Aurora picked out the white press on the skin. Nervous too, though perhaps in a different way than Deepak.

The stakes here rested on his shoulders, and someone wouldn't be very happy if he failed.

"I'm sitting," Aurora said. "What do you want?"

"No," the officer replied. "The question is who. Who do we want?"

The message in the cell on Dynas gave filled any gaps. The officer wanted anyone who knew about Kaia, the little girl that, so far as Aurora knew, was the only living survivor of Helix's adaptable virus.

"You already have them," Aurora said. "Us. Sever."

"Wrong," the officer said. "That's not all."

"What, you want the two guards? Lani, the Defense-Corp agent that flew with us off-world?" Aurora said. "We don't know where they are."

"That was it?" the officer said. "Nobody else?"

Aurora could've been cagey with the intel, but she wasn't playing some tricky game here. She didn't have a weapon, was outnumbered and outgunned, and didn't have anything to hide. If giving the man what he wanted would let her out of this room and get her squad off this ship alive, well, she'd tell him everything.

"Anaskya. Kaia's father Kashmal. That's really it."

Aurora sat back in the hard chair, shot Deepak a glare to make sure he understood she wouldn't forgive him for not mentioning this little ambush. "Looks like you might be a paranoid man, so let me tell you that we're not in the business of making friends."

The man, at least, laughed at that, "No, no you're not. We had trouble finding anyone on this ship aside from Deepak who even cared that your squad deserted. It's quite hard to make a profile of people when nobody knows who they are."

Aurora didn't say anything. There was nothing to say.

The officer's smile trembled in the silence. Deepak, taking the chair next to Aurora, looked down into his lap like a child about to be scolded.

"Do you know why DefenseCorp doesn't chase many deserters?" The officer said, breaking his clasped hands and laying them flat on the table, as if about to reveal a surprise. "Because most aren't worth a damn. The few that are, we find a sweet enough reward gives us what we're looking for."

"Nobody cares that much about us," Aurora said. "Anyone who does, wouldn't know where we are."

Sai and Rovo had families. They'd sent messages on Wexer, but a few days wouldn't be enough time for those beams to get halfway home.

"That's true. Lani, however, does care quite a lot about herself," the officer said. "She didn't want to die, and she didn't want to go back to Dynas. Instead, she gave us you."

Anger came easy, Aurora killed it easier. Lani bought her life by helping Rovo survive the escape from Dynas, by giving up Aurora's power armor. Sever could've spaced the DefenseCorp agent, but they'd played it right.

If she ever saw Lani again, Aurora would pull the trigger. That thought was enough to keep anything from showing on her face, and once again the officer's grin shook, faded when Aurora didn't give him the satisfaction.

"Nothing surprises you," the officer said. "I suppose that's a sign we do train our soldiers well."

"He did," Aurora said, nodding towards Deepak. "You don't."

"Him?" The officer laughed again, an annoying, squawking noise that Aurora attributed to the man's obvious facial operations. "He does what he's told, just like you will. Lani mentioned the girl, this Kaia. You know where she is."

"I don't."

The officer held up one finger. Both officers drew their pistols, aimed them at Aurora.

"According to Lani, you do," the officer said. "And Lani's been right about everything else so far."

"We ditched them on Wexer," Aurora replied. "They took a transport somewhere. Not my problem."

"It is your problem, because I'm making it your problem. Either you give me a solution, or they will erase you now, just like I am erasing all of your colleagues at this very moment."

Wait. What?

Almost all of Sever had left the *Prisa* after Deepak's introduction. Aurora could see them all splitting up. Could see more agents like these two tracking them down, one by one. Outnumbered, attacked by surprise in the one place Sever would consider safe?

"Say that again," Aurora said.

"You tell me where Kaia is, perhaps I'll call off the assignments," the officer said, now, finally, getting his chance to gloat. "Do hurry, though, because you are running out of time."

Was he bluffing? Would he stop these attacks, even if Aurora knew where to find Kaia?

Did she really want to spend another minute listening to this guy?

The *Nautilus* maintained, through its mass and magnetic fields, enough gravity to keep feet on the ground, to keep most things working as nature intended. Try to press against it, though, and you'd find yourself jumping to the ceiling.

"Deepak," Aurora said, "I'm tired of this. Aren't you?"

As the officer opened his mouth, likely to spew some threat or another, Aurora flipped the table.

The big, faux granite thing went right up and over as Aurora pushed it, smashing into the officer and driving him into the wall behind. Deepak picked up on Aurora's tactic and proved he wasn't playing the officer's game by putting his body between the two guards and Aurora, causing their rapid shots to fizzle into the room's floor.

"Sorry," Aurora said, pushing Deepak into the left guard, then squatting as the right lined up another shot that flashed over her head.

Low gravity assisted again when Aurora sprang from her crouch, a move that would've netted her a nice little hop on most planets, but that, on the *Nautilus*, sent her rocketing into the right guard's chest. As Aurora drove the guard back into the door, she looked and grabbed his pistol-wielding hand with her own left.

The other guard pushed Deepak to the floor, clearing the way for his own shot, only to find his comrade, courtesy of Aurora's snappy grip, shooting him. Aurora pressed the trigger two more times while driving her elbow into her victim's gut, getting grunts that meshed quite nicely with the shouts from the thrice-shot guard.

The fourth blast killed the yells.

Aurora, pinning the other guard, pressed her foot into the ground at the intersection of door and floor. Twisting her shoulder, using her waist, Aurora flipped the guard over her, pulling the pistol free with the move and sending the guard to the ground. The man hit the floor with a gasp as the air left his lungs, eyes popping open and seeing his own pistol aiming right in his eyes.

"Move again," Aurora said, "I dare you."

The guard stayed real still.

"Smart man," Aurora continued. "Deepak, mind seeing if our friend's still alive under there?"

The admiral, after taking the pistol off the burned down guard, hesitated before clearing the table. Threw Aurora a look that said here was a moment made for mistakes.

"Don't shoot him," Deepak warned.

"But I really want to."

"I know, but Renard's the only one that might get us out of this alive."

A name at last, but not one Aurora recognized. Not a public DefenseCorp executive or officer, though Aurora didn't exactly study the huge company's ranks. Whatever. Names didn't matter, actions counted more.

Aurora cocked her head, "Pretty sure he's the one that's trying to kill us, Deepak."

"There's a bigger story here," Deepak countered. "Just, don't fry him. Not yet."

Aurora waved the pistol towards the table, "The longer you make me wait, the more likely I am to start burning holes in it and seeing what happens."

That, at least, put Deepak into action. The man stepped over the surrendered guard and pulled back the table. Renard, so arrogant a moment before, had one hand over his nose trying to stop blood from leaking out, while the other held his own small sidearm like a wriggling fish. Even Deepak winced at the view.

Aurora adopted her best shark impression.

"Drop it," Aurora said, keeping her pistol on the downed guard, "or your buddy here takes one to the heart."

She felt the odds were even that Renard gave a damn about the guard, but Aurora worried more that the guard might try something if death vanished from his immediate future than the officer getting off a good shot with his little limp gun.

"You're all brutes," Renard snarled, the cocky spice dying fast into a sniveling brew. "As if violence can solve all your problems."

"Sounds like it created them," Aurora said. "Might as well end them too. You were saying my friends might be in trouble? You might want to elaborate, before I melt you and take my chances."

"Aurora," Deepak warned, and Aurora badly wanted to send the admiral some angry replies, but kept her focus on Renard.

Why the hell was Deepak defending this officer? What did Deepak know that he wasn't sharing?

"You want to save your friends?" Renard said, dropping his sidearm. "Fine. Take me to the bridge and I'll broadcast the coded message. All around the ship, they'll stop. Your friends will survive."

"You can't do that from here?" Aurora said, then glanced at Deepak. "He can't do that from here?"

"The *Nautilus* doesn't let you broadcast ship-wide from anywhere." Deepak, without getting Aurora's permission, helped Renard stand. At least the admiral kept his pistol ready. "That'd be chaos. The bridge is the closest place we can use."

Fine. Facts were facts, and Aurora wouldn't fight that one anymore.

"What about this guy?" Aurora said, nodding down at the guard who'd done a great job holding to her don't move order. "And his cooked friend?"

Deepak offered up a decent solution. The three of them left the conference room, Deepak using his admiral's security to lock the room behind them while sending out a security alert to resolve the situation.

"Keep your weapon holstered," Deepak told Aurora as they left the room. "Someone sees you walking with a pistol pulled, there's going to be trouble."

"Because there's no trouble already."

Renard laughed, a weak thing, "For you? It's just beginning."

Aurora rolled her eyes at Deepak, "Sure we can't just shoot him?"

"Aurora," Deepak sighed, "If you kill this man, then there will be nothing I can do to keep you alive. To keep me alive."

And Aurora's hard face slipped at Deepak's words, not because of what he said—any mission put Sever's lives at risk, this wasn't much different—but because of how he spoke, how he looked.

Despite having Renard disarmed, bloodied and in their custody, Deepak seemed very, very afraid.

SEVEN

Knife Fight

THE CIVILIZED CONVERSATION lasted until the guest quarters door slid shut behind them. A full-sized bed sat to the door's right, with a small desk alcove topped by a dark monitor past that. On Sai's left, a thin closet sat closed. Gray dominated.

The *Nautilus* was not a luxury hotel. It was, however, a good place for a fight.

With the door's click, the young man who'd followed Sai all this way slid a short, slim knife from a pocket up his sleeve. Sai backed away as the man advanced, the assassin taking his time to ensure Sai had nowhere to move.

Behind the crimson uniform, the man looked fit. His hair frizzed a little more than expected for a DefenseCorp regular, but the black stripes running up the sides now seemed to mean something other than a squaddie. Certainly no regular recruit would carry a thin stabber like this one.

More ominous, the man's smile stayed light and fixed. His eyes bright. As if killing Sai was his day's feature event.

Well, the man would be disappointed.

The thrust came with a twitch, a straight jab at Sai's neck that would've finished things at a stroke. Would've, except the man's eyes betrayed him, falling from Sai's face just before the strike, verifying the target, the aim, the speed.

Sai sidestepped into a shoulder charge, feeling the blade knick his neck. Sai's ram hit harder, pushing the man off his feet. As he fell, Sai grabbed the man's knife wrist and twisted, feeling tendons strain and seeing the blade drop to the floor. With his foot, Sai stomped on the blade, trapping it.

Pain shot through Sai's gut, and he looked down to see the man recoiling for another jab, the man's left hand flattened out like an arrow.

Not happening.

Sai heaved, whipping the arm he held and sending the man careening up and into the room's ceiling, courtesy of the *Nautilus*'s light gravity. Back first, the man grunted as he struck, his head cracking back as Sai let go the captive hand to seal the move's momentum. When the assassin dropped, a little slower than what Sai would see on thicker worlds, he had no way to control his descent. No way to do anything except fall straight down. Right onto his own knife.

The assassin had missed Sai's neck.

Sai didn't.

He sat on the bed. Looked at the red wet on his hand, then wiped it off on the dead man's uniform. The crimson didn't quite match the blood, but close enough. Sai felt his heartbeat slow down, his breathing come back to a normal pace. The fight had been so fast the adrenaline came rushing in after it was over, spiking as Sai tried to find a next step to take.

Of all the places in the galaxy, for years, the *Nautilus*

had been safe. Nobody would dare assault a DefenseCorp cruiser, and even if assassinations or shadowy plays swept the civilized world, Sever Squad never had the standing to warrant a target on their backs.

Until now, apparently.

The man's wristlet didn't offer any clues. Its screen had gone dark, and no matter what Sai did, the thing wouldn't wake up. Sometimes, the more fanatical tied their wristlets to their bio signatures, wiping the machine if its owner died. Maybe that happened, or the wristlet locked itself. Either way, Sai wouldn't be getting answers there.

The tiny drive in Sai's pocket, though, offered a better chance. Sai could plug it right into the monitor, but staying in a room with a body seemed like a poor call. Someone would walk in, whether to use the room or to clean it, and seeing Sai using a computer instead of getting help might get a bad reaction.

"Thanks for the help," Sai said to the corpse as he stood up.

A peek back into the guest room hallway confirmed it empty, so Sai went across the hall and down a room, leaving the body shut away behind him. A nasty surprise for someone.

Sai winced. A nasty surprise? Was that how Sai thought of bodies these days? Had he really seen so many deaths that they rolled off his conscience like water rinsed off his katana's blade?

In a mission's middle, suited up with enemies all around, allies to rescue and objectives to accomplish, Sai could turn to those distractions and keep on going. Push through to the end and then on to the next before placing what he'd done and seen into the right mental context. Even in those weeks post-Dynas, hunting a destination among the stars, Sai and Sever had tossed the time away together talking, laughing, surviving.

Standing in the guest room, immaculate and without personality, Sai realized he was really alone for the first time in too long.

He wavered.

Doubts clawed in the silence, telling Sai that his choices had caught up with him. That his whole plan—take the higher paying Sever role to guarantee his family's livelihood—wasn't working anymore, not when he'd left behind DefenseCorp's death payout and the better gear to prevent that death in the first place.

Here he was stabbing out assassins, considered a criminal by a powerful enemy, and sitting alone with a drive on it containing who the hell knew what.

Sai reached into his pocket, pulled out the little thing. Deepak wanted him, or at least someone on Sever to find it. He rubbed his finger along the drive's plastic surface, eyes pulling to the dead monitor.

He couldn't leave now. Those choices were made. If, though, Sai made it out of this one?

Take what cash he could get from his accounts and go back to his family. See what time he could get back, if any.

The monitored played nice with the drive and pulled up its contents. File after file splayed out, dozens. Sai figured someone had dumped everything they could on here. The file names themselves didn't offer clues: all cryptic, random letter and number series that spoke to a code Sai didn't have time to break.

Clicking on a few at random, Sai stared. The first offered up equations, a formula series leading to what appeared to be a component configuration, like what Sai might expect to see if he built a new explosive. The next showed off blueprints for a strange new suit, codenamed

Casparian. Unlike most power armor, the suit seemed small. Light.

The last offered up a hierarchy. Sai recognized the face, one of two at the top. The officer from the video back on Wexer. The other, a dark-haired woman Sai didn't recognize. Beneath them, a half-dozen on the second line. There wasn't any title, no official DefenseCorp layout.

Whatever this organization was, it lived outside the standard channels.

He yanked out the drive. Slipped it back in his pocket. Sai could've kept browsing through the files, and would, but a safer place to do that would be back on the *Prisa*, where he could make sure no other assassin would be waiting for him.

Or anyone else.

The assassin had followed Sai from the Quartermaster, but he hadn't been looking for Sai specifically. At least, it didn't feel that way. Sai had been the target because Sai had shown up where the target would be. If someone had hunted him, odds were good there might be more.

The woman had said to be careful.

If Sai had gone running towards the Quartermaster, he took his damn time getting back towards the *Prisa*. Looking out for the crimson uniforms with those black stripes, Sai took the moving walkways slow and watched. The *Nautilus* and its continual commotion that'd been so nice upon arrival held a different bent to it now, one that screamed a hidden enemy in every sound, every action.

Was that call for medical to respond to a critical event in the med bay an accident, or an intentional act? How about the overhead banger a minute later calling for a security check-in not all that far from the *Prisa*'s docking bay?

What about the dinner special flashing on all the monitors? Were meatballs a coded sign for a mutiny?

Sai shook his head, laughed, and drew some curious looks. No way the assassins were using the food menus to communicate with each other. There were dangerous people on the *Nautilus*, but maybe they just wanted to off Sever as deserters. Nothing more than a plot to get the crew back where DefenseCorp could take shots at them.

No need for a vast conspiracy.

Except the *Prisa*'s docking bay had blood on its floor. Smelled like charred clothes and burned flesh. Sai stood in the doorway and saw a ship that had its ramps up. That, going by the glass bits on the floor around the ship, had taken a few hits from something.

"Eponi?" Sai called, heading into the bay and letting the door shut behind him. "You there?"

Sai could see the *Prisa*'s cockpit from the ground, its windshield showing nobody in those seats. Maybe Eponi had left. Maybe she'd been taken.

Dashing to the lead strut, Sai lifted a small, hidden panel that revealed a square number pad. Most ships had these, emergency entry codes to get in if you lost your wristlet. Sai tapped in the code, which Eponi had set to Sever's squad band frequency. The panel chimed and the ship's ramp descended.

Sai wished he'd searched the assassin for weapons and taken any. The body and its messy demise had thrown him off his game. Now he looked up the ridged ramp and wondered if he was running right to another fight.

Well, he wasn't going to leave without his sword. Not to go back into the damn *Nautilus*.

Sai stalked up the ramp, taking the metal slow. Anyone paying attention in the ship would've felt the ramp going down, but that didn't mean they had to know exactly where Sai was, exactly how fast he moved.

At the ramp's top, Sai went into the *Prisa*'s central chamber. The rectangle space wasn't huge, but the couches were nice. Seeing them made his skin itch from the burns he'd taken on Wexer, ones that hadn't quite healed yet, even with the fast-acting cream sloughed over them. The stuff worked miracles, would—

Another crimson uniformed man dropped from the crew quarters above, landing poised in front of Sai with his rifle drawn, aimed, and ready to fire.

Then the man exploded.

Sai hit the deck as laser fire poured through the man's remnants, burning them away. A few stray bolts struck the *Prisa*'s insides, marring the clean copper color. Standing behind the man, back towards the cockpit and holding her rifle high, was Eponi.

"Hey," Eponi said as Sai looked at her from the ground. "What's up?"

"I think we're in trouble," Sai said, before remembering he'd lowered the ramp. Scrambling, Sai slapped the button to start it going back up. "And, nice shooting."

"Helps when they're standing still," Eponi said. "He must've thought you were me. So, thanks for that."

"I do what I can." Sai leaned down, picked up the man's rifle. "Did you cause the mess out there too?"

Eponi slashed a grin, "They tried to take my ship. Not happening."

"Yeah, well, they tried to kill me in the *Nautilus*, so I don't think it's the ship they want," Sai said. "Have you heard from anyone else?"

"Not a peep."

"Okay," Sai slung the dead man's rifle over his shoulder

and went into the *Prisa*, heading up towards his locker. "Better get ready then."

"To go rescue our friends from a bunch of strange killers?"

"Damn right."

EIGHT

The One Rule

GREGOR DIDN'T MAKE it ten steps from Rovo's bed before one of the bots blocked his path up and out from the descending med bay rings. The robot, a secretarial machine, accosted Gregor with questions about Rovo's name, age, and various personal habits that Gregor dished off with one head shake, shrug, or *I don't know* after another.

"Look it up," Gregor finally said when the robot started going in on Rovo's health history. "I gave you his ID."

Rovo had to have a health history with DefenseCorp. Had to. You didn't make it all the way from hiring to a squad like Sever without a scratch. For a second, while the bot considered his statement, Gregor wondered whether he still held the *Nautilus*'s record for most infirmary visits without dying.

Deepak had given Gregor a scrapped together medal reading "Get Well Soon" for the occasion. It'd been in the power suit lost on Wexer. Except for his hammer, Gregor's possessions tended to burn up or get blown away.

"Record located, thank you," the bot chirped, and Gregor suppressed a sigh at the obvious outcome. "How should we contact you about his condition?"

Another momentary stump. No wristlet, no private quarters on the *Nautilus*.

"There is a ship, the *Prisa*. I'll be there."

"Recorded. Have a nice day!"

As the bot whirred away, Gregor made for the stairs. He took one look back towards Rovo, the rookie's body hidden by his room's confines. Doctors and surgical bots continued to flow in and out, the reds on their gloves pulling Gregor's frown deeper.

These were the best of the best. Rovo's wound had looked bad—lasers to the lungs tended to be rough—but if any crew could pull the rookie from the brink, it'd be these.

And they'd have more victims to treat if Gregor didn't get a warning out to Sever soon.

Gregor hit the concourse, brushing past another stretcher coming in. A cloth sheet over a body. Gregor caught a leg, the crimson uniform, the black stripe.

"Where'd you find that one?" Gregor said as they wheeled the body into the med bay.

"Guest quarters," replied one of the wheelers.

"Alone?"

"You want to know, go find security." The wheeler delivered the reply and kept on going, the cart vanishing down the med bay's ramp.

It didn't pay to accept coincidence. Not on this ship, not right now. If another black-striped body came through, then Gregor had to assume someone else in Sever had been attacked. Had, going by what he'd seen, won.

Good. Served whomever had sent these bastards right.

The concourse didn't look like it cared. The med bay's end, beneath the bridge and above the weapons center

Gregor had just left behind, held foot traffic going to training rooms in the area and little else. Squads, loosely formed, jogged into designated centers for physical or simulator exercises, while officers chatted outside, some watching the events on viewing screens designed to show off what happened inside.

The public is always watching. Another DefenseCorp slogan hammered in through practice.

Another thing hammered in? When the lights change, stop and listen.

The concourse's mellow white lighting flickered, flashing over to a soft blue. Gregor, habit taking hold, stopped his walk—running seemed likely to attract the wrong attention—like everyone else in the corridor. Blue wasn't a dangerous color like red or yellow, but it meant a message from the bridge, something to pay attention to.

"This is your admiral speaking," Deepak's voice came heavy over the intercoms, as though he were announcing a death of a close friend. "As many of you know, the *Nautilus* has seen many newcomers in the last week. Our itinerary has been changed. Now, so has our role within DefenseCorp. To ease this transition, we are asking that all active troops return to their barracks and await further orders. For the rest of you, carry on and expect further details soon."

The blue lights flickered back to white, the change coming with loud yells as commanding officers barked their soldiers out from the training rooms and into jogging lines heading back towards their barracks. Gregor found himself stuck as the concourse filled with salaried soldiers fulfilling Deepak's command.

A strange, suspicious command. The order would clear the *Nautilus* concourses of armed soldiers, ones that might know Sever, that might help seeing someone get attacked.

Or, on the other side, it might be a straight recall before a major shift in how the ship organized its force.

Gregor, having just survived a surprise attack, chose the more dangerous proposition. And with the concourse clearing, he—

Two hands, different ones, landed on his shoulders from behind. Two stinging sensations hit his waist, firing up and down his nerves. Shockers, meant to spasm out his muscles until they gave up and left Gregor limp. An attack that should've brought down most troopers in a few seconds.

Gregor hit the floor, watching the last retreating troops fade away down the concourse while his eyelids twitched, while his arms and legs hit themselves on the ground. Then those same hands landed on Gregor again, turning him over. Two people, a Casparian and a man, both clad in DefenseCorp's medical uniforms, looked down at him.

Another attack. Another ambush. How many enemies did Sever have on this ship? These two didn't have the crimson-and-black uniforms on, but they had Zaydi's look to them: people on a mission, following orders they very much believed in.

"Fight," the Casparian said, its willowy white body seeming to shrivel and reform beneath its clothes, like a cloud caught in a net, "and we will finish what Zaydi could not."

The man's eyes flashed at Zaydi's name, and he knelt down next to Gregor's head, "Give me a reason, Gregor."

The Shocker had its uses, but the flares faded fast if the victim had enough will, enough strength to push back. Gregor bought into the tremors even as the pulses died, keeping his arms moving, his legs jerking as best he could. Aurora always said Gregor wasn't much for stealth, but when it counted, Gregor could play dead.

"Don't encourage him," the Casparian said. "Let's move him inside before someone comes back."

Gregor held his look on the Casparian while the two moved to try lifting Gregor. The aliens had specialties, none of which played out in open combat. So far as Gregor knew, Casparians in DefenseCorp played ancillary roles, supporting squads or working in the clandestine arm of the company.

The clandestine arm. The agents on Dynas. Gregor flipped back through his brief time with the agent trio on that swampy mess of a world. They'd been so interested in the idea of a successful virus. They'd forced Gregor to fly out and show them, had been sorely disappointed when it hadn't worked out.

Only one agent had made it off Dynas with Sever. Lani, who'd said she had no plans to go back to Defense-Corp when they dropped her at the trading station.

But plans could change.

The Casparian and the man tried to lift Gregor and failed. He made it a few centimeters off the floor before the Casparian dropped Gregor's feet and swore.

"He's big," the Casparian admitted. "Let's drag him."

Deepak said he'd exchange Sever's freedom for Kaia's location. Give up the only living example of the working virus. Deepak himself hadn't ever shown an interest in genetic enhancements. He was a by-the-books admiral, fulfilling contracts on the way to a comfortable retirement on some resort world.

There were holes here Gregor couldn't fill. The message back on Wexer suggested DefenseCorp wanted to know about anyone Sever had spoken to about Kaia, about Dynas. They wouldn't get that information by killing Gregor, Rovo, and the rest.

Something had changed, and as the Casparian and the

man dragged Gregor back into the med bay, Gregor tried to figure out what.

Rather than drag Gregor down towards the med bay's crowded middle, the two pulled the big man off to the side, into a low grade level meant for longer recoveries. Most beds here weren't occupied, a sign that the *Nautilus* hadn't been doing many major missions lately. The two dragged Gregor past three empty beds, getting him well away from the main ramp, before pulling him into a room and dropping him.

"Eyes on him," the Casparian ordered. "I'll confirm whether we can eliminate."

"On it."

The man drew a pistol, stood in the room's doorway while Gregor laid on the floor. He watched Gregor, a cloud sticking to a face that moved between gritted teeth and a deep frown.

"You can kill the act," the man said. "Guy your size, the shock should be off by now."

"You've trapped a beast," Gregor replied, indulging the man's command and sitting up. "Can you keep him caged?"

"I'd rather kill him."

"Because of Zaydi?"

The man's eyes narrowed, "She didn't deserve what you did, but no. More than that."

"Tell me?"

A laugh that belonged to the lost came from the man's lips, "Don't think so. You'll be dead in a minute anyway."

"Then why not explain?"

The man almost, almost looked like he would start talking. The mouth twitched up from the frown to a small smile, the victor's look. The Casparian, though, came back at that moment and ruined it. The ghostly face sneered Gregor's way.

"Lucky for you," the Casparian said. "Your commander doesn't know where to find the girl. We're not killing any of them yet."

The man swore. Gregor shook his head. Not only were these people dangerous, they were idiots. Who would kill off the ones that knew what you needed to know?

"Do you?" The man asked Gregor. "Do you know where the girl is?"

"Maybe?" Gregor didn't have a clue, but the man still had his pistol on him. "Why would I tell you?"

The morons had already blown their best threat. By showing they were ready to kill Sever, any urge to give up information went away. They'd kill Gregor anyway, so why talk?

"Can I?" The man asked the Casparian, taking his eyes off Gregor for a critical second. "We'll just say he tried to escape."

Gregor curled and jumped for the Casparian, moving to the side enough that the man's pistol shot missed by millimeters. Gregor didn't bother going for a grapple, trying anything fancy. He just slugged the alien hard with his right hand, lifting up as he did so. With the *Nautilus*'s gravity, the Casparian flew back and up from the force, dropping down to the next level and landing on another room.

The man recovered enough to aim his pistol Gregor's way, just in time for the room's walls to shift red. A loud beep squawked, throwing off the man's aim just enough for Gregor to keep on running from his Casparian punch. The emergency button did its job, sending the room into a flaring panic. Bots swarmed as Gregor made for the level's corridor, the mechanized hosts flying, walking, trundling by and blocking any shots the agent might be able to take at Gregor's back.

Gregor wasn't one to run from a fight, but the man had weapons. Had positioning.

Hitting the med bay's main ramp offered a choice. Gregor could head back up to the concourse, resume running towards the *Prisa* and his hammer. Doing that, though, would leave Rovo alone down in the med bay's pit. Sever's primary rule?

Don't abandon your squad mate.

The agents had weapons, but as Gregor broke right down the ramp, then dashed onto another level, hiding between the beds, the bots, and the hanging equipment, the big man knew he had something almost as good:

Surprise.

NINE

To The Rescue

BLOOD SPLATTERED her ship's floor. Its walls. Admittedly, the mess came at Eponi's own hands, pulling the trigger that turned the intruder into so much goo.

Still. Eponi had only scoured this ship a few days ago, before the assault on Wexer.

Everyone had their triggers. Some didn't like getting embarrassed. Others couldn't handle losing a game. Eponi didn't give two craps about her personal appearance, but her ship?

"I know you're going to tell me we can't clean this up right now," Eponi said to Sai as they looked at the mess. "But can I clean this up right now?"

"No."

"Damn."

They'd heard Deepak's message while Sai showed her the drive's riddle. Eponi hadn't made much sense of the three lines either, and the overhead broadcast drove the riddle from her mind. None of the others had come back yet, and Deepak clearing the halls of any neutral party that might help in an attack by one of the black-striped killers?

Sai led the way down the ramp, katana out and ready while Eponi brought up her rifle to cover. Upon hitting the bay floor, Eponi sent the ramp scurrying back up, locking the *Prisa.*

"I'll come back for you," Eponi whispered as they went to the bay's door.

"Bridge first," Sai said. "We know Aurora's with Deepak, or he'll know where she is. Gregor and Rovo should be able to handle themselves."

"You think the rookie could take these people?"

"I think Gregor can cover."

Fair, though Gregor didn't have his hammer. Would he still fight, even without it? Was that even a question?

Gregor would fight with anything he had. Fists, teeth, toes. If anyone could make it out of an assassination alive, it'd be him.

Outside the bay, the docking berth concourse had its usual bot array. Non-trooper staff continued their rounds, though they all stopped at the sight of Sai with his katana out. At first, the pause confused Eponi: DefenseCorp soldiers regularly had weapons visible on the ship.

Oh. The uniforms. Neither Eponi nor Sai wore any. They looked like civilians, ones covered in weapons and Sai, at least, had blood all over his clothes.

"Uh," Sai said, his katana grip faltering under the stares.

"Ignore us," Eponi announced. "There's a threat to the ship that we're handling under Deepak's orders. Carry on."

She'd used that voice before, talking to fans after kart race victories. Injecting authority and a little bit of puffery to keep people listening, trusting what she said. Only this time, instead of promising future wins for her team, she hoped to get a free pass carrying arms right into the *Nautilus*.

"Move," Eponi whispered to Sai. "And maybe sheath that sword."

The demolitionist did as Eponi asked, her words piercing his paralyzing veil. Sai went and Eponi followed, moving up the concourse and passed the first few workers. Eponi met eyes, issued solidarity nods, and, when nobody died, the berth crews went back to it.

"I'm impressed," Sai said as they went on, transitioning to a moving walkway beyond the berths to speed things up. "How'd you know they would listen to you?"

"Because I am amazing, and I know it."

"Right . . ."

Beyond the berths, the concourse smoothed into an emptier expanse. The missing troops should've filled these halls, meant for briefing rooms and strategy meetings for upcoming and current contracts. Instead, panels next to every door declared the spaces open and cleaning bots held sway. At the corridor's end, lift banks would take them up to the bridge, or down to the med bay and the mess hall.

"Any ideas who these people are?" Sai said as they went. "I didn't get much chance to talk with mine."

"I'm going to go ahead and guess that they're Defense-Corp," Eponi replied. "Also, that they're jerks. They shot out the *Prisa*'s cameras."

"And tried to kill us."

"Right, that too," Eponi frowned. "We know they're wearing official uniforms. They're on the ship and can get around. I think they overpowered a security detail too."

That earned a look from Sai, "So they're not just going to hurt us?"

"I don't think they care."

"Indiscriminate. That's not in our books."

Sai meant the DefenseCorp regs for squaddies. Unnecessary casualties, particularly civilians, were to be avoided unless, and it was a big unless, any accidents would support DefenseCorp's goals. Whether or not their enemies considered taking out a security detail excusable was a question Eponi couldn't answer.

"We don't have any books anymore, remember?" Eponi said. "You just have to live with yourself."

"Maybe not for much longer."

The lift pushed the duo up to the bridge, popped them out into another corridor. Almost empty again, save for the ever-present, disc-like cleaning robots scurrying across the floors. To those machines, the missing people must have been a huge opportunity.

"Glad something's enjoying this," Eponi muttered as they turned towards the bridge.

"What?"

"Nothing."

If the *Nautilus*'s mid-levels were functional, kept straightforward so the troops and docking bay workers could focus on their jobs, and the lower levels like the mess hall and med bay adopted some individual character, the bridge and top-level facilities played to their dual roles as operational centers and showcases.

Any big visitor would spend their time up here—there were special guest quarters for anyone too important to get shoved into the barracks—so Deepak had the walls decorated with actual art. Weaving color lines, a red, blue, cream, and black combination representing DefenseCorp's major branches, played along the wall's middle all the way down the concourse. Major DefenseCorp players had their pictures plastered up every so often, mixed in with critical ships from the company's past.

The color weave held Eponi's attention. The four

worked in concert. Red, DefenseCorp's active-duty squads, worked contracts and did the heavy missions. The blue were DefenseCorp's stabilizing forces, a group both Sai and Gregor had spent time in, taking contracts to keep worlds under control. The black held the agents, Defense-Corp's spycraft arm, taking more subtle contracts and helping to find intel for big missions.

The cream contained everyone else. All those support staff in the berths, the Quartermasters, the cooks.

"Look at this," Eponi said as Sai went bridgeward. "See anything interesting?"

"The colors?"

"Yeah, the colors," Eponi replied. "Crimson and black. Those were the uniforms."

Sai looked at the lines, "You're thinking they're agents."

"Always knew you were smart."

"Eponi, of course they're agents," Sai threw her an eye-rolling headshake. "C'mon. Who else was going to get onto the *Nautilus* and act like this?"

Sai started off again and Eponi went after him.

"Wait, you knew and you didn't say?" Eponi sped up to catch Sai, who seemed like he wanted to make up for every lost second speaking with another lunging stride.

"I thought you'd made the connection."

"But, down below, you—"

"The question is who's agents," Sai said. "Who's running this operation?"

"Oh. Next time, be more obvious."

"Will do."

The bridge did not respect their urgency. The big doors, with their downward and away slanting angles, stayed closed as Sai and Eponi approached, red-glaring security lights declaring locks that neither Sever member could open.

Sai and Eponi stared at the obstacle, waiting for someone to come or go. The bridge should've been a hive, even during whatever emergency Deepak had been getting at with his overhead announcement. People should've been running in and out, carrying messages, equipment, or just themselves from one place to another. Instead, nothing moved.

"This is strange," Eponi said. "Then again, everything's strange right now."

Sai reached up, tapped his katana's hilt, "Wonder if I could cut through . . ."

"You do, and I'm going to stand way over here so when you get gunned down, I can say it wasn't my idea."

Sai pulled his hand away, nodded. There had to be another way on, some way to get those doors open. The demolitionist went right up to them, pounded a few times with his fist. The metal reverbs echoed down the corridor.

The lights died again. All the white gone, sending everything dark save for emergency reflective squares along the concourse edges.

"Now look at what you did," Eponi said.

Sai didn't get a chance to put together a comeback. The lights came back on, but shifted into a deep, hot red. If Deepak's order had prepped the *Nautilus* for a lockdown, this was the natural follow-up: invasion.

"Really, Sai, I think we had enough problems," Eponi said, bringing up her rifle to ready status and splitting seconds turning left, right, and behind to look down the central concourse. "You had to trigger this?"

"Knocking on the bridge door?" Sai drew his katana. "You think they're that paranoid?"

"Someone's scared," Eponi replied. "Maybe you did the scaring."

"Then maybe I'll earn it."

Going invasion meant those same troops that'd gone into lockdown would get new orders. They'd be reporting to critical points on the ship to ensure the *Nautilus* stayed in DefenseCorp control. One of those points, naturally, would be the bridge, where two armed people with no identification, no uniforms, currently stood.

Sai reversed his grip on the katana, then plunged it into the door. The blade struck the metal, sparked, and bounced off. Turned out DefenseCorp put some real strength into the barrier protecting the *Nautilus*'s most valuable space.

"That's not going to work," Sai said, looking at his katana as if the sword had disappointed him in the most devastating way.

"Then we run," Eponi said. "Now."

She didn't wait for Sai, but took off straight down the center concourse. The sooner they put ground between themselves and the bridge, the less likely they were going to get shot by a squad of their own allies.

"What about Aurora?" Sai said, pounding up behind her as they went by locked administrative rooms. "She's still in there!"

"And she'll stay that way a little longer," Eponi shot back. "Can't help her if we're dead."

Though they weren't going to help their captain by running either. They needed an objective, something that could help them get onto the bridge.

"We could blow the door," Sai said, "if we found enough explosives."

"Oh yeah, that makes sense." Eponi snatched looks at the signs they passed, marking off the ship's zones with big letters. They were about to leave the bridge's administrative area and head into the VIP residences. "Bombs on spaceships. I thought you knew how that worked?"

"Look, trust me," Sai said. "I can rig it up so that we'll be just fine."

"That tone scares me."

"It should."

If they were going to get explosives, there was only one place on the *Nautilus* that'd have'em. The Quartermaster.

They stopped running at the central lifts, Sai slapping the call button while Eponi kept up her vigilance. The concourse, though, was quiet. Bots would've been recalled to their home stations with a lockdown, and any cream team members ought to have gone back to sheltered positions. Soldiers dispatched from the barracks might take a while to get going.

"The call button's not working," Sai said. "I don't have a wristlet, and the lifts aren't free anymore. We have to wait for someone."

"We might get lucky," Eponi said, daring to let herself think something in this disaster might go right for once.

Before a minute passed, with Sai trying to think up another way to the Quartermaster, the lift dinged, the doors opened, and a dozen armed squaddies stared out at them.

So much for luck.

Post-Op Treatment

HOTFIX. If any word defined DefenseCorp's attitude towards medical care, Rovo would choose that one. Staple the person together until they could wield a rifle and send'em back out. He'd read over the studies, the analyses back in his prior role, and Rovo saw the raw data stating most DefenseCorp troopers would retire or die before the accumulating effects of rushing someone back to the line took any real toll.

In other words, churn and burn.

Yet, lying under a light anesthesia as bots and doctors did their work, Rovo appreciated the rapid fashion in which the drugs nuked his pain, the healing gels sloughed off and replaced the burned skin, and the surgeons with their hand-held lasers, excised and rebuilt his charred lungs.

"You'll be weaker for a week or so. I'd recommend rest during that time," one of the doctors explained, his voice filtering in clouded and dreamy to Rovo's consciousness. "By then, your body should have itself back to working order. Not a hundred percent, mind, and I'd strongly advise against taking another unprotected hit to your breathables, but you'll be able to return to field duty."

Rovo would've said something in reply, would've mustered the strength to thank the surgeons for their efforts, but the line between his brain and his mouth had gone missing.

"If you're trying to talk, don't worry. You should get your voice back soon. We'll be keeping you here for the next day to make sure everything's going right. You'll be back in the barracks tomorrow, which I'm sure you're excited to hear," the surgeon said, Rovo catching a grin's ends in the man's cheeks.

Barracks that had no room for Rovo. The med bay staff would figure out who he was eventually. Did a potential criminal deserve the same treatment as an active duty DC soldier?

That question lingered as the providers wrapped up, the human members dwindling until only bots hovered over Rovo's body. They finished sewing Rovo up, and when the last vitals check came back green, the bed shuddered as a nursing bot attached his stretcher to its link and rolled him away.

The whole operation had taken less than thirty minutes from start to finish. With a simple stim, Rovo could be thrown into combat now, though he might regret it later. An efficient procedure meant to keep soldiers taking and giving laser beams as much as possible.

The nurse bot took Rovo to the second level, one away from the center and the med bay's most critical patients. The ride went smooth, supernaturally so, as was anything done by bots. No hesitations, no questions, no concerns by Rovo's caretaker, not even when a face that looked like it'd gone over to the day's bad side caught up to the bed.

"Tell me you're Rovo," the man said, the bitterness

that comes with being wronged lacing his voice. The man's uniform, that crimson and black stripes, gave reasons why that might be. "Don't lie, now, because I'm good at catching those out."

Rovo blinked. His throat scratched now, and his hands and legs twinged with nervous potential, but odds were the man didn't know that. If Rovo had to pick a side of the intelligence spectrum for the guy, he'd lean towards the idea the man had been recruited for throwing punches.

"That'll work," the man said, "if you can't talk. Blink it. One for yes, two for no."

Rovo blinked.

"Now we're rolling," the man continued as the nurse bot found Rovo's room and wheeled him in. "Listen carefully now, because I'm not gonna want to repeat this. Don't have the time."

Little stings punctuated the man's words as the nurse bot attached various IVs to Rovo's arms. Monitors around the room lit up with numbers Rovo couldn't parse, but the various greens, reds, and yellows suggested the rookie wasn't quite at health's pinnacle.

Yet.

"Here's the thing," the man sat on the end of Rovo's bed, cradling a pistol in his lap. "I've heard tell that you're the one that might have the answer we're looking for. You know what I mean?"

Rovo blinked twice.

"Figured you wouldn't. You grunt types never were quick to pick up on what's been happening under your feet this whole time." The man gestured towards Rovo with his pistol. "Always so focused on fightin' you missed what you were really fighting for."

Rovo didn't blink, didn't do anything except test out the nerves to his fingers, his toes. The IV flushed Rovo warm, but the tingling ends told Rovo he could move, could do something if it came to that.

Although, Rovo really, really didn't want to get shot again. Once today was enough.

"You're here because we need to know some things," the man dropped into a speechifying tone, as if Rovo were a student and the man a wise teacher. "There's a little girl we're out to find. I'm forgetting her name just now but I believe you know who I'm talking about."

Lie, or not? For all the man's words, he still sounded roughed up. Looked a little that way, now that Rovo caught a better look, propped up on the bed's angled headrest. As if the man had taken a punch or two. Risking a frustrated blasting didn't seem worth it if the man already had the right information.

Rovo blinked once.

"Good man, good man," the interrogator leaned towards Rovo. "Between you and me, the name's Conyers. Figured I'd make things fair, seeing as I know yours." Conyers scratched at his nose, looked outside the room into the med bay's neon-splashed dark. "The next part of this session, and it's the big one, is the girl's whereabouts. You have 'em?"

Rovo blinked twice.

Conyers nodded, "Suspected as much. They threw Zaydi after you two because she's an eraser, and they wouldn't have done that if you'd been clear you knew where the girl was. Unfortunately, that means we're not on great terms anymore."

The agent, assassin, Rovo wasn't entirely sure what to call Conyers, held the pistol vertical in front of his face and sighed. Rovo tried blinking once. Then twice. Conyers, though, wasn't looking.

Conyers leveled the pistol at Rovo's face in a slow motion. Shifted a finger to the trigger.

Now or never.

Rovo tried to move, tried to explode up from the bed, and found his legs flopping, found his arms able to twitch up enough to earn a Conyers laugh.

"My friend, it's going to take you longer than that to spring back," Conyers said. "Don't worry though, cause if I miss, they'll just patch you back up. Best place to get shot in the entire ship, right here."

Again the pistol leveled out, that black barrel looking Rovo right in the face.

With Zaydi, the attack had been quick. An instinctual contest to survive that prevented any real introspection until afterward. No life flashing in front of Rovo's eyes back there, and here? Rovo didn't have the time for it.

He kept trying to push his muscles to move, and the nerves responded, saying they were trying with all they had, but the muscles missed the motivation. No chance. Rovo closed his eyes, took in one more sanitized breath and savored the medical scent as it went down to his burned lungs.

Conyers didn't fire.

Rovo cracked an eye. The man still had the pistol aimed at his head, but Conyers flicked his eyes around, kept quiet. Waiting, or looking for something.

"On top!" came a voice from outside, bruised and lined with a Casparian's misty tinge.

Conyers took his eyes up to the room's ceiling, brought the pistol with the look. A bang rippled through the room, shaking Rovo's bed and sending the IV bags swinging. Was the *Nautilus* under attack? Had one of the nurse bots gone rogue seeing the pistol and come to Rovo's defense?

The second bang came with a crack, came with the

room's thin ceiling fracturing and falling. Conyers fired, the shot fizzling into the collapsing ceiling.

Sparking an entrance.

Gregor rode the rubble down, landing on Conyers, on Rovo, and tilting the bed up and sending all three men piling together at its base.

Rovo tumbled, feeling the IVs yank free, and rolled over Gregor to land on the room's floor. Right in the doorway, with his head past one side and his feet past the other. Gregor struggled with Conyers, both delivering punches to each other as they tangled with the bed, the sheets, and the ceiling pieces.

His hands and legs coming back to life, Rovo turned, watched the struggle, and noticed Conyers's pistol had slid near Rovo's head. If he could reach it, then maybe . . .

"Give it up, you monster," said the Casparian, stepping over Rovo's prone form and holding another pistol at Gregor. "You stop fighting now and we won't kill your friend."

Gregor delivered another good socking to Conyers, then stopped, giving the Casparian the dead-eyed look of a warrior who knew his next victim. Rovo kept trying to reach for the pistol. Conyers pushed himself a meter away to the room's side wall, wheezing through some battered breaths.

"You won't kill my friend because you will not get the chance," Gregor said.

"Bold words," the Casparian replied. "Conyers, who's the one that knows the girl? It's not him, right?"

Rovo twitched. A centimeter more. His left arm had itself cocked now. Just had to raise the shoulder and he'd have the pistol.

"Shoot him," Conyers said. "He's an ass."

"Not what I asked," the Casparian said. "I know he's

an ass. What I want to know is whether we'll be in trouble if he winds up dead."

Another twitch. His fingers had the grip.

"We won't." Conyers heaved into a coughing fit, speaking into the gaps. "He knows nothing."

"Good."

The Casparian went for the trigger, and Rovo fired. His shot went low, missing everything except the sheets crumpled at his bed's end, which took the laser's hot energy and burst into blue-orange flame. The Casparian startled, Gregor didn't.

Casparians as a species are light things, held together more by ethereal goo than bones. When Gregor delivered one of his trademark haymakers, his strike almost passed right on through the Casparian like a fist through jelly.

Almost.

The alien flew back through the doorway, its feet kicking Rovo as it went by. The thing didn't even manage a shout. A one-hit **KO** that would've drawn a cheer from Rovo if his mouth could manage it. Gregor turned to Conyers, the sheets now really going and sending up smoke, signaling alarms from the bay. Med bots, security personnel, anyone around would be here fast.

"Next time," Gregor said, then pushed the bed onto Conyers, trapping the man. "Rovo, time to go."

Rovo would've nodded, but instead he held on tight to the pistol while Gregor picked him up, left the room, and ran for the med bay's exit ramp. Not exactly following his doctor's orders, but Rovo was alive, and sometimes, that was enough.

ELEVEN

Infestation

THE BRIEFING BEGAN EXACTLY on time, while Aurora still had the lab-spun breakfast burrito in her mouth. The other DefenseCorp officers tended to be slapdash with their timings, particularly when it came to Sever. The squad would get dropped into the disaster's middle with simple, dangerous objectives. They didn't need the care and tending other squads, other fleets required.

But Deepak always chained himself to the clock.

Aurora suppressed a smile as Deepak went into the next assignment, a clearing house contract on a junkyard world its owners wanted cleansed before listing up for sale. Enough people didn't want to budge, enough bots had gone feral with corrupted programming, that DefenseCorp had been brought in to clear it out.

Sever would, of course, be sent into the teeth. An enclave filled with disgruntled dissidents, with weapons manufactured from scraps left after the planet's strip-mining.

As Deepak laid down the routes, he threw a wink Aurora's way, then planted Sever Squad square in the back. Reserve duty, a low stakes, low reward position that promised time spent watching the fighting from afar. Not what Aurora had signed up for, not the role that'd fill her accounts with bounty cash DefenseCorp awarded for performance.

Sever's captain, next to her, huffed under his breath, and Aurora could only agree. Deepak saw her look, took a big gulp in the middle of the briefing, and when it concluded, when Deepak hung around to talk, Aurora didn't.

THE BRIDGE PROVED to be a bad idea. Deepak and Aurora escorted the grumbling officer through the big double-doorway into the *Nautilus*'s shining space. A giant curved bubble carved into the asteroid's side, the bridge glitzed with its sweeping space view. Like so many ships, the bridge shot forward its floor, with descending sides giving space for thousands of officers and engineers to handle all the minute-to-minute work required for the *Nautilus* to stay flying.

At the bridge's very front, the helm loomed large. Two pilots worked in sync to keep the *Nautilus* moving, their screen arrays blending into the glass bubble, with data projecting up and onto the transparent barrier. Energy levels, course corrections, and who knew what else flew across their view.

Spreading away from the central split Aurora and the others walked on, the bridge fell away in staggered levels arranged by their importance to the admiral. Communications came first, its mezzanine-like design flowing out. Below that, levels dedicated to various systems transitioned to mission-specific sections meant to handle incoming questions and requests from in-action squads.

Sever probably had one of these while they were on Dynas, not that Aurora had a way to contact the *Nautilus* for most of that mission.

Few eyes turned to regard the incoming trio, and those that did made the quick decision not to play a part, returning to their tasks without a shout, a question, or any concern.

Cool air swirled in the broader space, filling in the quiet gaps as Deepak and Aurora carried the officer towards the bridge's middle, where several consoles sat at standing height for the admiral. Comms chatter picked up, questions cutting through the bridge carrying hints that the *Nautilus* wasn't quite right. A body had been found in the guest quarters, and a security detail had gone missing.

None of that made Aurora's nerves spike.

No, that came when Deepak pushed the officer into the consoles, where the man steadied himself. Deepak drew the pistol he still held from the guards, and pointed it at Aurora.

"Sorry," Deepak said, leveling the weapon at her while the officer brushed himself off. "I have too many lives on this ship to throw away for you."

"You're losing them already if you think he's going to forget what you did back there," Aurora countered.

"I don't need to forget," Renard stood, leaning on a console for support. "Deepak understands where his career comes from, and who can guarantee it." He shook his head when Deepak started to speak, and the admiral kept his mouth shut. "If you'll both stay quiet for a moment, let's check in and see whether I've made a terrible mistake."

While the officer turned back to the consoles, splashing up

the communications screen and dictating names to contact, Aurora reverted to what she'd done back in the meeting room. Analyze the situation, find weaknesses, and exploit them.

Deepak's drawn pistol had attracted eyes, but not the sustained alarm a weapon on the bridge should've caused. Aurora saw frowns, saw some head shakes, but most everyone kept themselves down and busy with their jobs. Either Deepak had told them what might be happening, or they'd already decided to join Renard's team.

But then, everyone on the bridge was an officer. Not a squaddie dropping into contracts on dangerous worlds. Deepak said he had to save his people's lives. Maybe he meant this group, maybe he meant these lives.

"Five people, Aurora," Deepak said. "That's all. When he came to the *Nautilus* and asked us to head after you, what was I supposed to do?"

"They wouldn't kill everyone," Aurora countered.

Deepak had the pistol, but he hadn't disarmed Aurora. She couldn't draw and fire while he had her under gunpoint, but with a distraction or a sudden change, Aurora might be able to pull something off. She'd just need to pay attention.

"This is a different side of DefenseCorp. I don't know what they're capable of," Deepak said. "I don't even know how many are on my ship. On this bridge. He threatened me with my crew's lives, and I believe him."

"Then you're doing exactly what he wants."

Deepak half-shook his head, when Renard turned around, a glower dominating his face.

"Bad news?" Aurora said.

"Quite," Renard replied. "Apparently your squad is very capable. You should be proud."

"I am."

The officer nodded, then held out his hand towards Deepak, "Your weapon, admiral."

Deepak hesitated.

"Don't make me ask again," Renard said. "Circumstances are changing. The *Nautilus* is to be considered a war zone until Sever Squad is dispatched. You will lockdown this bridge and order your soldiers to return to their barracks while my people complete the mission."

This time, Deepak didn't wait. He went past the officer to the consoles, and triggered the lockdown process. This time Deepak didn't wait. He went past Renard to the consoles, and triggered the lockdown process. A single alarm let out a shriek as overhead lights flashed. That drew enough attention that Deepak had to tell everyone not to worry, a statement, with Renard aiming the pistol at Aurora, held so little truth to it that she couldn't suppress a laugh.

"You think all this is funny?" Renard said. "Because I find it deadly serious."

"I'm sure you do," Aurora said, "and trust me, you'll still feel that way when we're stuffing you out an airlock."

"No doubt."

Deepak followed up the lockdown with a broadcast telling all the soldiers to head back to their barracks to wait for assignments, a ridiculous order but one Aurora knew would be followed. All these people depended on Defense-Corp for their cash, and who would risk that by questioning a command?

"Now," Renard continued, "I would like you to do something for me."

As if.

"Please, tell me what it is so I can tell you to go—"

"Aurora," Deepak said, cutting back in from the console. "For once, think about the ship. Do what he needs, and you might get out of this alive. All of these people might get out of this alive."

Who knew Deepak was such a coward? Aurora hadn't figured the admiral to have that small a spine.

"Listen to your admiral," Renard said.

"Not my admiral anymore."

"I can see why. You clearly lack the discipline to make a good DefenseCorp soldier, but perhaps you can help your squad anyway." Renard pointed towards the console. "You will issue a broadcast throughout the ship ordering your squad to station outside these doors. Once they arrive we shall have a discussion, determine the girl's location, and end this conflict."

In Aurora's experience, nothing about what Renard just said would come anywhere close to ending the conflict. Sever would smell that trap coming. But giving Aurora the comm would give her power. She couldn't let that go.

"You won't kill my squad?" Aurora asked.

"Clearly that's not very easy," Renard replied, still keeping that pistol level. Not at all like the limp hold in the briefing room. Either Renard had played a weakling, or he'd recovered from the table-flipping. "My mission is the girl. You are nothing."

"Fine." Aurora looked past the officer. "Hey, Deepak. You done over there?"

The admiral stepped aside, and Renard gave Aurora a path past him towards the comm. She took one step, then another that brought her even with the officer. Her eyes caught Deepak's, and he must've recognized that fire, that determination, because the admiral's went wide, his head started to shake.

Too late.

Aurora went hard left, twisting as she turned to take her body away from the pistol's aim. Renard didn't get a shot. The man's trigger finger wasn't ready, his mind still thinking he'd won this round. Aurora caught the officer's wrist, sent a jab into the man's throat that sent him choking.

With a hard kick, Aurora sent Renard flying back off the bridge, falling the two meters down to the lower level. As the officer fell, Aurora let her hand slide up the man's wrist, tearing away the pistol and flipping it into her own grip as the officer crashed into the consoles below. Continuing the motion, Aurora brought the stolen pistol to bear on Deepak while she drew the one still on her belt.

Evening out the aim to put a weapon on both, though Renard looked like consciousness had fled, Aurora allowed a small grin to kiss her face, "Sorry, Deepak. The opening was there."

"Aurora," Deepak said slow. "Look around."

Chairs shifted, a few curses flowed as staffers across the bridge stood from their stations. Several drew pistols of their own, and at least two pulled rifles from beneath their consoles. As Aurora swept her eyes across the bridge, she counted at least a third holding weapons aiming at her or the other crew members.

"Like I said," Deepak sighed, "this isn't just one guy. It's an infestation."

No cover. Nowhere to run.

"Drop the pistols," said a rifle-toting woman, climbing up the steps around the bridge's main platform to its center stage. "I won't ask again."

"Do it, Aurora," Deepak said. "They've been taking over the *Nautilus* for months. There was nothing I could do."

Aurora had been disarmed with a gun to her face twice already today, and a third time made for a maddening experience. She wanted to turn, snap off a blast and take out the one holding the rifle, then run-and-gun through the bridge to get all the rest.

That's what her emotions told her. The part that read the situation with a squad captain's mind said Aurora wouldn't live past a few seconds.

"All this for a girl?" Aurora said, bringing down the pistols.

"All this for what she is," Deepak replied. "All this for what you saw on Dynas."

"Dynas was a mess. A failure."

The woman came up to Aurora, took away the pistols. Others began tending to the officer, who groaned as they pulled him off the desk he'd used as an improvised landing pad. Aurora hoped he still had a few glass shards stuck in him.

"So you said," Deepak put a hand on Aurora's shoulder. "Apparently they see things differently, and they see you as a threat to their plans."

"Good." Aurora looked over at the comm. "Guess I get to make my announcement now?"

A cough came from below. Renard standing, with help from one of the other turncoats. He offered Aurora a plastic-faced glare as he limped towards the stairs. Aurora couldn't do much except watch Renard make his slow way around. To make her feel better, Aurora took a long look at the rifle being held in her face, then matched the agent's eyes holding it, and shook her head long and slow.

The agent's puzzled look warmed Aurora's heart. Hopefully the agent would think something was wrong with her rifle, or even the way the agent held it. Always fun to mess with your captors.

As Renard reached them, several loud knocks came from the sealed bridge doors, drawing Aurora's eyes and everyone else's. One man from below said two armed civilians stood outside.

"Don't approach those doors," Renard croaked, his voice a mess after Aurora's strike. "They are hostile, and will be dealt with once we are ready. As for this one, I've changed my mind. Take her to the airlock and shove her outside."

TWELVE

Old Friends

Two AGAINST TEN didn't make for good odds. Especially when those ten squaddies had their vests on, rifles ready, and looked like they wanted nothing more than to rumble with an invading force. Sai and Eponi, armed and unarmored, were not an invading force. They weren't even an invading duo.

They were just unlucky.

"Sai?" said a voice near the front as the troops raised their rifles and the Sever two lowered theirs. "What're you doing here?"

The squaddie's commander, a graying, strung-out man who'd been blitzed by a thousand battles and kept coming back for more, emerged from his group with one eye squinting. Jarret Jones, or JJ to the ones he hadn't cared to melt with his rifle, had made a name among DefenseCorp officers as a rank-and-file guy.

JJ liked the mud. He'd stay in it all his life.

"Long story, commander," Sai said. "Could say we're dealing with a problem."

"That problem have anything to do with the alarm?" JJ

said, then noticed the arms up on his squad. "Beacon squad, fan out. Check the corridor and hold the path to the bridge. These two aren't the enemy."

Beacon, a bigger group than Sever and one designated for missions that needed more boots on the ground, took JJ's words as gospel and went to it. For a second, Sai felt like he was a rock placed square in a river's rushing path as the troops washed from the lift and headed towards the bridge.

"Tell me I'm not making a mistake with that order," JJ said, hands flat against his waist, looking up at Sai. "Then keep on talking, because last I heard, you'd bit it on a mission I had no rights to look at."

"You know this guy?" Eponi broke in, eyes flicking back between Sai and JJ.

"First officer I served under with DC," Sai said, "and a damn good one."

"That why you left?" JJ sounded like he needed a cigar. "Beacon too good for you?"

"Beacon didn't pay enough to feed my kids," Sai countered. "Nothing to do with you."

JJ nodded, eyes glimmering as he ran them over Sai and Eponi's arms, "Here's the deal. You two are going to walk to the bridge with me. Beacon's been tasked with making sure we hold it back from any of these jokers attacking our ship. You tell me your story on the way, and make sure to include why you're holding that sword in civilian clothes."

There were people in DC that Sai wouldn't trust with the truth. Ones that would take whatever Sai spilled and find a way to turn it into more cash for themselves, or a possible promotion, or just to nail a deserter. Sai, though, had shared the trenches with JJ. Had ridden alongside the commander into the plasma rebellion on Condor Three.

Had put down an insurrection from the native species on Reader Four.

You don't survive engagements like those without learning a lot about the man beside you.

With Eponi following behind and offering occasional commentary, largely about how much work she'd have to do repairing and cleaning the *Prisa*, Sai described the attacks that'd happened since Sever had found their way back aboard the *Nautilus*.

"So you're telling me our agents, DC agents, are after your squad," JJ mused as they went down the red flashing concourse. Ahead, Beacon, broken into trios, checked and cleared closed meeting rooms with sharp shouts. "Before you get to the why, I don't want to know."

"You don't want to know?"

JJ's eyes flashed forward and he gave the smallest nod towards the squaddies in front, "You keep your place in a company like this by not getting above your pay grade. All these boys and girls are looking to me to keep'em safe, Sai. I'm not going to do that by learning the thing that's getting targets on your back."

"But we didn't try to learn it either," Sai said. "DefenseCorp sent us to Dynas, JJ. It wasn't like we had a choice."

"Bad luck, then," JJ said. "Point being, sounds like you're in a tricky spot. You know I've got no love for the sneaks, Sai. Nobody here does, but they've been infesting our ship like stellar rats lately. It's either we work with'em, or we find a knife in our necks."

Sai could get that. Aurora had mentioned the same philosophy to Sai plenty of times. Keep the squad alive above all else, a responsibility that fell on the commander more than any individual soldier. Except, sometimes, keeping the squad alive meant doing more than what sat immediately in front of you.

Back in the missions-for-money days, Sai had embraced the DefenseCorp mold and kept to his lines. Sever offered harder missions for more money, but otherwise kept things the same: you trained with your squadmates, healed up while in transit, then dropped into a few days of hellish combat before repeating. There hadn't been any reason to look beyond the current objective, no need to think about DefenseCorp's bigger machinations.

"That's not going to work anymore, JJ," Sai said. "Whether you want to believe it or not, DefenseCorp's changing."

"Is it now? Because you happen to be on the outside?"

"Yeah," Sai said, "because I can actually see it now."

"Enlighten me," JJ replied. "If you can do it without getting me killed."

"DC wants you to be better soldiers, but they don't want to do it with equipment," Sai said. "They want to change you, turn you into biological weapons instead of mechanical ones."

JJ laughed, "You just read a book or something? The Raider project ended a long time ago."

Sai'd heard about those, the original super soldier gone far awry. All the maniacal violence, none of the control. Hard to tell if Dynas aimed at something similar, but Helix and DefenseCorp definitely wanted to play with their force's genetic code.

"Don't know about that," Sai said. "Can't tell you much more without spoiling your ignorance, but I'm starting to think DC's preparing to make a play that'll change everything."

"And when it does, I'll react to it," JJ said. "Till then,

how about you two stick with me and we'll get this whole thing sorted out with the admiral?"

JJ asked it like a question, but the real meaning hung in the sentence's shadow: former squadmate or no, if Sai tried to break away, he'd meet with a laser to the back.

They reached the bridge's sealed door, several squaddies forming up around JJ while Beacon's other members continued clearing rooms down the other concourse to the left and right. JJ told Sai and Eponi to sit in the intersection's center, and to keep their rifles down, while he went to the comm panel outside the bridge and tapped his wristlet to it.

"So is your buddy going to bail us out?" Eponi said. "Because from the way he was talking, it sounds like he might bleed DC crimson."

"He's a good man," Sai replied, "but I'd keep your trigger finger twitchy."

"Oh great. Because look at these odds. I should've stayed on the *Prisa.*"

Sai didn't have much to say to that. Didn't have time to say much either, because when JJ stepped away from the panel and his quiet conversation, the bridge doors shuddered, then slid open as the lockdown disengaged.

Aurora stood in the doorway's middle, two crimson-and-black-striped agents behind her with pistols ready. Limping around them came an officer Sai didn't recognize until Eponi hissed that the face came from the video they'd seen on Dynas: plastic and, as Gregor put it, masking a whole lotta fear.

The admiral kept his distance. Deepak stood a ways back into the bridge, talking to some of the staffers. His voice kept things measured, the words saying Deepak was more concerned about the *Nautilus*'s system status and its current direction than the hostage taking happening right outside his bridge.

JJ knew Aurora, maybe not as well as he knew Sai, but the squad commanders all had their own events, their own meet-ups to keep the ship's officers in harmony. Sai wanted, hoped, to see an outburst from JJ, but the stolid commander kept quiet. Stepped back near Sai and Eponi and judged the situation with his granite passivity.

"Commander Jones," the limping officer said. "I don't believe we've ever met? The name's Renard Phyce."

JJ took the offered hand, pumped it once, let it go, "Can't say I've seen you around, sir. Mind filling us in on what's happening here? That's a fine squad captain you have at gunpoint."

There were six Beacon soldiers around them now, all with hands on their rifles. Two agents plus the officer. Sai and Eponi. Without knowing what side JJ and his soldiers would take, Sai couldn't move to slice Aurora free. For her part, Aurora looked a little battered but okay, and she offered Sai a quiet look that said she was fine.

For the moment.

"Nothing less than insubordination, insurrection, and desertion," Renard declared. "Aurora took her squad away after they completed their mission, and now they've returned to take the *Nautilus* with them."

"What?" Eponi said. "Take the *Nautilus*? You're insane."

Renard eyed Eponi, stretched a glistening frown over his lips, "Am I? Aurora tried to assault me on the bridge. She already murdered one of our men. There's no insanity here, just evidence." Renard turned back to JJ. "I assume, commander, that you have good reason for leaving these two traitors armed?"

"Didn't realize they were traitors, officer," JJ said. "We'll get that straightened out. Sai, Eponi, mind setting down your weapons? Don't want to make things spicy now."

"JJ," Sai warned. "This isn't the play to make."

The intersection seemed frozen in space, faces fading to the background as Sai locked gazes with JJ. He tried, by virtue of the telepathy that existed between deep friendships, to convey how bad siding with Renard would be. How wrong.

"Not my choice, Sai," JJ said. "Not that I'm happy about it, but a soldier's a soldier. I'm not in this to make these kind of calls."

The Beacon soldiers came forward, Renard's smug face watching the whole time as JJ's force cleaned out Eponi and Sai. Again, Sai watched his family's katana stolen away from its sheath, taken into the hands of a squaddie that looked at and held the blade as if he had no idea what to do with it.

"Thank you, commander," Renard said. "I have one more request for you. If you would send a couple of your most loyal troops to assist my agents, here, I would like to send these three out the airlock. A summary judgment for their crimes."

"No trial?" JJ said. "Most—"

"Summary judgment, commander," Renard repeated. "In case you've forgotten, the *Nautilus* is under threat. This is not the time to get bogged down in particulars. Defend your ship, defend your admiral, and defend your employer."

"Of course, sir," JJ said, waving over several Beacon soldiers. "I will escort them myself."

"Oh, I don't believe that's necessary," Renard said. "The airlock isn't far. I would rather you remain on the bridge with the admiral and I to ensure we're as safe as possible. There are, I believe, two more Sever members somewhere on this ship.”

Sai saw JJ war with Renard's request. JJ straightened, gave Renard a level look that said he wasn't stupid, then barked the order to the four Beacon soldiers that'd formed around Sai and Eponi.

“Sai,” JJ said as the soldiers took Sai's arms in their own. “It's been an honor. Sorry that things had to end like this.”

“Me too, JJ. Me too,” Sai said as the soldiers formed them up into a line with Aurora.

Together, the three marched towards a nearby emergency airlock, one meant to help evacuate officers if the *Nautilus* fell to enemy fire. One about to be used to send Sever to a frozen, eternal death.

“At least it won't hurt,” Eponi muttered. “Better than what I expected, coming here.”

Sai, though, wasn't paying much attention to Eponi's grumbles. Rather, he had his eyes on Aurora's hands. She kept them loose in front, fingers working ever so slightly in a language few knew, sending a message Sai was all too happy to read:

Be ready.

Diplomacy

GREGOR STOOD INSIDE THE LAVATORY, waiting to the door's left while the squad outside hustled past, heading back towards the med bay. Rovo sat on the toilet itself, taking slow breaths. Fast ones, full ones, hurt the rookie's repaired lungs, so he said.

Carrying Rovo like a child, Gregor had made it away from the medical bots, the curious doctors—one surgeon, apparently realizing Gregor wasn't going to stop, had shouted 'be careful!'—and the two agents after them. The red-lit concourse implied what was about to happen, and after a few seconds clanking down the empty hall, a lift's opening *whoosh* sent Gregor heading into a squat lavatory.

"Hiding in a toilet," Rovo said, coughing as he spoke. "Can't say I pictured this one."

"We do what we must to survive." Gregor looked at himself in the mirror, nodded at the scuffed look. He'd earned those bruises. "Now we have to make a plan."

"A plan?" Rovo braced an arm over his chest. "In case you haven't noticed, this whole ship's in lockdown. The squads are combing the halls. There's no way we'll get back to the *Prisa*. If everyone's even alive anymore."

"They are."

"How do you know?"

"Because we are Sever," Gregor said. "We are better than the ones chasing after us."

"I repeat, we're hiding in a toilet."

"Smarter, too."

The rookie, though, did have a point. Gregor wore beat up civilian clothes, while Rovo still sported a sky blue med bay gown. The rookie didn't have a weapon, didn't even have shoes. Getting anywhere without questions would be difficult. Answering any questions that wouldn't get them shot would be impossible.

Unless.

"We go back for the suit," Gregor said. "Down below."

"Say again?"

Rovo stared at the floor, and Gregor wondered if the rookie was about to evacuate his stomach on the smooth gray tile.

"Back to the labs," Gregor said. "Directly below us. We take the closest lift down one level, and we are there."

"We don't have a wristlet or an ID," Rovo rushed the words out in a burst, then clamped his mouth shut.

"Leave that to me," Gregor replied. "You stay here."

"Can do."

Gregor, never a man for subtlety, neared the lavatory's door and blinked as it whisked open on its own. The red-splashed concourse greeted Gregor, filled with the sounds of a ship in mild panic. Boots clambered along the hallway, their staccato echoes picking up metal tones as they mixed and matched with shouted orders and the occasional over-head broadcast calling squads to their stations.

The big guy had to make a choice when he stepped

outside the bathroom. Either try sneaking, making dashes from one place to another in hopes nobody saw him, or embrace the moment and act like Gregor was right where he ought to be.

Behind him, Rovo groaned.

Now was not the time to learn spy-craft.

Gregor went into the concourse, keeping his arms clear, his shoulders level, and his face patched over with a loose, nervous smile. Like what a civilian caught outside their section during a raid might look like. At least as well as Gregor, a strapping dude who looked like he belonged in a uniform, could pull off.

The nearby lift's bright sign glowed a natural green, radiating near the concourse's ceiling. Beneath it, two soldiers stood with rifles ready. Their eyes scanned the hallway, their arms taut.

Gregor could forgive them the attention. The invasion alarm hadn't been cleared yet, and Deepak's announcement made it seem like the enemies could be anywhere.

"Hello," Gregor said, heading towards the lift and accenting the greeting with a high, friendly wave. "I'm a bit confused. Was in that bathroom there, then I come out and everything's all red?"

The two soldiers looked at him, the farther one walking from his post to join his partner in a visual inspection. Gregor felt the crawling eyes, the analysis taking in his torn shirt, his battered outfit. The soldiers would be creeping towards suspicions Gregor couldn't let them have.

"I know what you're thinking," Gregor said. "That I look like shit. I do, there's no denying, but sometimes we have bad days in the labs."

"The labs," the nearer soldier repeated. Both were low ranks, their protective vests and standard-issue equipment putting them in DC's ground squads. The ones meant for larger engagements. Not quite fodder, not far from it. "What're you doing up here then?"

"Had to visit a friend in the med bay," Gregor said. "Bad timing."

"I've seen better. Do you have any identification?" The soldier directed a pointed stare at Gregor's bare wrists.

"Sorry, no wristlets with the tests we're running. What we're doing would fry them."

Not a bad lie, there. Maybe Gregor ought to try this stuff more often.

"Right," the soldier dragged the word, as if playing out how Gregor would've come up here without the device. "Who's testing with you? Anyone we can call for verification? The ship's under lockdown for potential intruders. We can't let you wander around."

"Okay." Gregor needed a name, any name. His mind went blank. "Gregor, Gregor Evanoff."

The soldier raised his wristlet, started tapping in the name. Gregor took another step closer, mumbling that he could help find the right one. The other soldier did exactly as Gregor hoped, taking the opportunity to look off down the concourse.

As the soldier typed the name—Gregor's own, the only one he came up with in the moment—a different question splashed in. Gregor had been planning a swift punch or two, knocking out the soldiers, followed by a running escape for him and Rovo to the lift and down below.

These soldiers, though, weren't his enemies. Gregor wasn't being paid to beat up random DefenseCorp troops, ones simply doing their jobs as ordered. As Gregor would have been years earlier, during his own early stints with DC.

Back on Wexer, the DefenseCorp forces there had come to take out Sever. Gregor had been fighting for his life and the lives of his friends on that rock ball. Here, that same threat existed, but not from these two.

"That right?" The soldier asked, breaking Gregor's zone.

Every letter held the right position.

"Yes," Gregor said.

The soldier tapped his wristlet. The screen changed as the wristlet searched the *Nautilus* directory, hunting for someone with Gregor's name. After several seconds, the screen flashed red. Nobody in the records with Gregor's name.

An active DefenseCorp trooper for more than a decade, and now Gregor didn't exist.

Before Gregor could reply, behind him and down the concourse, a *whooshing* noise accompanied by a falling body's fat splat on the floor. All eyes went toward's Rovo's form as the rookie propped himself up on an arm, looked their way, and coughed.

"Sorry," Rovo said, his voice carrying and sharing enough weakness to propel the soldiers forward. "Not the entrance I was going for."

"Thought you said you were alone in that lavatory?" the first soldier said to Gregor as they went towards Rovo together.

"I was wrong," Gregor said, "apparently."

The second soldier stopped, took a step to distance himself from Gregor and raised his rifle, "Look, man, this game has been going on too long. You're going to wait there and I'm gonna call someone who can tell me whether or not to shoot you."

"Ever hear of Sever squad?" Gregor asked, pulling at threads to see if anything stuck.

While he asked the question, the first soldier knelt by Rovo. The soldier took a good look at Gregor's wounded squadmate, and cut off any answer to Gregor's question by telling his fellow soldier to call for medical help.

"Don't know what you're talking about," the second soldier looked torn between continuing Gregor's interrogation and following his fellow's command, and Gregor used that indecision.

He knew a rookie when he saw one.

One long step put Gregor past the second soldier's firing field. Before the soldier could back up, Gregor grabbed the rifle's barrel and tore the weapon from the soldier's grip. The straps, left loose in the rapid scramble to get into position, let the weapon pull off the man's shoulders and away into Gregor's hands.

"Don't," Gregor said as the first soldier, recovering faster than his stripped friend, tried to bring his own rifle to bear. "We're not the enemy. Don't want to hurt you. We just need the lift for a minute."

Gregor had his new weapon pointed the right way now, had a clock ticking along in his head telling him it wouldn't be long till another squad happened along and interrupted this lovely get together. Time for Rovo to get rolling.

"Help him up," Gregor said to the first soldier. "He'll be okay."

"Who the hell are you?" asked the second soldier, being smart about it and not reaching for his sidearm.

"Already told you." Gregor back-stepped, put some space between himself and the two soldiers while the first followed orders and helped Rovo to a shaky stand. "Sever squad. We used to be DC."

"Used to be?"

"Mission went bad. We bailed." Gregor started walking backwards, towards the lift entrance. Kept that rifle pointed where business needed doing. "You ever get asked to choose between what's right and what's worth cash, you choose what's right and you'll end up here."

Now the soldiers looked confused, though the first did an able job getting Rovo from one step to the next.

"Here? The *Nautilus*?" The second soldier asked.

"No—" Gregor started, then the second soldier, using Gregor's answer as an opportunity, went for that damn sidearm.

Gregor shot. Pulled the trigger and sent burning energy streaming right at the second soldier's feet before the man's hand had his weapon free. The second soldier reacted the way a smart person would: let his hand walk away, kept his arms wide.

"Another tip," Gregor said, feeling the lift doors against his back. "Don't use the same trick I just used on you. It is boring." With his left hand, Gregor gestured at the lift's panel. "Call it, please."

The first soldier, still with his rifle strapped over his chest, still helping Rovo walk, though at least the rookie had his eyes open now, tapped his wristlet against the lift panel. Had a mouth that looked to be breathing, even if speaking seemed beyond the rookie.

Not a bad thing. Rovo always talked too much.

"You won't get far, you know," the second soldier, determined to stick with his bravado, said. "The *Nautilus* is awake now. Squads are everywhere. We'll find you."

"As I said, we are not the problem." Gregor felt the lift thrumming behind his back. Soon. "The ones in crimson and black are your real enemies. They are crawling around this ship, and will stab you in your sleep."

The lift shunted open behind him. Gregor watched the soldier's eyes to see if the lift had anyone on it, but their stares stayed on him. An empty vessel. Gregor sent his left arm out wide.

"Pass the boy here," Gregor said, and the first soldier obliged. Rovo took his freedom to half walk, half fall to Gregor, who backed into the lift.

The first soldier played it smart, didn't take the chance to reach for his rifle. A cooler head that'd live to see another day. Or at least another minute.

"Remember what I said." Gregor drifted to the lift's left side, where another panel waited for him to choose a destination. "Crimson and black. Those are the ones to watch."

When the lift doors closed, the two young soldiers still stood there, still watched Gregor, as if he and Rovo were ghosts in a story they didn't quite understand.

FOURTEEN

Vacuum Twist

YOU MIGHT THINK, growing up around space, jumping to the stars, leaping between worlds, and surfing the nebulas, that vacuum wouldn't be all that frightening. Like an omnipresent danger, it would fade into the background of her life, a whisper informing every action with a little extra caution. Don't mess up that repair, push that button, or open that hatch or you'd find all your air sucked away and your insides popping out like some horror show balloon.

And yet. And yet.

Eponi still felt her heart pick up whenever she thought back to the moment over Dynas, to the creeping along the gray tunnel connecting her kidnapped shuttle to Anaskya's ship and its salvation. The whip-sawing tube, the crackling as the oxygen feed from her ship to Anaskya's tangled itself up and threatened to rip Eponi loose.

So she had her mouth shut tight, her legs feeling locked as she walked in step with the four soldiers, two agents, Sai and Aurora towards the nearest *Nautilus* airlock. The standard deserter sentence: banished out into the cold dark to float until some gravity well burned you to cinders. A risk

Eponi had accepted when she'd bounced along with Sever in their desertion post-Dynas, one that, in the somewhat adrenaline-fueled heyday after escaping that damned swamp of a world, felt like it'd never arrive.

"How about we substitute the punishments?" Eponi said, as neither Sai nor Aurora seemed to be talking. The soldiers and agents, too, were quiet, and, dammit, Eponi couldn't take that anymore. "You can take these two out the airlock. I'm sure they'd love it. Go right ahead. But me? I'm thinking you still have a use for a skilled pilot. Shuttles that need landing and so on."

Nobody replied. The agents, the soldiers, didn't bother looking her way. They kept their pistols focused where they belonged as their booted steps marched through the red-lit concourse. Beacon squad expanded its reach around the bridge, clearing one room after another, and eventually the little death squad passed beyond their assigned radius. Alone, now, in their march.

"Do you all, like, not talk?" Eponi said. "Is this a new rule, that while doing an execution the victims don't exist?"

"Orders," one of the soldiers on Eponi's right said, and she, at least, didn't sound all that thrilled to be doing this. "The only reason you're talking with us is to argue for your life, or get us to make a different decision. By not engaging, we can preserve the objective."

"Oh, what the hell kinda words are those?" Eponi said as the airlock's signage came into view. "Are you a robot or something?"

"Just repeating the same guidelines you signed onto when you joined DefenseCorp."

"Well, they suck. And you suck for listening to them. If you're going to flush me down the cosmic toilet, the least you could do is give me one last conversation to enjoy."

Another soldier snickered, a laugh that cut Eponi the

wrong way. Yeah, she knew she'd been playing to a certain tone with her words, a certain carefree hopelessness at her journey's end, but actually getting a laugh punctured the veil.

If she was going to die, might as well make it count.

Eponi went for an agent first. The action didn't form as a coherent plan, more like an instinctual rush, guided by the crimson and black stripes walking a little ahead and to her left, pistol out and pointed Sai's way. The soldiers walking behind were the insurance, the agents the drivers.

Training directed her attack, a simultaneous jabbing with her left arm while her right pulled at the agent's second pistol in its holster. The agent shouted—squawked, more like—as Eponi made contact, her left arm doing a dirty stick into the agent's side while her body served to block the agent's pistol from making any decent aim at her.

Rifles rose, zeroed in as Eponi yanked her new pistol up against the agent's chin. The agent himself froze at the barrel's touch to his bare skin, a reaction Eponi considered eminently sane and utterly useless. She'd been expecting a fiery death and instead wound up in a hostage situation, one Eponi had no chance of winning.

Seven faces watched her, five of those with weapons aimed her way, each one trying to gauge whether or not they could hit a shot between her eyes that wouldn't turn the agent into smoking ruin. A truly tricky dilemma.

"Sorry, friends," Eponi said, snuggling up close to the agent and making as little daylight between his uniform and her beat-up civilian crapshoot as possible. "I've never been known to go quietly. Couldn't make this one an exception."

Her sardonic look, a half-smile and playful, maybe manic eyes danced among her audience. Eponi caught a slight hitch when she made it to Aurora and Sai, the ones who should've been on her side, but who now looked like she'd broken the rules to some game. Annoyance ran rampant over their features, and the sobering dose did what it could to quell Eponi's enthusiasm for her wicked way out.

"You're going to let him go," said the other agent, in a voice that said it'd done far too many interrogations with pliant prisoners. Eponi ought to fold, that voice said. Ought to accept fate because she deserved it. "You're going to drop the pistol right now, and when you do, you'll get what's coming to you and no worse."

"It's not a bad way to go," the soldier who'd talked with Eponi said. "I've seen it enough times. Quick, painless."

"Oh, you know it's painless?" Eponi said, choosing to engage with the soldier, with the one that sounded, a little, like she had a soul. "You ever interview someone who's sucked vacuum?"

"You know what I mean."

"Do I?" Eponi jammed the pistol further into the agent's chin, drawing out a heated grunt from the man. "Do I look like someone who knows what you mean?"

The other agent adjusted his aim, moved his body to his right, and Eponi lurched the agent that way. The move exposed her right side to the soldiers, and they knew it. Time was up.

"Drop the pistol or we shoot," another soldier said, a command this time.

Blast to the side, or vacuum? Eponi had to choose here and now and you know, faced with those options, there was only one way to go.

So Eponi pushed the agent away from her, dropping the pistol away from the man's chin and, in the same movement, aiming towards the other agent and pulling the trigger. The bright red bolt flashed, caught the other agent in the shoulder. Sent him burning to the floor.

No shots hit Eponi in the split second after, so she sent her aim rightward and blasted her former hostage in the back, sent him spilling to the deck. Two for one so far, not a bad deal. Now time to face the overwhelming odds and get herself sent along to the next life.

Sai pulled Eponi's arm down, leaving her to face four raised rifles without a weapon.

"Stop, you maniac," Sai said, keeping Eponi's arm at her side. "Don't make them shoot you."

"Make them shoot me? Isn't that their job?"

Eponi struggled against Sai's hold until Aurora went between the pilot and the soldiers. Rather than making a panicked lunge for the soldier's weapons, or getting into a fistfight looking for a miracle, Aurora seemed utterly calm.

"Thanks for holding your fire," Aurora said as Eponi relaxed, as Eponi started to think she might *not* be reduced to ash in the next few seconds. "She's a spark."

"You talking about me?" Eponi said.

"I am, and you'll be quiet now, before I let these soldiers shoot you," Aurora replied, before turning back to the foursome. "You understand what you're doing?"

"The *Nautilus* doesn't belong to them, commander," said the woman who'd been batting it back and forth with Eponi. "It belongs to us. We're going to go back to JJ and report mission accomplished."

"And if Renard asks about the agents?"

"They left," the soldier replied. "Didn't say where."

"Exactly," Aurora said. "Get to it."

Three of the soldiers picked up the agents and carried them over to the airlock, after Aurora re-armed herself with their pistols. A soldier returned Sai's sword. Eponi watched the whole dance with increasing confusion until

Sai and Aurora steered her down the concourse, away from the bridge and towards the *Nautilus*'s fighter bays, situated above the bigger berths for ships like the *Prisa*. The fourth soldier followed them, rifle loose and matching the smile on the man's face.

"Okay," Eponi said as they went. "I've kept quiet as long as I think is reasonable. What the hell was that?"

Aurora and Sai looked at each other, before Aurora took the lead, "You haven't been in DefenseCorp all that long, Eponi. And you jumped right in as a pilot, right?"

"Right. Pay was way better doing that than the grunt route."

"Exactly. DC has its divisions, and they work together when they need to, but there's not much love between the backstabbers and us."

"The backstabbers? Really?"

"Really," Sai said. "Bastards always have something awful in mind."

"So, you're saying—"

"Beacon, like most other squads on this ship, knows better than to trust what's going on here," Aurora said. "Deepak told me agents have been infesting *Nautilus* for a while now, before we even went for Dynas. Which means Renard's whole thing isn't just about us, but something bigger. The soldiers don't want to play his game."

"Isn't that insubordination?" Eponi said. "Couldn't they get launched from the airlock, same as us?"

"Deepak's their admiral," Sai replied. "Renard's not even in their chain of command. He can say what he wants, but the soldiers don't have to do crap unless Deepak says. It's right in the agreement we signed." Sai cocked his head as they reached a lift. "Or didn't you read the fine print?"

"You did?"

"DefenseCorp's not a government, is the thing. We're private employees, signing on to work in a branch of our choosing," Sai explained, in that patient voice he used whenever he wanted to be Sever's dad-in-chief. Eponi normally hated the tone, but here, stuck in the whirlwind after nearly getting vacuumed, the gentle facts wrapped her like a warm, reasonable blanket. "Aurora and I couldn't tell whether the soldiers would hold true to that or not, but when they didn't shoot you right away?"

"We picked our side," the soldier finally spoke up. "JJ made it clear back in the barracks. We work for Deepak, not the damn agents." The soldier tapped his wristlet against the lift, calling the transport to their level. "You all good from here? I can't be gone long or it'll be noticed."

"We'll be fine," Aurora said. "Thanks for the assist."

The soldier dashed off a quick DefenseCorp salute and jogged back down the corridor. Matching that departure, the lift door swung open, offering Sever their own escape. The three piled in, and Aurora punched the docking bay level.

"Okay, so we're not dead," Eponi said. "Which I approve of. And there's a sort of rebellion going on in here, which is great. Still have to ask, though, why are we going back to the docking bays?"

"Because the *Nautilus* is under attack," Aurora said. "Time to make it convincing."

FIFTEEN

Paper Thin

SKINNED KNEES. A broken wrist from a bad fall off a bike pedaling around the neighborhood. Rovo hadn't suffered a worse injury until he came all the way to DefenseCorp, where within a matter of months he'd taken training and then real lasers to the chest, to the back, to knees and arms and to the face. Power armor and protective vests had blunted most of those, and what made it through had been patched up by the *Nautilus*'s medical staff, much like this one.

Except he'd never taken a shot to the lungs like this. No protection aside from his casual shirt, the wound hurt more than the rubble falling from the collapsing tower on Wexer. The med bay's drugs blunted the sting for a while, though their side effects twisted Rovo's other insides into knots, blurring his vision until his every glance felt like it'd been smeared with oil.

Every breath scratched and burned, as if the oxygen Rovo inhaled had to push through a charred, spongey forest.

What Rovo needed, wanted was a bed and a long week to recover.

Instead, Rovo had Gregor's thick arm hooked under his shoulders, holding him up as their lift opened back onto the very floor that'd earned Rovo his blast wounds.

"Oh hurrah," Rovo said as the doors revealed the familiar, warning-sign filled concourse.

Like the one upstairs, like all the hallways on the *Nautilus*, this one glowed red. The invaders might make it down here too, steal some big DefenseCorp secret and make off with it. Dastardly pirates, taking what didn't belong to them.

Of course, the pirates were them. Sever Squad, a bunch of thieving malcontents. That's what Rovo had been reduced to, his glorious—

"Focus." Gregor pulled Rovo from the lift, into the concourse and towards the doorway to the very particular room, *Weapons 3*. "Not much farther."

"For you, maybe," Rovo said. "For me, this is a marathon."

"Then run it."

No sympathy from this guy. Gregor always seemed so hell bent on the mission. Couldn't be bothered with an iota of compassion.

"You hate me, Gregor?" Rovo said. "Cause, like, I'm not a fan of this gruff attitude."

Gregor didn't stop moving. Though Rovo found it hard to find distinct shapes with his warping vision, it didn't seem like anyone had yet claimed this concourse. No squad running through here. Perhaps because the weapons labs were about as deep within the *Nautilus* as you could get: if invaders made it this far, they probably had the ship.

"You are delirious," Gregor said. "Walk. It will be easier."

Sure, easier for him maybe. As Gregor reached the door, he let Rovo stand on his own while the big man puzzled over the *Weapons 3* door. Already a notice hung outside, closing off the room due to an accident. The badge scanner, hunting for a wristlet, shone its angry red at them, a hue that matched well with the concourse's current color.

Wonder if they'd coordinated that, whomever designed all this.

"Hey," Rovo said, tottering towards the wall and catching himself with a flimsy arm. "You think this was all planned?"

"Yes," Gregor said. "From the moment we broke out from the facility on Wexer, I believe whomever commands these agents decided to bring us to the *Nautilus* with the best bait they could offer. Maybe they really want Kaia, but more, I believe they want us dead."

"Sure, that's what I meant," Rovo said, chasing the connections Gregor made like a dog jumping at falling leaves. He caught one or two and let the rest go. "There's no way they think they can keep Dynas a secret. Too many people."

"Not forever," Gregor said. "Just long enough. We deserted, they panicked."

"Because we'd ruin their party?" Rovo leaned full back against the concourse wall, stared across the way at a poster that demanded safety first with a vested-up scientist holding a thumbs-up to the camera. "Like, why?"

"Fear makes people do stupid things."

Rovo could agree with that. Not that he'd known real fear, not really. Even on Dynas, the chaos and alienation of the whole mission trumped any fear for himself. Wexer, well, Wexer had been a desperate scramble for the Talpa. Even here, even feeling his lungs struggle through every breath, fear wasn't at the top of his emotional list.

Didn't mean Rovo couldn't do stupid things, though.

"You going to get through this door any time soon?" Rovo asked as Gregor continued to stare at the panel.

"I am not sure," Gregor replied. "I had hoped to find another person down here to leverage."

"Why not use that rifle?"

"Shooting the panel won't work," Gregor said. "They are protected."

"You know that, huh?"

"The movies are the movies. This is reality, rookie."

Rovo nodded, a motion that slung his head forward and back farther than he expected. Muscle control still lacking. He plastered both palms against the concourse walls to steady himself.

"Then how about you shoot the door?" Rovo said. "Try the very middle."

Gregor stepped back from the panel. Inspected the door. Seemed skeptical.

"Listen, man," Rovo said. "There's budgets for every-thing. They're not gonna blast proof every door on the ship, and why do it to these?"

"Because these are weapons labs?"

"Yeah, and you can secure these with blast doors, but I don't see them on right now." The thoughts came flowing from some inner mist, an epiphany series made possible because Rovo no longer felt any idea was dumb, was too far-fetched. "Like, who'd bother if there's not an active experiment going on inside?"

Gregor issued a combination growl-sigh that carried withering contempt Rovo's way, but the rookie, flush with the invincible glow of the nearly dead and drugged, shrugged it off and pulled himself another meter away from the door. Gregor backed into the concourse's center, aimed the rifle, and, with one last eye roll towards Rovo, pulled the trigger.

Ten blue bolts blitzed into the door's silver body, sinking into the barrier and leaving charred holes. Thin metal not designed to handle energy and heat curled away along the bolt edges, leaving a riddled portal begging to be kicked in.

"What'd I tell you?" Rovo said.

"Perhaps I give you too little credit." Gregor went up to the door and delivered a full kick.

The weakened panel crumpled and swung in, its leftward ties clinging with enough strength to prevent the door's total collapse. Even so, the wreck could no longer be called a barrier.

"See?" Rovo said, once more adopting his position on Gregor's shoulder. "I'm always right."

"Are you?" Gregor questioned seconds later as they stood in a cycling room that, believing the main door open—a correct belief, really—kept its inner portal shut. "Then, what do you say to this?"

"If it worked once, it'll work twice?"

Rovo wouldn't call himself a genius—at least, not out loud—but whatever those surgeons had given him had turned his brain to straight fire. He sat on the little chamber's floor and watched Gregor laser some more shots over him, laughed a hoarse chuckle as they punctured the inner door just like they had its outer brethren. Gregor delivered another solid kick and they were inside.

The huge power armor hung down in the room's middle, unchanged. Blast scars littered the floor behind it, where Rovo had struggled for his life. The control center sported its own additions, blacked and sparking as Gregor's shots pierced the door and carried right on through.

"Can't say I wanted to see this room again," Rovo said.

"Then don't."

Gregor, a born comedian.

The twist came when Rovo, fully expected to be Gregor's dragged-along load for this venture, found his muscle-bound sidekick lifting him up and carrying Rovo towards the armor.

"Hate to break it to you, friend, but I'm not going to fit in that thing," Rovo said as Gregor propped him up in front of the open suit.

"It will adjust."

"That'll take a lot of adjusting."

"Be quiet, rookie, and stand still."

Well, fine then. Rovo would wait for the suit to prove Gregor wrong. With his blurred vision, Rovo found the green-lit scanning lights a wince-inducing trip. The suit hissed, clanked, and popped as its various slats, gears, and bolts adjusted to accommodate Rovo's more, uh, svelte form. While the armor's full size stayed the same, inner layers pulled in tighter, finally blinking ready with a bright chirp wildly at odds with the armor's purpose.

"In you go," Gregor said, and pushed.

Rovo didn't have time to protest. He fell into the armor, his lungs taking a painful bump as Rovo's body settled into creases. The armor registered his approached, snapped into place. The visor came to life, and strange lines began scrolling across the screen over his eyes. Lines reading about adjustments to the pilot, compensating for his injuries, for his altered vision.

His mouth dropping open as much as the helmet would let him, Rovo felt the armor deploy its own medical advice. New pricks dotted Rovo's skin as the suit injected him with emergency fluids, with adrenaline to keep him alert, with further numbing agents to keep away his recent surgery's pain.

"How?" Rovo asked when the suit settled into its steady operating state, leaving Rovo feeling, if not incredible, then at least functional.

"I noticed the evaluation before," Gregor said, standing right where Rovo had stood before Zaydi went all assassin on him. "The suit, I believe it is meant for endurance operations. Long term, little reinforcement."

"Keep the soldier going." At first, Rovo admired the ingenuity, then he realized what it would actually mean. "So they could send us out further, for longer."

Gregor nodded, "Perhaps it is good we retired when we did."

"Retired? Sure."

Rovo and Gregor continued talking over plans while the rookie felt out the suit. The control center's blast-bolt scarring didn't prevent Gregor from releasing the power armor from its restraints, and Rovo waddled, then walked, then even lunged across the room with it. For all its fancy life-saving enhancements, the power armor still felt familiar: kinetic boosters, weight compensators for every limb, and a visor that would pick up potential threats and splash them across his screen.

That last pronounced itself as Rovo completed another loop, making sure he could move both the legs and arms simultaneously without passing out. Despite the power armor's assistance, the damn stuff was still heavy, and definitely not within the surgeon's medical advice for Rovo's recovery.

The visor splashed red behind, and then, as Rovo turned, in front. Red tended to mean weapons out and pointed at the suit, or close enough that the suit's billion cameras could consider them threats.

This time, those threats belonged to two agents, their crimson-and-black uniforms clogging up the small doorway Gregor had blown apart.

"Company," Gregor said as Rovo put himself square between the agents and his squad mate. "Your lead?"

"For once, yes," Rovo agreed. "Can you handle me protecting you?"

The agents, both looking too fresh-faced to know what they were getting into, had pistols raised. While they'd looked about to come running into the room, seeing Rovo prompted a hasty retreat, followed by a shouted threat to disarm and surrender.

"I do not need protecting," Gregor replied, "but it would be amusing to see you crush them."

"So we're not surrendering?"

"I think not."

"Okay then."

Rovo stomped towards the small chamber, twisting sideways to let the armor fit through. Even with the turn, he mashed off the door remnants, cracking through into the concourse with a drunken buffoon's grace.

The two agents had split apart, one facing Rovo's back, the other his face. Both fired their pistols, the measly bolts splashing off the armor without the slightest effect. Despite his burned lungs, his bruised bones, and a drug-dulled headache, Rovo swung up a cocky smile, reading the suit's kinetic boosters for combat.

He might have some fun today after all.

Behind The Glass

IT TOOK a week after the mission, but eventually her captain told Aurora to do something about Deepak hanging around after their training sessions. Aurora laid it out for the junior officer, told Deepak straight out that Sever, like all the other squads, was here for the cash.

"And we're damn good," Aurora continued as they shared another mess hall lunch. "Give us what we've earned."

Deepak didn't back down from the criticism, didn't try to toss it off but met Aurora's suggestion with the seriousness she put into it. He set his fork and knife down, stuck out a hand, and Aurora, after giving it a quizzical eye, shook it.

"You want a starring role, you got it," Deepak said. "You're right, you can handle it."

The next job would be a few weeks away, and Sever spent those weeks jazzed up, training harder than before. In the hours between training sessions, Aurora tweaked her power armor, went to extra briefings for anyone interested in squad leadership—and the extra cash that came with it, and kept running into Deepak.

Lunches, dinners, and some nights burned on the *Nautilus* observation deck, talking shop and a little bit of everything else. Aurora didn't even have trouble admitting she liked Deepak, his cheery devotion to duty, and the man did have a way of getting the best wines on the cruiser. She found the fastest, least traveled routes from his cabin to hers and back again, a mission for two.

And when the assignment came, and Deepak dropped Sever right where they wanted to be, he didn't wink Aurora's way this time. Instead, Sever earned Deepak's trusted look, and Aurora matched his steady stare.

Ready.

Finally.

THE WALK TO THE AIRLOCK, where Aurora, Sai, and Eponi were supposed to be cast out in to the black ether, proved to be a fertile opportunity to delve for ideas. When you're steps away from death, there's a freedom that sinks in, shaping the possibilities and letting the creative ones rise up and gain purchase.

Renard, the bastard that'd infiltrated the *Nautilus* with his swarming agents, felt he had control. He could snap his fingers and have a cadre of undercover gunners burst forth and demand his desires at rifle's end. Even so, the *Nautilus* held thousands upon thousands of DefenseCorp squaddies. Soldiers that owed their allegiance to the admiral and to DefenseCorp's boots-on-the-ground division. Most squads had commanders that, like Aurora, kept DefenseCorp's clandestine arm at, well, arm's length.

All too often, the pre-mission intelligence had turned

into a strategy of soaking the adversary in bodies until they gave up. Those bodies were never agents.

"Which is why, if we make it clear to this ship what's going on, we'll get the troopers on our side," Aurora said as they headed down the red-lit concourse towards the docking berths. "We'd outnumber the agents, and we could kick them off this ship."

"Still don't get why you think they'd all fight for us," Eponi said. "What's Deepak going to do when Renard tells him to ignore your order?"

"He won't have a chance," Aurora replied. "Because you're not going to give Deepak or Renard a choice."

"Sounds like I'm not going to be thrilled with what you say next."

As if Aurora cared. Eponi would pull off what her commander needed her to, not because Aurora had any real standing in their post-DefenseCorp hierarchy, but because if Eponi did anything different, she'd wind up dead.

After dishing out the details to the pilot, Aurora dropped Eponi and Sai off at the *Prisa*'s berth. Aurora took their weapons, excepting Sai's sword, and with a promise to contact after carrying out the plan, set off on her own.

Convincing a ship that the attackers weren't coming in from the outside but were, instead, seeded from within wouldn't be easy. The change had to be hard, had to be total. Make every squad treat anyone else as a threat.

And bet that the agents, once threatened, would give themselves up.

The *Nautilus* had its massive bridge, and most communications routed through there. But not all. Ships this large needed a back-up base, a place that could become the de facto command deck if the bridge were incapacitated by enemy fire or accident. The *Nautilus* had its comm center on the second level, by the Quartermaster and above the engines.

Opposite the bridge, with maximum protection.

Walking the corridor, solitary in the red, tangled with her memory's expectations. The *Nautilus* existed to be loud. To be active. For its concourses to churn with business being done. With every echoing step along the clear floor, the ship's wrongness increased. As if Aurora had transplanted away from reality to a cleaner, more terrible fiction.

Deepak's own actions added to the corrosion. He'd been Aurora's sometime friend, always respected colleague, and yet, he'd twisted Renard's knife. There were a thousand things the admiral could've done to warn Aurora, to warn Sever. In the quiet corridor, Aurora counted them off as she walked, from secret secondary transmissions, to written notes, to squad codewords that the agents watching him might not understand.

"Was it really because you care so damn much about this ship?" Aurora asked herself as she passed the last berth, where the *Nautilus* transitioned from shipping to everything supporting the big craft.

The idea didn't make any sense. The agents were always a tighter, smaller force. They could never take the *Nautilus* unless Renard pulled every agent from everywhere and stuck them on the ship, an impossibility. Deepak had to be misreading the situation, or he knew something big Aurora couldn't guess.

Ahead, after a brief section allayed to rapid refining for volatile materials taken off visiting vessels, the Quartermaster's glowing letters pulled Aurora forward. Still nobody, which seemed odd, considering the invasion order. *Nautilus* squads should've been pressing the berths, securing places like the Quartermaster that could be valuable to an attacking enemy.

But if the troopers weren't here, then where?

The Quartermaster's ten window slots were shut, presenting a long wall without much else going for it. At the far end, Aurora could make out the transition, with blue flagging banners, to the secondary comm center. Thus far, the deserted march had been eerie, but hardly dangerous. After nearly getting spaced, Aurora wouldn't complain.

The peace lasted till she passed by the third window. Aurora kept her pistol drawn, held down by her waist, so hard it whipped up and ready as the blind retracted. Her trigger finger exercised restraint when Aurora saw an older woman standing behind an assistance bot, using the thing's spindly arms for cover.

"Don't tell me that was an accident." Aurora etched her words with knives.

"No, no," the woman replied, "I have to talk to you before you make a mistake."

"Then talk."

The woman shook her head, "Not here. They're waiting for you now, but they'll come looking soon enough." To Aurora's left, between the fourth and fifth window, a service door whisked open. "Come back, where it's safe."

Behind the Quartermaster's counters? Even discounting the current situation, Aurora hadn't ever been back there. The place had so many safeguards, security, and audits that any squaddie dumb enough to go digging would find themselves busted back to guard duty in seconds.

Curiosity, and the woman's hinting at an ambush much

further down the line, pushed Aurora to the service door and through it. Caution kept Aurora's pistol raised.

After a meter long entryway, Aurora found the secret kept behind the closed windows and the counters and the bots: the Quartermaster's storage spaces were beautiful. Goods stacked atop shelves went back as far as Aurora could see—or, at least, that's what the crystalline lighting made it feel like. The item menagerie required to fulfill the *Nautilus*'s staff's myriad needs clustered in long rows, criss-crossing here and there as deemed appropriate by whatever gods controlled this packaged paradise.

The flowing compliments advancing through Aurora's impressions spawned from the rainbow brilliance decorating each row, each section, each container. As if cloaked in flickering wisps, every spot stretching in every forward direction from Aurora seemed to catch a luminescent fire, the shelves aglow, their items little miracles to be chosen by the lucky bots.

"A bit much, isn't it?" The woman who'd invited Aurora said, now freed from her bot shield. "I see you're having the same reaction most do when they come back for the first time." She laughed once, a pin prick thing. "It's all pretty when you see it once. Try staring at it for hours and days and years."

"But . . . why?" Aurora couldn't help but ask. That such a resplendent space had been hidden back here all along, and Aurora was no beauty admirer, seemed a crime. "What's the point?"

"Oh, it's all for the bots. The reflected lights tell them at a distance precisely what items among our millions are located where. It's all very sophisticated."

Aurora knew a hint when she heard one. The woman hadn't called her back here to discuss the Quartermaster's intricacies. With effort, Aurora turned her eyes away from the shimmers and focused on the woman, on the still bots behind her, waiting at closed windows for customers that wouldn't come.

"So I'm here," Aurora said, remembering she still held her pistol and choosing not to hold it in the woman's face. The Quartermaster staffer had on her uniform, had her hands visible, and looked about as threatening as a furry Talpa back on Wexer. "What'd you want to tell me?"

"That your plan won't work."

"And you know my plan how?"

The woman cocked her head in the look given by the patient to their lessers, "You should be dead, and instead you're here, heading towards the comm center. It doesn't take much to discern your intentions."

Aurora shrugged, "So?"

"So perhaps you ought to change your tactics," the woman said. "I gave an associate of yours a little drive. On it, there is information that would help you. Did he give it to you, by chance?"

"An associate?" Aurora said. "And no, I don't have any drive."

"Of course you don't." The woman clicked her tongue, waved back at the shiny inventory. "All of this is going to be turning against us very soon. DefenseCorp is making changes, and when they're finished, you and I and every other soldier aboard this ship will be unnecessary."

Aurora stepped back from the woman, bought space to bring her pistol to bear, "You're not just some Quarter-master aide, are you?"

"Look what we have here," the woman said, more to the bot on her left than to Aurora. "Rare are such smarts in the squads."

The squads? Every slur had its origins, its home. Squads, said that way, was no different.

"Agent," Aurora said, this time bringing the pistol right up and ready. "Cut the cryptic words and tell me why I shouldn't burn you right here?"

If the threat had any effect, the woman didn't show it, "Tell me, Aurora. Why did you choose to join Sever squad?"

"Don't play games," Aurora replied. "My friends are in trouble, and I don't have time."

That, at least, seemed to get a respectful nod. Maybe the agent figured Aurora didn't know much more than guns and runs, but at least Aurora stuck to her priorities.

"Fine. Not all of us want what Renard's after," the woman said. "If there's any part of DefenseCorp that would have a hidden group working against it, it would be ours. The *Nautilus* is on the front line of a larger plan, one you stumbled on by accident because that scientist couldn't take Dynas any longer."

Aurora trimmed through the words, looking for the meat behind the fat.

"So you want us to stop Renard," Aurora said, "from whatever he's planning. Already on it, in case you hadn't noticed."

"Oh, not just Renard," the woman said. "DefenseCorp is at an inflection point. Cash is no longer enough for some who see an opportunity in a galaxy without competition. We must remind them that the punishment for power is too severe for their ambitions."

"Talk straight."

The woman sighed, "You want your objective? You want your insurrection on this ship? Then let me help. Perhaps we can both get what we're looking for in the end."

"Great. Glad you're in," Aurora started back towards the door and the concourse on its other side. "Coming?"

"One moment," the woman said. "Before we go rushing off into the enemy, why don't we make sure we're prepared?"

Aurora looked at her pistol, a standard-issue thing with a power pack good for a few dozen shots before dwindling to empty. The agent might have a point.

"Okay, but quick," Aurora said, then snapped her left hand's fingers when the agent started back towards the stacks, drawing the woman's look her way. "And what's your name?"

"Vana," the woman replied. "Though you won't find anything if you go looking."

Aurora shook her head as they headed back into the stacks, hunting weapons. Always like an agent to assume an agenda.

Vana wasn't wrong, but Aurora didn't care about her. She had more important agents to destroy, squadmates to save.

Follow The Plan

THE *PRISA* SAT where Sai and Eponi had left it. A stain still marred the docking bay floor leading from the doors to the craft's boarding ramp, now sinking down to meet them after Eponi entered in the unlocking code on the *Prisa*'s front strut. Unlike the concourse, the docking bay kept its silver-white lighting, its quiet sounds, its empty feel.

"For a ship being invaded, it's real calm," Sai quipped as the *Prisa*'s ramp touched down.

"Aren't we supposed to change that?"

Aurora had mentioned the scare tactic as the plan, and the trio had discussed a way to do it. A way that sounded difficult in conversation and loomed even worse as Eponi and Sai stepped up to put it into practice.

"It's not going to be easy," Sai said as they went up the ramp. "You ever lead an attack on a ship before?"

"Sai, I'm a kart racer." Eponi threw a disgusted look at the charred bits still clinging to the *Prisa*'s center floor. "Besides, when was the last time DefenseCorp sent us into a space conflict?"

Not for a long time. Sever had its role to play, one tied

to ground-based assaults. The *Nautilus* wasn't a nimble vessel out doing pirate hunts or clamping down on any feisty corporate fleets daring DefenseCorp's space security dominance. Rather, Deepak's mammoth force slugged its way from world to world, hanging in the skies and sending its doom-dealing waves planetside.

"Guess we'll have to learn quick," Sai said. "Which turret do you want me in?"

"Neither." Eponi kept going towards the cockpit. "Less accurate, but you can control'em both from here. If we get into an actual dogfight, we're done anyway, so you might as well stay where I can blame you when things go wrong."

"I'm thrilled."

"Bet you are."

The *Prisa*'s cockpit presented four seats in a two-by-two formation, giving the pilot and co-pilot front and center while the back two offered views and consoles for systems management. Coming from a career in drop shuttles, where Sai spent his time locked into a gunnery system in the back, sitting somewhere he could see much of anything felt novel.

"You ever done this before?" Eponi said as Sai pecked at the consoles, flipping them between engine power, shield strength, weapons.

"Actually, no." Sai swiped, found both turrets and split their controls to his screen's sides. "I literally use the fingers to point and shoot?"

"You literally do."

"This is going to be terrible." Most gunnery systems gave you handles, a smooth glide to send your barrels pointing where you wanted them. Sai tried aiming right there in the bay, and getting a fixed look at the doorway took multiple swerving swipes. "How could you hit anything like this?"

"I'll have you recall what I said a minute ago. If we get into a dogfight, we're gonna lose," Eponi said. "If that actually happens, I'll flip the turrets to automated control till you get back to one. But let's hope Aurora's plan sticks and we don't have you play laser jockey."

"I'm good with that."

Sai didn't want to consider going automated. Setting a computer to run the targeting sounded like the best thing, with the fast reflexes, precision calculations, and all that. Instead, turning the shooting over to an AI meant teaching it, in the middle of the fight, whether a target was an enemy or a friend, whether to go for the kill or disable it, how much energy to spend. A complicated nest not worth tackling while someone else shot hot laser into your hull.

The *Prisa* floated off the bay's floor as Eponi activated the engines. The struts retracted as the comm system bubbled with the first outreach from the *Nautilus*. Eponi glanced at the incoming hail, and when she didn't answer it, Sai did.

"Don't want them to trap us in here, do you?" Sai said.

"Oh, you're going to charm them with your smooth talking?" Eponi fired back.

The officer on the comm system's other side coughed, a loud one with a single purpose. Sai and Eponi shut up, though she rotated the *Prisa* so its nose faced the closed bay shield leading into space. The blank metal wall presented the primary barrier to vacuum, supplemented by the commonplace magnetic shielding meant to keep oxygen from blowing out every time a craft came and went.

"Uh, *Prisa*, we're under lockdown at the moment," the officer on the comm said. "We have to keep the doors shut until the situation returns to normal."

"Do you know what the situation is?" Sai asked as Eponi charged up the weapons, sending energy that would be pushed to the *Prisa*'s engines into the batteries that'd turn it into scalding light. "Because I guarantee it's not what you think."

"I'm not sure what you mean," the officer replied after a long pause. "The codes are clear. There are dangerous—"

"And what if the people calling the codes are the dangerous ones?" Another long pause. Sai muted his end, turned to Eponi. "Are you thinking we burn our way out?"

"I'm thinking we give this guy one chance to save his ship some painful scars."

Sai nodded, unmuted himself as the officer finished up some rambling excuse. There were always those, the excuses. Anyone who didn't want to see could find ways to stay blind.

"Here's what you're going to do," Sai said, "and you're going to do this not because it's in your code list, or because a superior officer told you to. You're going to follow my directions because a little ship like ours can't hurt the *Nautilus* from the outside, but in here? We're plenty dangerous."

Nothing like threatening your former home.

The officer, apparently unfamiliar with assaults coming from inside his own docking bay, went dark again. Sai gave him two heartbeats, then went back to his turrets.

"Ready to go?" Sai asked Eponi. "Odds are they're sending a squad our way."

"Oh no," Eponi replied. "I'm so scared."

"I didn't come here to kill DefenseCorp soldiers, Eponi."

"Wish they shared your attitude." Eponi centered the *Prisa* on the exit wall. "Fire away."

Sai closed the call with the officer, tapped on the console, and watched as the *Prisa*'s turrets unleashed a jagged green torrent. The lasers superheated and boiled away the metal barrier as Sai directed the cannons to carve out a hole big enough for the *Prisa* to fly through. Inside the craft, beyond the light show, the destruction offered no sound, no smell. Like watching a movie.

"There's that squad," Eponi said, frowning.

"How can you tell?" Sai continued blasting. The lasers closed in on carving a wide enough gap. "There's no working cameras left?"

"Our rear shields are getting hit," Eponi said. "It's cute, how they think they can break through."

"Let's not give them any more chances than we have to." Sai pointed at the yawning, orange and black burning hole before them. "Think you can fly through that?"

"Might leave a scratch, but if it's what I've got to work with?"

"It is."

Eponi goosed the *Prisa* forward and the ship jumped like a coiled spring unleashed. Sai closed his eyes as the craft rammed right through the damage he'd caused, a few rending shrieks spilling through the inside as Sai's turret-work proved lackluster.

But they were outside. In space. Among the stars.

"You know those repairs are coming outta your accounts," Eponi said as she swung the *Prisa* into a long loop over the *Nautilus*. "New paint isn't cheap."

"We live long enough to get this thing repainted, and I'll happily pay for it." Sai flipped his console over to the *Prisa*'s scanners. Clean and clear. The *Nautilus* was zipping along in transit. No need for escorts. "How long till they scramble someone after us?"

"Don't know, don't care," Eponi said, flipping the *Prisa* so that the *Nautilus* hung above their heads, like a giant metal moon in a starry sky. "I may not agree with Aurora's grand plan, but we're on the rails now."

Locked into a mission. How often did that happen? Sever tended to get an objective and find a way to get into a dozen other fights along the way, scrambling through one mess after another before emerging at the end with the prize in hand. That's how it'd been on Wexer, on Dynas, but here?

Controlled and pushed down corridors. Now Sai and Eponi had one shot, one path, and if they didn't execute, there'd be another short-lived, burning star around the *Nautilus*.

Aurora had to get this right. Had to. The play was a leap, but Sai hadn't been able to find a different option. Hadn't come up with anything beyond hacking their way through a few thousand soldiers to murder Renard, and even if Sai put the katana where it ought to go, they'd never get off that bridge alive.

So Eponi put them outside that big glass shield. Kicking up faster than the *Nautilus* to crest the giant craft's rocky front, head down towards the bridge, then matching the *Nautilus*'s velocity as Eponi flipped the *Prisa* around. Without gravity in this deep space disaster, nothing slowed the *Prisa*, letting the ship get nose-to-glass with the bridge and its thousands staring out at them.

"Wave," Eponi said, sending her hand in a slow back and forth.

They were small. So damn small. The *Prisa* a speck in front of the *Nautilus* and its bridge, so large that Sai couldn't see around. Like confronting the horizon. Like threatening a god.

"This is insane," Sai said.

If Sai felt blown away, like he'd gone far beyond regulations, expectations, Eponi didn't look the least bit phased.

Still waving, with a manic grin plastered across a face, a form that otherwise held a locked-in concentration Sai couldn't help but envy, Eponi seemed in her element.

"Oh yeah," Eponi said, not looking away from the bridge. "This is as crazy as it gets, Sai. I'm loving it."

With his hands moving, bringing up the comm and starting a direct hail right to the *Nautilus* bridge, Sai couldn't quite identify with Eponi's emotion. Loving it? His nerves pumped, he swallowed hard, and Sai knew he'd rather slice through a thousand soldiers than go face to face with a ship in space.

"It's like kart racing," Eponi said, apparently oblivious to Sai's greening gills. "You reach a point where it's all or nothing. You have to go for it. It's sounds cheesy, but here we are, man. Here we are, laying it all on the line."

"Sure," Sai said through a dry mouth. "Call's connecting."

"You want to be the messenger?"

"Okay," Sai closed his eyes, shut out all those watching pinpricks on the bridge, and tapped open his mic. "Hailing the *Nautilus*, this is the *Prisa* with a simple request. If you do not comply, we will ram the bridge."

Sai took a breath, kept up the slate face, and with Eponi nodding encouragement, started a war.

Friendlies

THE ROOKIE DID HIS JOB. Gregor didn't have to pull his rifle's trigger, didn't have to advance beyond the doorway's cover as Rovo used the newfangled power armor, toothless though its weapons might be, to catch and bash in both agents, leaving them unconscious on the concourse floor.

"Can't deny, that felt pretty good," Rovo said. "Even better, since the rest of me feels like garbage."

"Yes," Gregor replied. "Bashing helps the soul."

"Never thought about it that way, but you might be on to something."

Whether or not Gregor's philosophies would stick, though, wasn't the moment's question. To the right, the experimental concourse continued towards the *Nautilus* bow, presenting rooms that could offer up weapons, equipment, or some clue as to what's going on here. Leftward lay the mess hall, more barracks rooms, and eventually the engines.

Without a wristlet and a working ID, they didn't have a good way to use the lifts. Gregor eyed an agent's body, wondering if he could use the man's limp bones and the wristlet attached to them as a key, but the small computer had gone dark. Locked up like the others.

"So do we have a plan now?" Rovo asked as Gregor confirmed both bodies couldn't be used. "I thought we were going back to the docking bays?"

"Hard to do that without a wristlet," Gregor said. "Do you hear anything?"

Rovo still had that Bug, the little device stuck in the rookie's ear. Gregor couldn't see the rookie listening to it without the power armor, read any expression, but when the giant metal arms shrugged, that provided answer enough.

"If they're talking, I'm not catching it," Rovo said. "Think we're still on our own."

"Then we make for the barracks." Gregor played the risks against each other. "We might find someone we know, or someone we can convince to get a lift for us."

Rovo didn't object, and the two stomped off in the red light towards the mess hall. Gregor's back itched without his hammer's familiar weight, and he didn't like the rifle's grip in hands without power armor gauntlets. Seeing Rovo clank ahead struck Gregor as strange, a reversal of positions. The rookie ought to be the one hiding behind Gregor's armored legs.

But missions made a mockery of the usual, and this mission had left normal so far behind that Gregor couldn't hold to it anymore.

"How'd I do back there?" Rovo said as they went past the ready rooms for the labs behind them. Lockers stacked with protective suits, all locked with red-glowing panels. "The suit's saying I didn't take a single real hit. Figure that's not too bad, right?"

"Why are you asking me?"

"Because you're the basher on this crew. I don't do

much up close and personal work. Did I get the feet moving right? How about the feint and jab move on the first one?"

"I don't know."

Rovo quit it after that. Gregor punched away a frown, leaving the usual impassive frame. He wasn't the rookie's instructor. Hell, the rookie wasn't even a rookie anymore. After Dynas and Wexer, Rovo had seen and done enough to earn his status as a full-fledged squaddie with Sever. The kid would have to take his own feedback, learn his own lessons.

That's what Gregor had done. From his first deployment to his last, Gregor had taken stock of every thrown punch, every hammer swing, and looked at how he could hit it harder, faster the next time around. So far, it'd worked.

"Hey," Rovo said as they neared the mess hall. "I'm catching something on the Bug."

Gregor took another look behind, confirmed no other agents, no other squads were sneaking up on them. The mess hall was locked down like every other chamber, but with Rovo's power armor, they could punch right through when they needed to move.

"From who?"

"Uh," Rovo said. "Not who I expected."

"Not an answer."

"Right," Rovo said. "It's from Kaia. She's saying they've landed on their new home."

Implications shrouded those words, but Gregor pushed them away, focused on the more important question, "Are you certain?"

"Definitely," Rovo said. "The message is a few days old, which would match up with when they left Wexer. Just caught up with me now. Means they didn't go all that far, either."

"I am not surprised."

Kashmal, Kaia's father and the dubious man that'd called Sever in for a rescue to Dynas and its swampy schemes, didn't have much cash when they'd landed on Wexer and split off. He'd planned to sell secrets from Dynas to float them over till Kashmal found another, less deadly, job. Gregor didn't know what it took to pawn off data about body-altering viruses, but he could guess it wasn't all that easy.

"Didn't Deepak want to know where Kaia was?" Rovo asked, standing stock still in the power armor. "Wasn't that his whole play?"

"Aurora thought we could tell them the freighter name," Gregor said. "DefenseCorp could track them from there. Perhaps you could offer them something better."

"Yeah, except we have an issue."

"We do?"

"The Bug's not exactly hooked into interstellar satellites. It pokes into relays when it gets close, scans the waves. It caught this message because the *Nautilus* found it first. My tag is still tied to this ship."

Tags. Set yourself up anywhere in the galaxy with a working satellite connection and your identity would proliferate across the stars, telling everywhere within humanity's reach precisely where you could be found. Any satellite that catches a message with an unknown tag would broadcast it out to any satellite in range, pinging data around the galaxy like a dog hunting for its owner. For Sever, *Nautilus* had been their longtime home. Gregor hadn't even thought about resetting his, not that he'd get many messages.

His parent's missives had stopped coming years ago.

"You said this is an issue?" Gregor asked.

"Deepak wants to know Kaia's location, right?" Rovo said, the questions sounding a little ridiculous coming from inside that big suit. "That was our whole lifeline here? Well, that message to me came through the *Nautilus*. Anyone paying attention to their incoming catches might see it."

"Encrypted?"

"Sure, but on a ship infested with agents?" Rovo turned back towards the mess hall doors and started towards them again. "How long do you think that'll last?"

"The bridge, then?"

"Not if we can help it." Rovo centered the armor on the mess hall doors, crouched into a charging stance. "The comm center will have, like, a tenth as many people. We can get the message there and delete it. If we're lucky, the bridge won't have noticed it. If we're not, then you'll get to do a lot of smashing before we die."

Always a silver lining.

"Lead the way, rookie," Gregor said, taking cover on the mess hall door's right side.

"Oh, I'm leading." Rovo kicked off, sending the armor into a shoulder charge at the big concourse-spanning doors.

The suit's kinetic boosters did their work, blitzing the suit into and through the doors with a hard, rending bang. Torn metal shrieked and snapped as Rovo plunged in, sending up sparks. Gregor followed quick, raising the rifle as he came, bathed in the concourse's red warning lights.

Gregor had been ready for a reception. If a squad, agents or otherwise, wasn't going to head into the weapons lab after them, then waiting to slay the Sever members under the mess hall's crowded cover made sense.

Overturned tables made makeshift barriers, their

chromed tops shining back at Gregor. The red lights played havoc with the mess hall's artwork, turning the designs into horror show outlines made all the more ominous by the rifle barrels pointing their way. At a glance, looking behind Rovo's raised arms, Gregor counted more than two dozen. At least a couple squads sent here.

Should take that as a point of pride: DefenseCorp rated Rovo and Gregor high enough to require this much resistance. Not bad.

Without any cover for themselves, there wasn't a fight to be had here. Gregor followed Rovo's lead and dropped the rifle, raised his hands. Waited for the squads to decide a kill order made more sense than playing nice.

Instead, a firebrand woman in the brighter blaze red uniform given to frontline bulwark squads, those who took the hard first drops into thick fighting to hold positions at all costs, rose from cover. With her rifle raised and pointed, she advanced to the mess hall's middle, closing with Rovo, her boots clacking on the metal floor, their traction tech sticking her with every step.

"Keep those arms up," the woman said as she closed. "I see them dip a centimeter, we're turning you both to ash."

"Good to see you, Lamya," Gregor said. "Too bad this isn't a simulation, or I would call your bluff."

Lamya didn't seem to share Gregor's opinion. Aside from the quickest flicker his direction, she kept her concentration on Rovo, "Eject from the suit, soldier. I don't know where you found that thing, but it won't hold up when we start shooting."

"Don't follow her orders," Gregor said, making a bet. Hoping it would pay off. "Lamya, we're not here for you."

"I don't care what you're here for," Lamya replied,

dropping her eye to her rifle's scope. "We *are* here for you. Leave the suit, now. I won't ask again."

"She sounds serious, Gregor," Rovo said. "I'd rather not get shot again today."

"Quiet, rookie," Gregor said, then started walking towards Lamya. "If you stop us here, then we're all going to lose. The agents will win."

"The agents?" Lamya laughed. "Gregor, you always sound crazy, but now you're in another world. Tell the kid to get out of the suit."

Three choices. If Rovo left the suit, they lost their advantage. Gregor and the rookie would find themselves prisoners, locked away in a holding cell and waiting until someone decided to cook'em or cast'em out into vacuum.

Gregor could fight. Maybe he'd make it to Lamya before the squads burned him down. Rovo, without a single power pack for his weapons, would get a couple lumbering swings in before lasers melted him away.

Which left . . .

"Before you shoot," Gregor said. "Call the bridge. Check with the admiral. Aurora should be there. They'll clear us. Vouch for what I am telling you."

"And if they don't?" Lamya said. "If they tell me you're the same damn intruders that we're supposed to be handling?"

"Then we're right back here. A trigger's pull away."

Diplomacy. The words felt slimy in his mouth, weak and sad. Begging for his life, trying for miracle tactics to survive. Every minute on the *Nautilus* save the scrap in the med bay had been a crap sandwich. Rovo, though, didn't deserve to die this young. Gregor could grit through this for the rookie. Just this once.

Lamya, holding the rifle one-handed, brought the wristlet to her mouth. She started speaking into the computer when the overhead lights flashed. The red warnings blinked away, returning to their usual silver-white. As the squad leader that ought to have torched Gregor and Rovo lowered her wristlet, a shaky voice crackled over the *Nautilus* intercoms.

"Stand down," Deepak announced. "The intruder alert has been canceled. All squads are hereby ordered to disarm and return to regular duties. The threat to our ship has been neutralized."

The admiral repeated the order a second time, and Lamya's incredulous face grew more and more suspicious as she heard the words. Gregor would've felt the same, would've figured some trick had been pulled. But when something breaks your way, you have to push the advantage.

"You heard the admiral," Gregor said. "We're not the threat, Lamya. Let us go."

The squad leader gave Gregor a stare hard enough to crack granite, then dropped her rifle.

"All right, Sever," Lamya said. "You have your chance, but we're coming with you. Things turn out like I think they will, there's going to be shooting."

Gregor couldn't agree more.

Threats and Bets

EPONI HELD onto the bravado like a star that would grant her every wish. The rush suffused her twitchy hands as they gripped the *Prisa*'s flight sticks, her eyes as they blinked from the scanners to the systems and back again, searching for a flaw and knowing they would find none. She listened to Sai say the words Aurora had set for them, putting a fatherly spin into the demands that Deepak would have to carry out, and every damn sentence pushed Eponi closer and closer to the edge.

You did not desert DefenseCorp without consequences. Those were dire enough. But threatening to ram a DefenseCorp ship? An *Odin*-class cruiser, with man-hours and material tons by the millions, no less?

There would be no coming back from this. Eponi wouldn't fly a kart again, no matter how much cash she made—not that she'd live long enough to make much. No racing team, no bank-rolling brand would risk angering DefenseCorp.

A deserter could be let go. An enemy would be killed.

"I think that was it," Sai said, letting go a long exhale as he wrapped up the list. "Did I get it all?"

Eponi filtered Sai's speech back through her own haze, "Let's see, you had'em pull the lockdown, declare any agents to be hostile, and clear our records? That about covers it."

"How much you think they'll do?"

"Better be all of it," Eponi said, "or I'll goose these engines and poor little Deepak's gonna be so much space dust."

Sai nodded slow, looking not too thrilled with that potential outcome. And why wouldn't he? Man had a family, chose to leave'em, in a decision that Eponi could never reconcile. She'd been forced to play this game, swing laser smut all across the galaxy at the behest of a dangerous dealer, but Sai? He could've stayed home. Could've tucked his kids in every night and whistled them awake with the morning light.

Eponi's jealousy had bled away to pity over the missions, and she couldn't let go of the feeling now, watching him watch the too-small faces on the bridge through its giant glass bulge. He'd chosen to dance with a devil that wouldn't ever let the song end.

Maybe Sai knew that and didn't care.

The comm crackled and Sai tapped its broadcast open. This time, Sai's left console fluttered and morphed into Deepak's clear face. No transmission jaggies here, seeing as Eponi calculated Deepak's nose sat fifty meters away from her cold metal cockpit.

"I've done as you asked," Deepak said, and Eponi could swear the man had aged a few years between the time she'd seen him in the bay and this moment. Renard stood behind the admiral, free and frustrated on the bridge, an obvious counterpoint to Deepak's assertion.

Sai's low sigh showed he noticed the bastard too. "What are you both going to do? And where is Aurora?"

Sai seemed to be at a loss. Man wasn't ever much of an innovator if the problem didn't involve slinging two wires together to make something go boom. Eponi swiped away the system status on her console, joining it into the call and plastering up a wild smile she'd used to strike nerves in her kart racing opponents.

"Here's the thing, Admiral," Eponi said. "You're a liar." Deepak opened his mouth and Eponi waggled a finger. "Ah ah ah, nope. Keep that trap shut for a minute. See that man behind you? Don't know if you were listening when Sai read off the instructions, but that space roach there is an agent, and ought to be in stun cuffs. You want real points with us, you'd be sending him out the airlock right about now."

Deepak, and the admiral caught a smidge of praise from Eponi here, kept himself together. Gave Eponi a full three seconds to consider whether she wanted to add an appendix to her verbal takedown.

"Are you finished?" Deepak asked when Eponi kept things tidy. "Renard, along with the other agents on board this ship, are not mine to arrest. They belong to Defense-Corp as much as I—"

"Okay, I'm going to stop you there," Eponi interrupted. "We're not concerned with who's got the right to do what. We're looking for results. I'm not seeing any." Although Eponi did see Renard looking ever-more angry, and that brought with it a perverse pleasure. Given that Eponi would be blown to pieces whenever *Nautilus* decided to get its fighters in the air, she'd take that joy. Would revel in it. "So I'm going to count to five, and if that man's not on the ground with cuffs on his wrists, then we're going to have a party."

Sai's eyes had made it to about moon size as Eponi started her count. Deepak sputtered, but two of the troopers behind him had better ideas. Renard didn't fight as they slipped the cuffs over the officer's wrists, binding him up and pushing him closer to the camera so Eponi could see the job had been done.

"One," Eponi said, leaning into the camera as if to take a closer look. "Admiral, looks like your own staff have a better play on things than you do. Now, tell me you'll put the target on the agents like Sai kindly asked you to?"

The big play, this one. Aurora didn't think Deepak would do it, wanted Eponi and Sai to ask anyway, put the heat on the admiral and get all those mild-mannered officers running coffee on the bridge to wonder if their lives were about to end because Deepak decided to protect a bunch of spies instead of his loyal staff.

When Deepak refused, Aurora would hop on through the *Nautilus*'s back-up comm center and declare the admiral a traitor to his own staff. She'd call for an uprising, and boom, they'd have a spark on their hands. Eponi and Sai would fly back in, offer support, and help kick all the damn agents off the ship.

Easy.

"You understand the choice you're giving me?" Deepak said. "If I agree, this ship will be torn apart in the fighting."

"If you don't, it'll be torn apart right now," Eponi replied. "Choose a side, admiral. I'm getting bored out here."

More importantly, Eponi kept one eye on the scanner up on her console, watching for those red blips indicating something had been launched to come find them. The dots hadn't shown up yet, but Eponi had no doubt they would. Whether Deepak scrambled fighters or Renard's agents found their own ships, no way the *Prisa* would be left to hold the cruiser hostage all that much longer.

Deepak stepped back from the camera spitting his image into Eponi's eyeballs. Big decisions had to weigh on the minds of those who made them—one of many reasons why Eponi tried to stay away from the things—and Deepak didn't look any different here. He swept a long look over the levels spreading out beneath him, and Eponi wondered whether he'd get angry looks in return, hopeful, pleading faces, or the firm resolution from people prepared to die to . . . what, defend the agents?

Eponi couldn't believe that. The spies held a certain respect among the squaddies, mostly because they came up with the contracts that kept cash rolling in, but everyone knew a friend that'd died due to bad intelligence. Everyone knew the agent's operating principle: the ends justify the means.

"Okay," Deepak said, flipping away the begrudged tone that'd stained his earlier talks with the formal command Eponi recognized. The king putting on his crown. "Broadcast this throughout the ship. Any and all agents are to report to loading bay C-17. For the safety of this ship, its soldiers and its crew, this order goes into effect immediately."

Eponi muted her mic, kept her mouth shut, but failed at keeping the surprise away from her cheeks, her eyes. Deepak had actually done it. Hadn't quite put the agents in chains or kicked them out an airlock, but he'd split the ship.

"I'm stunned," Sai said, echoing Eponi's own thoughts. "Didn't think the admiral had that kind of spine."

"Would've lost a lotta cash on that bet," Eponi agreed.

Deepak looked more than a little drained after delivering his speech, but he approached the camera again.

Opened his mouth like he was about to deliver a stern warning to the ship holding him hostage, when the admiral's look twisted off to the side. Behind him, Eponi saw Renard, stun cuffs dropping away from his wrists as the supposed soldiers let him free, reach for a pistol.

"Behind you!" Eponi said, then realized she still had the mic muted.

Before she could tap it off, before she could repeat the warning, the feed cut. Eponi jerked up, looking through glass, space, and glass again to see what she could see. Flashes blitzed around the bridge, a light show punctuated by bursts as missed shots struck things with a tendency to explode.

Eponi and Sai had no way to tell who was winning the fight, no way to tell whether Deepak or Renard still lived. She tried punching another call through, but the hail went unanswered.

"Aurora said we would be starting a war," Sai said. "I guess that's what we did."

"Didn't think it'd actually happen."

"At least we're not dead."

Eponi would've agreed, would've said how relieved she was that she hadn't had to plunge this beautiful ship into the bridge. Eponi wouldn't have said that she wasn't sure she could've gone through with it, had Deepak called her bluff.

But she didn't have to make any admissions, because the damn scanners beeped out an alert that trumped the bridge's light show and its implications. Four small craft, lighting out from the *Nautilus* and spraying out in a wide sweep towards the *Prisa*.

"Those didn't come from the fighter bays," Sai said.

"Because those aren't our fighters," Eponi replied.

"Who wants to bet that Renard's people brought some insurance?"

"Not me."

"Coward."

They were done threatening the bridge. Deepak had put the flames into play. Aurora had to take the internals from here. Eponi punched up the engines, fed some power back into those laser-deflecting shields, and breezed the bridge as the *Prisa* kicked up and over the *Nautilus*. Those four dots flew around, forming up behind them.

"Mind going to a turret?" Eponi said. "Or were you going to play swipe shooter?"

Sai started, then picked himself up from the chair, "No, definitely not swiping. I'll get back there."

"Thank you."

The first ice blue shots whisked by as the dots closed. Eponi did a double-take at the laser color as she flipped the *Prisa* rightward, getting ready to loop around the *Nautilus* and use the big ship's bulk for cover.

Blue meant high energy. Burst cannons that'd deliver a helluva punch, but that sucked up energy like Eponi sucked up those cocktails on Wexer. These four fighters weren't playing for a long engagement, then. They wouldn't have much shields, much engines.

They wanted a quick kill.

"Sorry to disappoint," Eponi said to nobody.

Time to see whether the *Prisa* would back up her words.

TWENTY

Finding Kaia

So FAR, being housed in a hardened shell juicing Rovo with numbing, energizing chemicals had been a good experience. Turned out Rovo rather enjoyed not getting shot, squashing his enemies, and the clank clank clank as his heavy feet slammed along the concourse towards the comm center.

Lamya, Gregor, and half her squad followed—she'd left the other to watch the weapons labs—and the ensemble had Rovo feeling like a true leader, marching at the head of his soldiers to some grand destiny.

That grand destiny, after a lift ride, revealed itself as an understated, windowed wall. Unlike the bridge, which squeezed its bulk into a smaller and more defensible door, the *Nautilus* comm center parlayed openly with the entire ship. Rather than hardened steel, the comm center revealed itself to the concourse through a glassy wall broken into partitions, each one willing and able to swing aside for anyone who approached. Scanners peeked out from the lines between those partitions, hunting wristlets to verify.

Behind the glass, Rovo caught looks aplenty turning to see his clomping force as they drew closer. Rovo's suit had him almost hitting the concourse ceiling, his metal arms going wide enough to cover half the hallway's width. Imposing in any circumstance, terrifying in the *Nautilus* and its stellar confines.

Turned out the comm center hadn't been left without protection. Another squad, gathering together after Deepak's order to stand down, broke apart as Rovo approached, settling into a panicked scramble. Their commander, pulling at his rifle, slowed as Lamya went around Rovo and called for a halt.

"They say they're not the enemy," Lamya declared to the commander, to the squad and their itchy trigger fingers. "You heard Deepak's order stating the same."

"I heard him say we shouldn't trust the agents," the commander replied. "I don't know who that might be."

Deepak's second, stunning order had come through while Lamya's squad readied up to ditch the mess hall. Treat every agent as a potential threat, herd them all to a docking berth Rovo couldn't remember. Rovo figured that must've been Aurora's doing. Turn the tables on the bastards and send 'em running.

Good.

"Me either," Lamya said. "I do know, though, that we're not agents. Not the man in the power armor, nor this civilian here."

"I want to trust you, but . . . " The commander kept looking over Lamya's shoulder, at Rovo.

Maybe the rookie should speak for himself.

"Don't know who you are, commander," Rovo said, keeping the armor still. As unthreatening as he could. "What we're trying to do here is track back an incoming message. It has nothing to do with the *Nautilus* or the agents."

Not strictly true, not strictly false. The best kind of statement.

"Then why are you in power armor?"

"Because an agent nearly killed me," Rovo replied. "Without this armor, I wouldn't be alive."

Another bullseye strike on the veracity scale.

The commander took another look beyond Lamya, at the armed squad behind Rovo. The man's fingers left his rifle's trigger behind as he no doubt came to the correct conclusion that his squad would be on any conflict's losing side.

"Okay," the commander said. "We're not even supposed to be here anymore, anyway." The man took in a breath, assumed the straight posture that came with confidence in his decision. "Squad, let's head towards the docking bays. See if there's somewhere we can help."

The commander's soldiers embraced their leader's directive to save their own lives and headed off, not a one bothering to look back towards Rovo. When you'd escaped Hell, why would you linger?

"Thanks for the help," Gregor said to Lamya as the group approached the comm center's glass. "I wouldn't have wanted to hurt them."

"I know," Lamya said. "I know you would have, though."

"Yes."

Rovo winced at that. Gregor had to figure out when the truth could do more harm than good.

Lamya's squad broke out around the comm center, watching the concourses as they intersected in front of the glass-walled space. Gregor and Lamya went inside, leaving a door open for Rovo, who'd have to abandon his power armor to fit.

Leaving his medically boosted cage didn't seem like the best idea. Someone else in the comm center could take and trace Kaia's message as well as Rovo could, without risking Rovo's own life in the process. He wasn't sure how many of his surgical fixes had ruptured—if any—but leaving the suit's comfort cocktail had him nervous.

"You coming?" Gregor said, returning to the entry while Lamya delivered a short speech to the crowd in the comm center, declaring precisely who controlled the space. Demanding any agents reveal themselves. None did. "Unless you trust someone else to find Kaia?"

That, Rovo did not.

He spoke the evac key command and the suit did as the suit was supposed to do, popping free its joints and letting Rovo half step, half fall into Gregor's arms. To say getting caught by Gregor felt a little wrong would've been, well, wrong. Way back, when he'd first walked into DefenseCorp, Rovo had been fluffed with the solo hero's toughness, the idea that he had to be self-sustaining at all times.

After a laser or two to the chest, that opinion had died its final death.

Inside, the comm center splayed out across a flat, oval space dotted with bland details. Everyone in here knew they played secondary roles to the bridge crew. Rather than a spectacular view into space, the comm center had a simulated screen coating the back wall, playing out pre-programmed backgrounds. Behind that screen sat some of the thickest hull plating on offer, fortifying the comm center for its real purpose as crisis command.

The bridge held thousands. The comm center had maybe a hundred clustered into pods grouped around a central platform, accessed via a small ramp going up from the comm center's entry. The admiral or whomever happened to be captain—if the bridge had to be evacuated, odds were solid the command chain had been blown up—would take that spot and try to save the ship.

Rovo didn't want that kind of attention. A volunteer noticed Rovo's uncertainty, standing and waving them over to his workstation.

"Need a break anyway," the man said. "Feel free to do what needs doing."

"Thanks," Rovo said as Gregor helped him to the desk.

Settling into the chair, ignoring the growing twinges from his chest as the suit's painkillers continued on their slow journey towards nothingness, Rovo punched up the *Nautilus*'s message queue. Filtering by his tag, Rovo found the list stored on the cruiser's vast drives, and felt his breath catch for a second.

With Dynas, with Wexer and all the garbage that'd been going on since Deepak had sent them on to the swamp planet, Rovo had forgotten about life's normal cadences. In the lines up there before him, Rovo read headlines from his parents, his sisters, and a few friends still milling away on the space station over his homeworld, locked in those stable lives Rovo should've been taking for himself.

The notes, sometimes coming in with videos, called out birthdays and successes. Questions about whether Rovo had seen the latest game or had any thoughts about this or that galaxy-consuming gossip. Before Dynas, Rovo spent downtime aplenty in his cabin, dashing back replies to everyone.

He'd been dark for weeks now, and while it would probably take a few more before anyone really worried—galaxy transmission times made everything uncertain—the pull to tap through several unread notes had Rovo's hand shaking.

They'd given up so much already. So much.

"Focus," Gregor said, the man's hot breath close to Rovo's ear. The move would've been creepy except Rovo knew Gregor had to be quiet, had to keep what they were doing a secret. "There will be time for this later."

Rovo doubted that.

Kaia's message sat at the top, the most recent. Her name wasn't attached to it, the sending tag had been marked as UNKNOWN. The girl didn't have any official record of her existence, and she wouldn't be old enough to care for a while. Provided she lived that long.

Rovo tapped the message. Read its contents. A short and simple and sweet paragraph talking about how fun the transport ride had been so far. That her daddy said they were going to Gillane Four. That Kaia would be so happy if Rovo would meet them there, because Kashmal had said they would be getting ice cream when they arrived.

Wouldn't it be amazing if they could all enjoy it together?

"That's what we need," Gregor said, reading the note over Rovo's shoulder. "Let's go."

Promising himself that he'd send replies as soon as the *Nautilus* moved on from death trap to a normal cruiser, Rovo again used Gregor to help him up. The two met Lamya's eyes and said they were ready to get going. Now that they had Kaia's location, they could bring it to Deepak.

There, Rovo would find out what they wanted with the girl, and how to protect her.

"We'll go with you," Lamya said, when Gregor informed her of the plan. "I'm still not sure where this mission of yours is going to end, but I don't trust it."

"Don't trust much, do you?" Rovo said.

"Rookie," Gregor warned.

"No, I don't," Lamya said. "Not when it comes to deserters."

Rovo would've continued flinging fire with Lamya, more out of petulant exhaustion than anything, but Gregor shifted Rovo to the side. Eyes rolling, Rovo looked back over the comm center and the people watching them. A few still handled calls, tapping away at their consoles or speaking into headsets. Others looked ill, watching the squad with wavering looks. Still more wore anger, frustration on their faces, mingling it with fear's tight lines. Swinging from lockdown to invasion and back again couldn't make for a stress free work environment.

At the workstation Rovo used, the man they'd kicked out returned to business. He tapped away too, as if the interruption hadn't caused the slightest problem. The man looked so focused. Good on him to . . .

"Hey," Rovo said, "I think I might've forgotten to log out."

"What?" Gregor asked, catching Rovo's meaning and looking towards the madly tapping man.

"I'm not all there," Rovo said as Lamya echoed Gregor's question without catching the point. "It's the injuries."

Gregor shuffled Rovo back towards the workstation. The man whipped his head around as they approached, his hand gliding across the console's commands and wiping the big screen. Nothing but a starry background waited when Rovo and Gregor made it over the man's back.

"Need another go?" the man offered.

"Just need to make sure I logged out," Rovo said. "If you don't mind."

"Sure thing, boss, sure thing," the man stood up again, left his chair and gave them some space.

Rovo sat, tapped open the message log program. Sure enough, his name still splashed across the top. His messages sat there, waiting to be read by whomever. Rovo reached for the log out button, ready to send the access into oblivion, when he noticed another program churning away on the console.

A quick tap brought up a correspondence application, meant to beam off any new messages to the galaxy's satellite. Gregor asked what Rovo was doing, and the rookie ignored him. The man sitting here had been tapping so fast, Rovo had to see, had to eliminate a possibility.

He flipped the correspondence application, had it list out all recent messages sent out. There, the top one, had a brief message and a briefer headline.

Asset

Gillane Four. With Kashmal.

Gregor cursed. Rovo's lungs burned as the shock spliced through the suit's remaining drugs. He'd done it. Given away the girl's location. Without that secret, Sever had no bargaining position. Without that secret, they'd—

"Too bad you had to go and look at that, boss," the man said, behind them. "Never been much for the bloody side, but you know how it goes."

Rovo didn't have to look far to see the drawn pistol, to see the sad, set look of an agent ready to earn his keep.

So much for not getting shot again.

TWENTY-ONE

Corporate Objectives

DEEPAK'S WORRIED LOOK, a clash with his still-spotless uniform, greeted Aurora when she woke up. A hazy awakening, given the anesthesia. The realization hit and Aurora tried to move her arms, legs, and she could, she could twitch her toes, curl her fingers.

"There'll be a scar," Deepak said, an odd tone around the words. "That's all."

"Hey," Aurora said, shaking off the fuzz. "We won, right?"

"You did."

"So the bonuses are good, yeah?"

Deepak shut his eyes, opened them with a pinched sigh, "The bonuses are good. The mission succeeded."

"And Sever? The rest?"

"There were losses," Deepak said. "But that's not important. What is, is that you're okay. Or you will be."

Aurora laid into her pillow. Ran through the names in the squad. Who might've been compromised, might've been hurt. The sadness, the apprehension clouded in, but the cash tinged its edge. Sever, hell, all of DefenseCorp knew why they did this job. The lump sum would be a start, a damn good start.

"It's the life we're living, Deepak," Aurora gave the man a smile, he looked so worried. "You're the one putting us into play, and we need to win the game. Then we all get paid. Sometimes, there's a price."

Deepak didn't have a smile to give her, though, and when the nursing bot came in and cleared her for discharge, Aurora couldn't shake the feeling Deepak wanted her to stay in that hospital bed, safe and secure.

BY THE THIRD AISLE, Aurora had herself all stocked up. She'd slipped goggles over her eyes, a tactical pair providing a simplified version of the power armor's display and that, more importantly, dulled the glittering tags. All that light served to dazzle in the first minute, served up headaches by the fifth.

The goggles went along with a belt holding flashbangs, thigh holsters stocked with pistols, and a smaller, anti-personnel rifle meant for dumping power packs with explosive light shows in tight quarters. Aurora had spare ammo too, hooked over the armored vest on her chest in classic bandolier fashion.

Vana took Aurora's crowd control and focused it on single target elimination. She'd chosen a banger set up to empty a whole power pack in two shots, with big red waves that'd roast anything within a few meters. She'd watched Aurora pick and choose with bemusement, leaving additional weapons for herself in lieu of more ammo.

"If we have to fight as many enemies as you're gearing up for," Vana said when Aurora slotted another flash bang on her belt, "then you won't live long enough to use all those toys."

"I'd prefer not to use any of them," Aurora replied. "The goal is surrender, not slaughter."

"Good luck with that," Vana said as they returned to the Quartermaster entrance. "Renard's people? They know what's at risk here. What they're fighting for."

"And what's that, Vana?"

"A better way to do business. Or so they think."

"They're going to fight fanatically over a better way to do business?"

"If that business is running the galaxy, yes."

Aurora settled into an unseen frown as she followed Vana back into the concourse. The red lights had disappeared, a change that brought back Aurora's plan and all its urgency. The Sever captain hadn't been rushing through because she figured Eponi and Sai would have to negotiate for a while, if they received any response at all.

But, if the lights had changed, if the lockdown ended, then they had a chance.

"We must have missed a message," Vana mused, looking around. "Nothing plays back in the stacks. Meant for bots only."

Those bots, though, must have heard something. While humans hadn't yet repopulated the concourse, bots strolled along carrying out their general duties. Floor cleaners whistled past, while supply movers trundled along with loaded carts heading this way and that. Even the Quartermaster's own machines had their windows open, ready to handle requisitions.

"If I'm guessing right," Aurora said. "It means I'm late. Let's go."

While they'd walked through the stacks, picking up their arms, Vana had divulged her history in the bits and pieces format agents tended to take. As if information were finger nails getting pulled off their hands or hair yanked strand by strand. Nonetheless, Aurora had fallen on her patient interrogator tactics, dipping into a fixed resolve that had Vana giving in before they'd made it through the first stack.

"If you're going to keep asking me questions," Vana said. "I guess I have to answer?"

"Good guess."

"Then I'll keep it simple," Vana replied. "DefenseCorp's giant. Wasn't always that way. It swallowed up organizations as it went, and most of us didn't fit in so perfect. Cash worked as a salve for a long time, letting people push aside their complaints and look to retire as an escape. Only not everyone wants to retire, not everyone wants to escape."

"And Renard's one of those."

"Not just him. There's a bunch of relics in DefenseCorp, some that made their way far enough up the ladder to hold real power. They haven't forgotten where they came from, and now they're trying to do what they couldn't before."

Vana delivered that last flavored with frustration. Whether that came from her anger at the situation or because she hadn't been able to do the same, Aurora wasn't sure. What the agent said next didn't do much to clarify.

"I'm here to protect what DefenseCorp should be. What the galaxy needs it to be," Vana said. "Peace and security, bought and paid for. Not a dictatorship, not an empire. A facilitator so worlds can have confidence they'll go on turning, so children can get their educations without being shot, so someone can fly a ship from system to system without pirates."

"For a fee."

"Yes, for a fee."

Vana's honest vision still left holes. The same holes that might lead to another Dynas, to another Sever squad seeing their employer going a meter too far.

Back in the concourse, Aurora kept herself a step behind Vana, kept her rifle ready. Regardless of what the agent thought of Renard, Vana still gave DefenseCorp her loyalties, and according to DefenseCorp regulations, Aurora ought to be shot and stuff out an airlock.

Up ahead, as Vana and Aurora, on a moving walkway, neared the comm center, shapes that'd looked like bots from afar resolved themselves into squaddies. The soldiers stood still. Way too still for any usual guard posting. As the walkway pushed Aurora and Vana closer, the agent made the move to get off the advancing treads.

"Something's not as it should be up there," Vana said as Aurora followed her into the concourse's central, static corridor. "Go slow, stay ready."

Aurora could've picked a bone with Vana over who had the right to command who in this situation, but she could set aside her pride. With her own squad scattered and risking their lives, now wasn't the time to be petulant.

The concourse didn't offer any cover, and anyone bothering to look their way would've seen two vested soldiers approaching at a slight crouch, weapons up and aiming. The squaddies, even when Aurora and Vana closed to straight shooting distance, didn't look their way. The troopers ahead kept their arms at their sides, weapons on the floor near their feet.

A sure sign someone had given them the order to drop the damn things.

But who? Aurora knew where Sai and Eponi were. On the *Prisa*, barking demands at Deepak. Rovo and Gregor, though, could be anywhere on board. Last time Sai had seen them, the two had broken for the cafeteria. Could they have gone to the comm center? What would've brought them there?

Kaia.

Rovo had the best shot of knowing the girl's location. The rookie had mentioned the cute goodbye gift he'd handed the child on Wexer. Maybe he thought he could get in contact with her.

Or maybe some agents had wrung that information from him and had brought Rovo here to send out a message.

"Feeling like my squad might have something to do with this," Aurora said.

"Is there a problem on this ship not tied to your squad?" Vana replied.

"Your attitude?"

Vana gave a fast, low laugh, "Stay tight."

The comm center's glass windows overtook the standard metal-and-rock walls combing the *Nautilus*'s hybrid concourses. Vana moved near the moving walkway's railing, deciding to use that as cover. Aurora followed, keeping her eyes and weapon trained on the squaddies. Almost a dozen soldiers hung in the intersection ahead, and they had to know Vana and Aurora were coming by now.

And yet, not a soul looked their way. Not a one reached for their floor-bound weapons. Instead, everyone kept their faces set on the comm center. Why?

Vana stopped so fast Aurora nearly trampled the agent. Would have, except Vana's curse gave Aurora a split second preview that their normal forward cadence had come to an end. Looking along Vana's eyes, Aurora saw a scene through the comm center's partitioned, glass entrances.

Gregor came through first, his bulk dominating any stage he happened to be on. He appeared past the comm center's middle, rising over a desk occupied by Rovo, whose hands tapped away on a console Aurora couldn't see. Behind them, mostly blocked by Gregor, she picked out another man in a classic pose that declared death to anyone who moved in his way.

The situation spilled out from that core, in a spastic recognition that brought Aurora deja vu from the nightmare back on the bridge. As if called to arms, more than half the comm center's staff looked to be standing with weapons drawn, pointed towards the squaddies and their fiery commander, Lamya, stuck in the middle with her back turned Aurora's way.

"Looks like we're a little late," Aurora said. "If we hadn't gone through the stacks—"

"Then we'd have been surprised, just like them," Vana snapped. "This isn't a crap fest yet, Aurora. We can fix it."

"Please tell me how."

"Distract and destroy," Vana said. "You're going to take me in. The agents here know I'm one of them. I'll play hostage till it's time to switch things up."

Risky, but Aurora could buy into the aggressive play. Trying to run through those doors with guns blazing would give the agents steps to set up a counter, would mean Gregor and Rovo would be blasted down before Aurora came close enough to make a difference.

Besides, taking an agent hostage, lie or no, felt pretty good.

"Drop your rifle, then stand slow," Aurora said, and Vana complied. "Walk forward."

With her rifle keeping a minimum distance from Vana's back, Aurora followed the agent into clear view. Now the squaddies looked over, unable to hide their curiosity. The agents saw them too, and the one holding Gregor and Rovo up called for everyone to stay calm, stay focused.

"And keep tapping," the agent told Rovo. "The easier you make this for us, the quicker we'll make it for you."

Aurora didn't have to ask what the agents would be speeding up for Rovo. They'd be doing the same thing to every Sever if they could.

"You can stop listening to him," Aurora said, guiding Vana through the doors. She felt a few pistols change their aim her way, weapons no longer pointing at the squaddies. "Lamya, been a while."

"It has," the squad commander replied. "Can't say it's a pleasure seeing you again."

"Might be we can change that," Aurora said. "Who's leading this pack of traitors?"

"Doesn't matter who's in charge," said an agent to Aurora's right, a tight-packed woman who didn't look like she gave two craps about Aurora's hostage. "You're going to put down that rifle and do whatever else we tell you, or your squaddie show ends here."

Ah, the moment before the first fire. A sweet time, filled with hope and possibility. Aurora had her targets, an optimal set going from her starting position, knew Vana had the same. There'd be a few seconds between the first shot and when the squaddies entered the fight. Survive that long, and Sever might walk away from this alive.

She'd seen worse odds.

"Sorry," Aurora said, and Vana ducked.

Aurora held the trigger as she took aim, using her weapon's fast fire rate to stitch lasers across the comm center and, largely, burn some solid holes in the big screen at the center's back. Aurora sidestepped as she fired, making the slightest difficulty for the agents looking to hit her. Vana drew her pistols quick, adding targeted shots to Aurora's spray.

The agents, however much Aurora wanted them to,

didn't sit and take it. They used Aurora's action to mean an open license to kill, and shot at the squaddies, at Lamya, at everyone. Laser fire and fast-growing smoke from shot things burning filled the space, along with cries for help, for vengeance, for mothers and fathers.

Aurora pitched forward into the blitz, leaning on the rifle's trigger until the power pack clicked empty. Hard to tell how many targets she'd hit as Aurora went into the desk maze. She felt heat from the vest where several shots had plunged into its energy-sucking material. Another hit or two and the thing would be compromised, too torched to hold anything more, but it'd kept Aurora alive enough to get out from the open.

With a click-hiss, the new power pack slipped into the rifle, and Aurora circled right, going for the agent that'd led off the discussions. Aurora found the woman still behind the console the agent had started at, snapping off shots towards the entrance. The damn spies. DefenseCorp didn't bother to give'em firefight training.

They'd kill you quick in the first few moments, but get past that and they didn't know to keep moving, keep firing.

Aurora did, and the agent went down without ever seeing who pulled the trigger.

TWENTY-TWO

Last Shot

KICKING around a spaceship in zero gravity wasn't easy in the best of times, such as during a long, uneventful star-viewing trip from one isolated outpost to another. Sai, trying to get to the *Prisa*'s left turret while Eponi dashed around the *Nautilus* in a twisting, spastic dance, hit his head, his legs, his knees on just about every surface until he found a grip on the handrails lining every hallway, every section.

Even then, as the *Prisa* turned, Sai had to modify his grip. Without gravity, Sai didn't rotate with the ship, just hung there as his world orbited around him. His stomach reacted like his brain, sending nauseating waves quelled only by the adrenaline spikes coming whenever the attackers managed a strike against the *Prisa*'s shields.

"You planning on shooting soon?" Eponi's voice rattled through the intercoms. "I'm not having fun here!"

"Me either," Sai said as he found his way to the *Prisa*'s left prong, the narrowing tooth lined with storage cabinets and ending with a single seat linked up to a twin-cannon turret.

As Eponi began another rolling maneuver cutting across the *Nautilus*'s side—which side, Sai had no idea anymore—the demolitionist gave up on the hand rails and pushed himself towards the turret chair with a floating leap. As Sai drifted by the silver-lined, yellow-signed cabinets, he saw space and ship splitting the window outside the turret.

The *Nautilus* played its horizon part, slicing against the deep black that space held for anyone making an interstellar jaunt. They'd turned away from Wexer so fast after boarding the cruiser, speeding core-ward. It'd be days before the *Nautilus* reached any intersection where it could turn towards another inhabited system. Weeks before it arrived in what anyone would consider civilized space.

That isolated locale hadn't seemed all that ominous until Sai made his way to the turret, saw the console scanner light up with the four fighters following the *Prisa*, and nothing else. No nearby traffic, no reinforcements, no escape opportunities.

If Renard and his agents planned to take over a DefenseCorp ship, this would be about the perfect spot to do it.

"Sai, please tell me you're getting there," Eponi said, electric and focused. "They're bunching up close, thinking they're gonna get some focus fire. On my mark, I'm gonna flip-drift and give you a wide open look."

"I'm ready to take it."

Sai settled into the chair, the *Prisa*'s systems scanning his height and calibrating the targeting sticks for his reach, the scanner to his eye level. The screen blocked out the real world, showcasing potential threats as small arrows against a basic screen. Enemies as red arrows, allies as blue diamonds—not that Sever had any allies out here—and their expected trajectories spidering out as faint green lines.

As Eponi started her flip-drift maneuver, Sai felt the engines kick in, punching the *Prisa* up from its bottom into the aforementioned flip. A dicey move that turned Sai and Eponi facing their followers, Eponi supplemented the maneuver with a hard energy shunt to the frontal shields, killing the engines in the process. Keeping up its velocity, the *Prisa* went backwards, giving Eponi and Sai a clear shot at their enemies.

"Line'em up," Eponi said.

The four pursuers came cruising around the *Nautilus* edge, swooping around in a loose formation that bespoke of limited cockpit time. Sai didn't know how to fly a damn thing, but he'd seen enough tight air combat around or over his head to know the wobbly group blasting towards him wasn't all aces.

Their scanners would've told them the *Prisa* waited around the *Nautilus* curve, but not that it'd turned around its lethal side. The foursome curled around thinking they were predators, but their prey had turned a deadly trick.

Holding down the gooey triggers, Sai sent molten bolts rocketing to the formation's left side, caressing the *Nautilus*'s shields while tracing his target. The fighter, a dagger shaped craft with its heavy cannon under its pointed nose, reacted as Sai wanted, jerking away from the oncoming laser surprise towards its wingmen.

Eponi lit up the *Prisa*'s central cannon, a gatling thing made to perforate any target dumb enough to sit in the ship's sights. The middle two daggers, leading their assault, broke left and right to avoid the laser stream. A smart dodge, considering the fighters had to get closer for their big hitting blasts to get within range. A dumb dodge, because Sai's target veered right into its middle-juking friend.

The two fighters, their proximity alarms no doubt screeching their imminent doom, panicked. Eponi's target swerved up, pulling into a slanting ascent that put the fighter on a hard collision course with the *Nautilus*. Sai's reversed its earlier move, getting back outside, right where Sai's turret, tracking after the fighter, found it.

Sai's bolts hit, punctured, and blew the fighter. Vacuum swallowed any fire before it started, creating a shrapnel burst as the craft popped all its joints and scattered into the mess. Its disaster buddy tried to swerve away from the *Nautilus*, a swaying move that didn't quite kill the fighter's speed before its aft made contact with the big cruiser's rocky hull. Panels, debris, and more than a few fighter chunks blew off as the speck hit the wall. Dead in space, the fighter ricochetted away from the battle, spinning into the black.

Before Sai could compliment Eponi on her choice flying, huge blue blasts filled Sai's view. The lasers themselves weren't all that wide, but their brightness created halos, as if comets streaked towards the *Prisa*.

The ship shuddered as the first shot hit, draining the *Prisa*'s remaining shields to zero and setting off grainy, squawking alarms that did nothing to calm Sai's nerves or set his focus to anything useful. The second blast seared the *Prisa*, a near-hit that left some blast scoring on Sai's windshield, as though a giant space bug had splattered black guts all over the glass.

"Keep shooting!" Eponi's shout carried over the alarms. "We got this!"

Where Eponi found that confidence, Sai didn't know, but he did as she asked. Swiveling the turret to the remaining pair, Sai joined in with Eponi's center cannon and a computer-operated right turret to burn the *Prisa*'s remaining power on an offensive salvo. The two fighters juked and dodged while their big guns recharged, closing to a range that meant certain death if either survived to another shot.

Lining up that fatal blow, though, required those damn daggers to stay still for a hot second. Still enough for Sai's shots to skitter along the outer fighter, already trying to dodge away from the *Prisa*'s right turret. Just like Eponi had done with the first pair, Sai caught the fighter forgetting the *Prisa*'s many guns, and his lasers burned off an engine, freewheeling the dagger to join its buddy in a forever journey to infinity.

Eponi had her sights set on the last fighter, but the weaving pilot, with more space now that his wingmen had been obliterated, avoided her streaming fire. The flyer wheeled right, putting the craft away from Eponi's danger, out of reach for Sai's turret. The *Prisa*'s right side peppered shots, but the AI couldn't keep up with the dancing, always shooting where the fighter had been rather than where it was going to be.

"Bring him left," Sai said. "I can't hit him over there."

"Working on it," Eponi replied. "Engines aren't too happy right now."

Maybe because she'd bet it all on the flip'n'shoot. Sai couldn't argue with the results, but it'd been an all or nothing play. They hadn't hit the last fighter, and now they were coasting in a line, easy pickings for a calm attacker.

The *Prisa* shuddered as Eponi tried to salvage her move, and Sai saw the power for his own shots drain away as Eponi gave everything she could to the engines. They'd poured everything into offense, and now they had to go the other way. Their velocity slowed and the dagger fighter rocketed towards them.

Sai blinked, realized Eponi had gone from one move into another. Get the dagger fighter to overshoot and pull another flip, giving the *Prisa*'s triple threat a perfect engine pair to light up.

"I see—" Sai started as the dagger fighter closed, its point aiming right for them.

As the dagger shot.

Eponi swung the *Prisa* as the blue bolt flashed, the shot crashing towards them. From Sai's view, the big blue bolt went right, and he would've believed too far right, except the *Prisa* jolted, a shaking rush accompanied by more pops, bangs, and concussions than Sai had ever heard.

Behind him, an emergency seal slammed into place, trapping Sai into his turret prong. Keeping out any potential leaks to vacuum, giving Sai the oxygen currently stuck in there as his time to live. Outside, the *Nautilus* came and went into view, the *Prisa* spinning as its engines struggled to compensate for the damage.

"Eponi, please tell me something," Sai said into the console.

Static came back. A sharp burst, then nothing. Not good.

Sai tapped away at the console, trying to bring up a system status list, trying to get some information on what'd happened. As he swiped, Sai found one red assessment after another. The *Prisa*'s power frittered all over the place, its engines barely sparking along. Like water rushing through a pipe with a thousand valves springing open, too little energy flowed everywhere.

As for the vacuum leak, the console put it between the *Prisa*'s right wing and the center core. A sheared hole that'd broken open.

"Sai," Eponi's words sounded different, fuzzier and

harried. "Had to switch consoles. Mine blew out with the hit. Far as I can tell, we're dead in space."

"By my count, we're still alive."

"That fighter's out there. He's going to come back and finish us off."

Sai swiped the console back to the scanner, saw the fighter's red arrow swooping back around. Lining up that fatal shot.

"You have any tricks left?" Sai said.

"I'm a pilot and my ship's not working right now." Eponi coughed. "Our power relay is busted. Even if that fighter doesn't hit us, we're gonna blow up on our own."

Like a bomb. Sai hooked into the reference, a puzzle he knew how to solve. Disarming an explosive often meant keeping two things from reacting, meant routing them away from each other or killing the connection. The *Prisa* kept trying to send power to the engines, to the right turret, and neither one worked. Eventually, all that energy might burn through something important, blowing the ship to atoms in what would be, with all the vacuum, a profoundly disappointing explosion.

"Route everything to my wing," Sai said. "Everything you can, push it to my side."

Eponi coughed again, but Sai could almost see the smile when she spoke, "You're a moron, Sai. You'll explode when you fire."

"At least I'll get him."

Eponi didn't answer, but Sai saw his console flash. With a swipe, Sai jumped back to the scanner, the turret reporting all the power it needed was waiting. The fighter had its arrow going right back towards the *Prisa* now, a slow walk-up as it lined up for the fatal shot up the *Prisa's* aft engines.

"Got one last thing to tell you," Eponi said. "Don't miss."

"Been a pleasure flying with you, Eponi."

Wheeling the turret around, Sai centered the cannons on the fighter. He whispered a quick prayer to his children, to his wife, and pulled the trigger.

TWENTY-THREE

Smokescreen

GREGOR REFUSED to let any surprise touch his nerves when he saw Aurora waltz into the room with an agent at pistol point. He hadn't seen his commander since she'd vanished with Deepak minutes after boarding the *Nautilus* and Gregor would be lying to himself if a big ol' part of him hadn't figured an agent had Aurora kissing vacuum by now.

Instead, in she came, bringing the thick pre-fight tension with her. Gregor decoupled his focus from Aurora as she spoke, locking instead on the distance between himself and the jackass behind him, the scum who'd played Rovo into dropping Kaia's location.

When Aurora's hostage dropped and his commander started laying waste with that intriguing rifle she had, Gregor's pre-loaded plan went into action. The agent behind him had both pistols drawn, aimed, and ready to shoot. Turning would take too much time, but Gregor had slid his feet ever so slightly so he could kick himself back at the first sign.

Like an angry trust fall.

The charge back knocked the agent off balance, sent the first pistol shots burning over Gregor's shoulders and into the ceiling. Gregor kept his feet pumping, working the ground to keep his back slamming into the agent's chest while Gregor's left hand fought to keep the agent's pistol arms from finding any aim.

If he could get the agent against the wall, Gregor's size ought to be able to mash the agent to dust.

If.

Gregor's ankle struck something hard as the agent swiveled, the smaller man using his size to get out from under Gregor and trip his opponent. Gregor fell hard, hit the comm center's smooth floor, and looked up into a double-barreled salute. Smoke blew up around the agent's twisted face, a seared look that said vengeance was very much wanted in that moment. Smoke couldn't hide that rage.

Didn't do much to hide the chair crashing in from behind, either.

Rovo swung the seat hard into the agent's head, a blow that sent the rookie tumbling after the agent. Both hit the ground, the agent glassy-eyed as Gregor tore away the pistols, and Rovo groaning that he'd torn something in his chest.

"Thanks, rookie," Gregor said, delivering a solid knock-out blow to the downed agent. "You going to make it?"

"Don't know," Rovo said, one hand on the chair, as if the furniture were his anchor in the madness.

"Then hold on till I get back."

Gregor would've helped Rovo right then and there, but with all the laser fire burning through the comm center, getting the fight finished would bring better odds for the rookie's recovery than a daring drag-out.

With Aurora and the squaddies occupying the comm center's front, Gregor used the smoke and desks to cover a stalking slide back towards the outer wall. Non-agent staffers followed DefenseCorp's protocol, huddling beneath their desks and praying to whatever gods they believed in. The agents themselves, and Gregor killed a noisy curse at their apparent numbers—the sheer laser volume gave a clue that the damned spies were everywhere—clustered towards the back, forming up an actual defense.

Between every desk, building little cubicles, stood silver-steel barriers. Thin and translucent, the cross-shaped constructs dotted the comm center, dividing the space into clusters. As the battlefield took shape, those barriers diluted lasers enough to pass for a shield, and the agents stacked up behind several towards the back wall. Passing through the smoke and staying low, Gregor went from one cluster to the next, approaching the agents from the side.

He reached the last row without seeing anyone, encountering empty chairs, burned out screens, and little else. Peering around the slat's corner, Gregor made out hazy outlines in the smoke, the agents fighting against increasingly poor odds. The squaddies had their rifles now, and Lamya's commands carried over the noise, setting her forces into an entrapping circle.

Why were the agents continuing to fight if they didn't have any hope?

Gregor understood going out in a glorious blaze, flinging every last effort you had into impossible odds. Agents, though, didn't seem the type. They played in the shadows, shifting allegiances and saying whatever was necessary to keep themselves alive, keep their mission going.

No way they would keep fighting unless they expected something to change.

Gregor reeled around, looking back towards the comm center's entrance and those windowed partitions. The smoke thinned out that way, and through its ashen cloud Gregor saw few squaddies left outside. Everyone streamed in, making their meter-by-meter advance towards the agents.

Another attack coming from behind would trap them all.

Best make sure that couldn't happen.

Gregor pushed against the cross near him, the barrier shifting as strength it was never meant to withstand shoved it forward. The cross groaned along the smooth floor as Gregor pushed, rotating with the force and having absolutely zero effect on the ongoing firefight.

But the idea bore out.

After another laser flurry buzzed across the room, Gregor made a lunging run towards the makeshift barriers the agents had erected. Their crosses served as cover, and Gregor, without a single shot coming his way—it helped that he'd kept his own pistols quiet, not drawing attention —crashed into the left cross. The agents had pulled together four of the things in a loose arc, and Gregor punched in one side.

Going full strength, his shoulders leading the way, Gregor hit as close to the cross's center as he could, lifting and pushing the barrier over. The entire thing went up on its side before momentum crashed it onto its top, hitting hard on glass that shattered with a crackling tear.

Leaving Gregor, without any cover, looking at a whole bunch of angry agents.

There were some fights you could win by brute force, some fights you could win by being smart. Gregor preferred the former, but now? He tried the latter. He dropped his two pistols, threw his hands up and hoped.

Across the galaxy, Gregor found honor to be a fickle idea. Most people, be they human or alien or somewhere in between, tended to think of themselves as on the good side. They wanted to do what they thought was right, what would preserve some moral integrity for themselves.

And shooting an unarmed man, arms raised in surrender, tended to fall outside that window.

So the agents hesitated, some turning back to their active firefight, the others glancing at their comrades and trying to figure out whether they could take prisoners in this messy crapshoot of a situation.

That hesitation proved to be all Lamya and Aurora needed.

Even with some agents breaking back to the engagement, the turn came too late. Squaddies collapsed from all sides, with Aurora herself popping up over a cross and laying down devastating repeater fire. In seconds, ones Gregor spent with his arms raised, his back to the comm center's wall, and his breath held, the agents were neutralized.

As the squaddies disarmed the spies, Lamya caught on to Gregor's notion and posted watches at the comm center's doors. No reinforcements had shown up yet. Whether they would at all now that the fight had been called, who knew, but chances wouldn't be taken.

"Nice play," Aurora said, giving Gregor a clap on the shoulder as they headed towards Rovo. "Know what saved your ass, though?"

"No?"

"Your giant head. Saw that standing up through the smoke and knew you'd be dead in a second if I didn't do something."

"That is the first time my head has been useful."

"Congratulations," Aurora quipped, then drew in a

hard breath as she saw Rovo, leaning against the side wall where he'd dragged himself. The rookie looked damn pale, like he'd seen a ghost while giving blood. "What the hell happened to you?"

"Long story," Gregor said, when Rovo shook his head. "He needs to get back to the med bay, but there are too many agents."

"We'll get him there," Aurora replied. "Find Lamya, have her call for a medic to make sure he'll pull through."

"What are you going to do?"

"I came here for a reason," Aurora said, nodding towards the workstations, some still undamaged despite the comm center's smokey ruin. "There's a message that needs sending."

Lamya's squad did indeed have a medic, and Gregor left Rovo in the soldier's hands. Aurora took over a workstation, after telling Gregor to get back into the power armor. The suit might be the most powerful weapon on the *Nautilus* right now, and Sever needed it under their control.

The hulking suit waited outside the comm center. Gregor accepted the scan, breathed through the snap-hiss adjustments as the suit replaced its Rovo build for a Gregor-sized setup. Getting back inside the power armor felt good, a comforting rush that coupled Gregor's existing strength with invincibility.

"Gregor, you in?" Aurora's voice crackled through the visor.

"I am." Gregor wiggled his fingers, watched the metal hands follow his commands. "Ready to go."

"Good. You're going to escort Vana to the bridge by way of the barracks. Pick up a squad or three and go reinforce Deepak."

"Reinforce?"

"I haven't been able to raise the bridge," Aurora said,

though the zero surprise in her voice had Gregor wondering what she knew that he didn't. "Renard might still be there, and that's not good."

"Renard?"

"Vana will fill you in."

Gregor saw the woman, vest sporting a few burns from hits, push her way into the concourse and throw Gregor a dry look. Apparently Vana wasn't all that impressed by the power armor. Her loss.

"And you?" Gregor said, zapping the message back to Aurora.

"I'll be coordinating the resistance."

"The resistance?" Gregor asked, as Vana went on by, waving for the Gregor to follow. With one clank after another, he did. "What resistance?"

"The agents on this ship just declared war on everyone else," Aurora replied. "We've got to find them, stamp them out, and then follow the chain on up."

Gregor took several steps to process Aurora's words. They sounded like a return to normal policy, that Sever was abandoning its mercenary run before it ever began. Gregor had no qualms about bashing the bad guys, but this felt less like a mission and more like Aurora had herself wrapped up in a cause.

The questions died before Gregor found a way to pose them. Now, on board a ship crawling with hostiles, wasn't the time to push Aurora. There were enemies to destroy, and for the moment, that would be enough.

"Aurora tells me you're the dangerous one," Vana said as they headed towards the *Nautilus* center and the barracks waiting there. "A man more likely to punch than pontificate."

"Not wrong."

"That's good," Vana continued. Gregor took a better

look at her. The agent carried ammo aplenty for a rifle held in both hands, but she didn't move like someone expecting fire. More like someone who had a plan, who knew she could accomplish it. "Where we're going, I'm going to need that strength."

"The bridge?"

"Eventually," Vana said, getting to a lift and pressing the call button. "Thing is, there's a reason Renard wants the *Nautilus*. Why he moved so many agents here over the years."

Gregor stayed quiet. Best to listen when someone starts revealing information. The lift arrived, and Gregor clomped in alongside Vana. She didn't hit the top level, but instead sent them hurtling back down. Towards the mess hall and the experimental labs.

"Renard's not playing this game with one hand," Vana said, as if describing a particularly dull picture. "Your little girl is a bonus. A surprise. We're after the real prize."

The lift opened, and Vana led Gregor into the lower level concourse.

"And what is this prize?" Gregor asked.

"Take a look at yourself," Vana said, lifting a coy smile Gregor's way. "You're wearing an early version. The latest prototype is on this ship somewhere, and we have to get it before Renard does."

"Or?"

"Or he takes it with him, and we're very, very dead."

TWENTY-FOUR

Jump Start

THE SHRAPNEL SOUNDED like steel rain. Eponi winced as the last fighter's remnants crashed into the *Prisa*, drifting unshielded and burnt out in the *Nautilus*'s shadow. Sai's shots had been true, had incinerated the dagger fighter on its final approach. Those saving bolts had also fried out the *Prisa*'s power conduits, the little cables sending coiled energy from the *Prisa*'s batteries to wherever Eponi needed them.

Right now, Eponi wasn't all that sure what she needed. Her butt sat planted in the *Prisa*'s primary pilot chair, and she'd just pried her hands loose from a flight stick grip so tight the muscles had locked in. In front, the *Nautilus* hung like a metallic moon, dominating the view with its running lights and reflective silver patches. The cruiser seemed frozen, but both it and the *Prisa* were hurtling along at a high velocity towards somewhere.

Even without its engines, outer space did nothing to slow the *Prisa* down.

And yet, the *Nautilus* did seem to be creeping ahead.

Eponi frowned, leaned closer to the windshield, as if a few centimeters proximity would help her discern relative motion. The lean in didn't, but the shrapnel wave blowing by around the *Prisa*, did.

Any impact, however small, would shave velocity. Any negative push, like the press from Sai's turrets when they blasted towards the dagger fighter, would kill off milliseconds. Not much, not many, but enough so that the *Nautilus* would outpace Eponi's damaged ship. Would, if Eponi couldn't find a way to get the *Prisa* moving, leave them stranded in remote space.

The odds of a pickup out here were too low to play with.

Eponi would've warned Sai about the situation, but the *Prisa* didn't have any functioning intercom system anymore. Hell, it didn't have *any* functioning systems that weren't tied to its critical battery back-ups: life support— air recycling, temperature control—would churn away as long as the *Prisa* held any energy at all.

So if the *Nautilus* made it away, Sai and Eponi could die real slow.

Eponi's pilot console sat dark, blown out by the first real hit to the *Prisa*. She'd used the copilot's one to contact Sai, but that had joined its sister in the great beyond after Sai's power-sucking shot. The pilot would have to leave the cockpit to save her ship.

"Fine," Eponi said as she scooped herself from the seat, her muscles twinging as they were called upon to move a weightless body into the air. "I'd like to see you try and kill me, space."

Taunting the interstellar void made Eponi feel better as she took a long look back into the *Prisa*. Beyond the four-seat cockpit, a short hallway whose floor doubled as the ship's quick lift opened into the *Prisa*'s central lounge area.

From her vantage point, Eponi could see her newly acquired craft would be stuck in a repair bay for a long, long time.

The seals on the lockers, spiked by the energy surges, had given way. Random tools, food packets, and Eponi's rifle drifted around, spending momentum on low-grade crashes with each other. Ruptures along ceiling panels revealed blown sensors and their attendant alarms. Chunkier debris floated in from the *Prisa*'s right side, where the ship had taken its hardest hit.

Behind them, the lounge sucked in little lighting, expanding more as a gray cavern than the *Prisa*'s core.

Eponi kicked forward, brushing aside debris as she made contact. Much as she'd like to see if Sai still lived, goal number one was getting the *Prisa* moving again, which meant kicking to its engines and linking them back up with the batteries. In the ship, the engines sat straight back, accessed by going down below the center. The same way to reach the main exit ramp.

Except everything went real dark once Eponi left behind the cockpit and its starlight show. Without a wristlet or a console, nothing gave Eponi more than a dim reflection. She'd have to navigate by memory, by touch.

The *Prisa* played its own disaster concert while Eponi judged her path and kicked off towards the center chamber's opposite side. The alarms had, mercifully, died with the power surge, but a scattered drum line rang throughout the ship as battered contents bounced around and off each other. Static wisps echoed here and there, intercoms connecting for seconds at a time before cutting out again.

All complemented by *Prisa*'s life-support systems and their comforting churn, a low-grade grind whirring throughout the ship.

Those sounds coupled with the cool, hard metal

touching Eponi's fingertips as she hit the chamber's far wall, sliding into the descending curl. Using the ceiling above her, close now that Eponi stood beneath the *Prisa*'s second floor and its crew quarters, Eponi straightened herself out. Felt with her feet to find the steps leading downward.

Without gravity, Eponi couldn't walk, so she propelled herself instead. Pushing off the ceiling, her wrists giving Eponi the angle she needed, the *Prisa*'s pilot ghosted her way down the steps. The descent wrapped, with the cut-out for the exit ramp halfway along. The leftover starlight died here, dwindling to utter black.

Eponi closed her eyes. Not because the darkness scared her—definitely not—but to focus, to pour her senses into her finger tips, her booted feet, and feel every centimeter as she went. The focus had a second purpose: to try and keep away the gnawing, feasting panic that they'd be stuck out here, left behind by a *Nautilus* crew that wanted Sever dead.

Everyone had their own nightmares, and Eponi's centered pretty square on getting caught in vacuum, on being left to die in space alone. She hated airlocks for that reason, and loved sitting in the pilot's chair because holding the flight stick gave Eponi some control over her fate. She hadn't been able to out-fly all four fighters this time, but she'd come damn close, and clinging to that fact kept her going.

It'd been a heroic effort. Worthy of the best pilots. And the best didn't give up just because someone clipped them with a lucky shot.

Eponi found the ramp's door, its ridged edge a signpost showing a destination not far away. The stairs flattened out into a level curl heading back towards the engines. Easier now to keep kicking forward. She kept her eyes closed, felt a hot whiff in the air as she came closer to where all that energy sat stuck.

Sai would've been useful. He'd come up with the plan to reroute the conduits to fire that last shot. Could probably do the same with the wired mess waiting down here. Eponi hadn't exactly done much repair work on ship guts —DefenseCorp had paid experts for that kinda thing—so this would be more guessing than a firm play.

But better to take a shot than die waiting for one.

When the steady churn washed out the random clanks, Eponi opened her eyes. Still no overhead lighting in the engine room, but various meters and small status screens cast enough yellow, red, and green glows to give a certain festive color to a situation that otherwise looked like disaster. Sai's power surge hadn't just blown things up above, it'd thrown things off down here.

The *Prisa*'s engines synced their power right up to the ship's big batteries, storage slates that charged when the ship landed, or from captured starlight sucked in by panels all across the *Prisa*'s surface. From what Eponi could tell, the surge, or the dagger fighter's shot, had shorted out all but one engine, a single cluster clinging to life.

Eponi leaned in, read the numbers, the status bars. Tried to run some mental math, a harder task than it should've been, but fear and rusted out habits—flight computers tended to handle the numbers—forced Eponi to claw through the equations a few times. Not having a surface to write on, a wristlet to record anything, didn't help either.

But, with all those caveats, Eponi figured the single cluster, coupled with the *Prisa*'s remaining velocity, could keep them within hailing distance of the *Nautilus* for a while. Except, for the engine to help at all, Eponi would have to flip the *Prisa* again.

The maneuvering jets, little things meant to shunt the *Prisa* one way or another, looked better off than their bigger brothers. Eponi had killed them after flipping the *Prisa* in the fight, sending their energy to the lasers, to the shields, and that might've kept the things alive. Now she had to get power going their way, and doing that meant tangling with the batteries themselves.

At her feet, the glow illuminated a grated floor. Beneath the oval patchwork sat the batteries, and the raw wires connecting their energy directly to critical sources, like the main engines and the life support systems. At Eponi's eye level, looking black and burnt out, the *Prisa*'s primary switchboard sat dead and done. Conduits, thick coated wires, came in from various sections and plugged into the board. Each one had been thoughtfully marked by the *Prisa*'s prior owners with their purpose.

"Guess what?" Eponi said as she found the one for the maneuvering jets. "We're gonna get out of this together. You'll see."

She'd talked to all her karts, too. Given them compliments when they'd pulled off a turn, passed a leader, or kept Eponi alive through yet another tumbling disaster. The words made her feel less alone, more like the ships were her friends.

As sappy as that sounded, in a universe like this? Friends were hard to come by.

Eponi unplugged the cord, reached down and lifted up the grate. Felt around to find the open slot on the battery's port, and gave the maneuvering jets free access to the boost juice. Immediately, a new hum rumbled through the *Prisa*, the ship waking up and realizing it could still be saved.

"I'll come back for the rest of you later," Eponi said to the switchboard and its torched lines.

Feeling her way back through the stairs, up and all the

way to the cockpit, Eponi saw the *Nautilus* had kept its advance, stretching out its lead. The flight stick felt dead in Eponi's hands, its assisting power gone with most everything else. But when Eponi toggled on the jets, when she pulled back hard on the flight stick, the links worked.

The *Prisa* flew.

TWENTY-FIVE

One Over All

ROVO WATCHED. For the first time in what felt like forever, he watched.

Lamya and her squad rounded up the agents, packed the twenty or so together and marched them off somewhere. The agents didn't look happy, didn't look sad. If Rovo had to guess, the dry expressions on their faces said they were thrilled to be alive, and not too concerned about the future.

Worrying, that. But then, so was the pain spreading out from his chest and leaking on down his legs, up around his shoulders. Nerves that didn't want to rest.

Rovo watched the skeleton crew manning the comm center, the loyal officers, ensigns, and various crew going back to their duties while dealing with the couldn't-be-fun realization that their co-workers, their friends, their fellows had been someone else the entire time. Rovo hadn't felt that betrayal before, but he knew how duty could distract, and Deepak's crew went back to sending along messages, handling called-in questions, and directing traffic around the ship.

Others set about cleaning what they could, or helping bots navigate through the wreckage to start repairs.

Aurora hooked Rovo's main attention, though. She'd picked the closest console that didn't have a laser hole through its screen. Rovo saw her tapping through, sending one message after another, each one reading the same thing.

As if feeling Rovo's eyes on her, Aurora stole a look his way.

"Still alive over there?" Aurora asked.

"Not sure I want to be," Rovo replied. "Getting shot sucks."

"I know. I'd take you to the med bay right now, but until I get word that it's clear, I don't want to risk it."

"You know I've been to the med bay today?" Rovo said. "Two agents tried to kill me there."

Aurora didn't look thrilled at that. Rovo must've ruined the joking mood. Set things on a different course, because Aurora pushed herself back from the desk and took the few long steps to sit next to Rovo.

"Agents tried to kill Sai and Eponi as well," Aurora said. "Me, too. Renard, that man we saw in the projection on Wexer? This is all his play. He thought I'd know where Kaia was, that's why he had Deepak separate me." Aurora's eyes narrowed, looked at nothing in particular. "Deepak made it seem like the *Nautilus* was at risk. That's why he helped Renard, or so he says."

"Do you believe him?"

"It doesn't matter," Aurora said. "We're going to fight for the ship regardless."

"Why?" Rovo replied. "We know where Kaia is. We should just get in the *Prisa* and leave. Who gives a damn about the *Nautilus*?"

The question came out easier than Rovo thought it

would. The little girl that he'd found, alone and largely abandoned in that Dynas apartment, made the ship, made all the agents and the admiral and their dueling agendas so pointless.

Here he'd joined Sever to become a battle-hardened soldier and now a girl's carefree love had thrown that dream away. And Rovo didn't care at all.

"Because if we let Renard win here, then he can focus his resources on us," Aurora said. "If we push the troops across DefenseCorp to fight the agents on their ships, on their worlds, then DefenseCorp's going to be too busy struggling with itself to care what we do."

Rovo blinked. Tried to catch on to Aurora's words and what they really meant.

"Those messages you were sending, what were they?"

"The truth." Aurora leaned her head against the wall behind her, and Rovo figured she must've been as exhausted as he was. "I sent exactly what happened here to every DefenseCorp ship in the *Nautilus* directory. They'll all hear that they shouldn't trust their agents onboard, that they need to act to prevent a coup."

"The agents might intercept those messages."

"Good. If some get through and some don't, that will make it look even worse. The more we turn DefenseCorp against itself, the better."

"You're sounding almost evil, Aurora."

"I'm protecting my squad, Rovo," Aurora said. "And I don't think turning more squads against Renard and whatever his plans are is evil."

"No, but . . ."

"C'mon." Aurora stood up, reached down to help Rovo to his unsteady feet. "Until the med bay's ready, I have something I need you to do."

Aurora set Rovo at the console. The messages Aurora

had been sending played out in front of the rookie, with plenty more ready to get passed on to still more ships. DefenseCorp had thousands, maybe millions, of vessels covering the galaxy, and Aurora wanted to send the message to every single one.

Rovo also noticed Aurora hadn't signed the messages as herself. The name attached to all of these belonged to the comm officer that'd used this desk before the firefight. A war started by someone that might already be dead, that would never know what they'd been used for.

"I'm not a communications expert," Aurora said, noting that she'd been sending the messages one by one. "You are. I'm hoping you can find a way to do this faster."

"If I don't die first."

"About that," Aurora said. "I'll talk with Lamya. Get a medic to take a look, and once we clear the med bay, you're going back in."

"What're you going to do?"

"We haven't heard anything from the bridge in a long time," Aurora said. "I don't know what that means for Sai and Eponi, but I want to find out. Vana and Gregor are heading up there, but I'm going to try and get some more information. I won't be far away, so call if you need something."

His commander left Rovo there, staring at a screen with the responsibility to tear a galaxy apart.

Back aboard his old space station, in his old career, with his old responsibilities, Rovo saw all the correspondence that shifted through his sector. Saw plenty of messages meant to undercut an admiral here or build up an officer there. Political maneuvering. Sides existed everywhere, and DefenseCorp often handled its internal disagreements with the victor sending the loser off on some distant assignment to a forgotten rock like, well, Wexer.

Rovo read the message Aurora had been sending, wanted sent. It didn't have the straightforward language drafted by a specialist, and it lacked the authoritative tone to command an immediate response. Instead, Aurora demanded action in simple terms, presenting the agents as a nebulous threat that ought to be apprehended to be safe.

Aurora wanted a war, but the way she'd written this thing would fall right within the usual DefenseCorp trappings. If anyone bothered to act on it, they'd slap the agents on the wrist until the agents convinced them otherwise.

The threat couldn't be nebulous. Couldn't be vague. The agents had to have an objective that would bring every squaddie to their feet in anger. That would have admirals putting stun cuffs on any agents they saw.

Rovo knew words that could bring that about. Clear evidence coupled with specific steps to negate the immediate danger. Add in some official dressing, and a message that could be dismissed as a strange superlative would get right to the captain of every ship. Would no doubt get some to take their agents in until the truth came out.

Enough agents would protest the action, enough fights would break out, that Aurora's plan might work for a while. Buy Sever some time.

Rovo felt chills, sat back from the console and looked around the comm center. Lamya had squaddies posted outside the partitions, watching for some attack that hadn't come. Aurora spoke with the commander, it looked like the two were arguing over something. Otherwise, the center hummed as those who still had working desks went back to it, while others helped bots with the clean-up. The smoke dwindled, though the burning smell permeated everything.

A sign that as fast as things could go back to normal, some things simply wouldn't. Couldn't.

Triggering a face off between DefenseCorp's two main divisions would do the same.

She'd come to the door when Rovo knocked. They'd communicated through a twisting knob, the slight shivers and tremors in the door. Rovo had carried Kaia through Dynas, pursued by the people who could've been the very same agents they fought here. Hunting for her, wanting to use Kaia, her blood, for things Rovo didn't want to imagine.

Yeah, he could send the message.

The work came easy once he'd decided to do it. Rovo slipped in the terms, re-arranged the focus, and then queued up the release to patch through networks on a repeated blast. Aurora had been sending isolated messages one ship at a time. Rovo had the *Nautilus* broadcasting the warning on a constant beat to any satellite in range, using a general DefenseCorp tag that any DC ship would snag and see.

It would take years for the warning to cross the galaxy, but the words would get there.

"It's done," Rovo said, making his slow way to Aurora.

"You look better," Aurora replied, looking up from her console. The words came bright, but Rovo saw worry. "Medic do his job?"

The medic had flushed Rovo with enough painkillers to keep him floating on a numbing cloud, yes.

"I'm all right for now," Rovo replied. "What's up with Sai and Eponi?"

Aurora tapped at the screen, blew up a scanner showing ships around the *Nautilus*, "The *Prisa*'s out there. Looks like someone decided to try and shoot them down. I'm not getting a reply from the ship, and it's falling behind the *Nautilus*. We can't slow down the cruiser without the admiral giving the order." Aurora's muscles tightened, a spring coiling. "If Deepak's even still alive. I haven't heard from Gregor and Vana either, which makes me worried."

"So we have problems, is what you're saying."

"Definitely problems," Aurora looked over Lamya's way. "Lamya's playing her orders. She doesn't want to leave the comm center, especially if there's a chance the bridge is compromised."

"Aren't there other squads on the ship?"

"That's the thing," Aurora said. "They're all getting pulled to guard critical points. We've already sent three to the bridge, and haven't heard back from any of them."

So why send more into the maw?

"Then, what do we do?" Rovo wished he had something smarter to say, but he hadn't exactly dealt with a total ship takeover before.

"You ought to get some rest," Aurora replied. "I think I can convince another squad to head to the bridge, and I'll go with'em this time."

"Because you'll make the difference. One person."

"One badass commander, you mean."

"This isn't a joke, Aurora," Rovo said. "I mean, Kaia's life depends on us getting off this ship alive. Sai and Eponi might need help. And, hell, I need help."

"And none of that matters if we can't take the bridge, or make sure it's destroyed," Aurora said. "Otherwise, they'll know anything we do. They can shut doors behind us, turn turrets against us, or worse."

Rovo leaned against the glass-topped cross, grateful for the support the thing gave his exhausted legs, his sore chest. The painkillers did a great job killing the aches, but the drugs sure left a lot of crap behind to deal with.

Aurora had it right: Rovo did need to rest.

Not that he could.

"If you're going to the bridge, then I'm going to the docking bays," Rovo said. "I'm going to get Sai and Eponi."

"You're a pilot?"

"For this, I don't need to be."

Rovo would've laughed at the look Aurora gave him then, would've if pushing that much air through his torched lungs didn't make the rookie feel like he was about to die.

But he hadn't.

Not yet.

Restless Warrior

THE NEXT ASSIGNMENT, Deepak threw Sever onto an edge. A placement guaranteed to see little action. Observe and protect. Aurora wasn't thrilled, but she gave Deepak room there. Sever had some new recruits to fill the losses from before. Good to ease them in.

But the one after that? After they'd spent the night watching a nebula spin by in its glorious purples and reds? Deepak threw Sever into the reserve again, playing guard duty around a collection of wealthy bureaucrats whose cash made them annoying and irrelevant to the riot suppression work DefenseCorp was really there to do.

By the third toss-off task, Aurora didn't even look at Deepak while he read off Sever's crap assignment. After the briefing, she didn't wait for him. When they returned, Sever not suffering a scratch, not even firing a blast, Aurora kept her mouth shut, her eyes looking elsewhere.

Only when Deepak waited outside her cabin, when he blocked her from going inside, did Aurora decide the time had come to talk.

"You're trying to protect me, and I don't need it. I

don't want it," Aurora said, opening the conversation with the hottest salvo she'd sent in months. "Sever doesn't deserve it. We're good enough for the hard work, we've earned it. Hell, our cash accounts make it seem like we're cleaning toilets."

"You're alive," Deepak said. "You're not hurt. Isn't that better?"

"Of course I don't want to get hurt, but that's the job," Aurora replied, sending her arm past Deepak to open the cabin. He followed her inside. "I'm not your delicate flower that you get to protect."

"Don't I?" Deepak's eyes flashed, and he leaned on the wall, trying to project a cockiness the man hadn't had any day in his life. "It's my job to make the assignments."

"It is," Aurora countered. "You're supposed to put DefenseCorp in the best spot to succeed, and that's not happening when we're in back."

"Maybe I don't care what DefenseCorp wants."

"Then what about what I want?" Aurora said. "Do you care about that?"

Again, Deepak fell into a faltering protest. Of course he cared about her, that's all this was. Of course he wanted her to do well, but not getting into danger. Of course he—

"This is a bad idea," Aurora said, cutting Deepak off as he delved deeper and deeper into pathetic territory. "You're a good guy, Deepak, but I'm not yours to save. Don't protect me, don't screw my squad."

Deepak stiffened, saw Aurora had no joke, no softness in her look. Words seemed to come and go from his mouth for several seconds, before he fell into a formal Defense-Corp nod, said goodbye, and left.

The next assignment, Sever found themselves dropping behind enemy lines. During the briefing, Deepak didn't look Aurora's way. Afterward, he didn't wait for her. And when they passed by another nebula, Aurora didn't watch it from the top deck.

But the cash in her account grew and grew.

SOME PEOPLE LEAPT over the edge, others had to be pushed. Deepak put himself in the latter camp, standing on the bridge with Renard. DefenseCorp's two divisions hung in the balance there on the *Nautilus*, the agents and the soldiers, facing off over the ship's direction, over the future of the company that, by now, had the galaxy's strength.

If one admiral gave way before Renard's pressure, how many others would follow suit?

Aurora couldn't know how much Renard infected. Whether the man spoke only for the agents he'd gathered on the *Nautilus*, whether he was only one branch of a larger web strung throughout DefenseCorp. Either way, she'd learned, she'd been taught, that you have to cleanse the disease wherever it appears, and prevent it from spreading.

That doing so would keep pressure off Sever's backs? A nice benefit.

Most of all, Aurora wanted to wipe that smug, plastic smile off Renard's face.

Sai and Eponi had agreed to the idea. Their role: provide the distraction, prevent Deepak and Renard from settling into their servant-ruler agreement. Spark a fight on the *Nautilus* that would give Aurora time to send the messages.

They'd succeeded. Now, Aurora had to complete the mission.

After helping Rovo get going towards the docking bays —two squaddies went with him for escort and assistance to keep him moving—Aurora counted Lamya and six squaddies left holding the comm center. Most of the others had left to escort the agent prisoners to Deepak's designated bay.

Not a great number to defend against an ambush, though Aurora felt less and less like any attack would happen. The agents, so far, had shown a desire to work from the shadows, to leverage surprise for their assaults.

Sitting here and waiting would make Aurora and the others easy targets.

"You're not going to the bridge too," Lamya said when Aurora said what she was going to do. "Can't let you."

"Let me?"

The squad commander, bearing a few laser burns on her uniform and a gray bandage across her shoulder, waved a hand around her, "This is, until we hear otherwise, the *Nautilus* bridge. We have to defend it, and I need to know what's going on. You're going to debrief me, and then we're going to set up here until we get more information."

"You're playing this like a normal engagement," Aurora replied. "It's not. We have to keep them guessing, moving. If we give—"

"We're not giving them anything," Lamya put a hand on Aurora's shoulder. "Our squads are securing every major system on the ship. Soon, even if there are more agents on board, they won't have power over anything. We can sweep each section in turn, validate identities, and net anyone suspicious."

Crawling the ship would take time. Something Lamya might be used to, in her squad's standard role securing a front line and holding it for days, for weeks. The idea of sitting in this comm center had Aurora twitching. She belonged in the action, not holding an objective. Especially after she'd achieved what Aurora needed.

"It sounds like you have it under control," Aurora said. "Deepak said to bring the agents to bay C-17? I'll head that way. If Renard's there, I'd like to ask him a few questions. Maybe fill him with a few holes."

"Aurora, I'm telling you to stay here."

"Lamya, don't know if you remember this, but I don't work for DefenseCorp anymore." Aurora turned, started for the comm center's doors. Lamya could shoot her in the back, could try to stop her, but Aurora had to bet Lamya wouldn't go that far. Had to bet that the mutual crisis mattered more than keeping Aurora here. "You ought to try leaving sometime. Very freeing."

In the windowed reflection as she left, Aurora caught Lamya's burning glare, but the squad commander didn't attempt anything else. A squaddie took advantage, went up to Lamya and started asking questions, and Aurora found her way back to the concourse unmolested.

The walk back to the docking bays—Aurora looked for Rovo, but the rookie must have taken a different route—went fast. More squads poured around the ship, moving in groups as they cleared rooms for suspected agents. Aurora didn't hear any firefights as she passed by the Quartermaster, no calls for back-up or alarms raised about an ambush.

Maybe the agents had given up, had realized their smaller numbers meant nothing against the more numerous, better armed and armored squaddies.

Aurora could hope.

The Sever commander caught up with Lamya's escort detachment as they neared bay C-17. The C-level bays were designed for larger troop transports, the ones meant for full-scale invasions. The big ships could hold a thousand or so frontline soldiers, sacrificing comfort for protection and space. They resembled long, flat arrowheads, coated with crimson-black solar paint. Aurora had never dropped in one of the things—Sever belonged in smaller, targeted craft—but she'd heard from others that the experience felt like purgatory: by the end, you tended to wind up in hell.

The first sign things might not be as clean as Deepak's order warranted came via the concourse itself. Those bot-cleaned walls picked up interesting smudges as Aurora caught up with Lamya's advancing squad. Dark burns and pink-red sprays said combat took place here, and the *Nautilus*'s strict cleaning regiment echoed that combat had happened recently.

Which would explain the squad's creeping movement. The agent prisoners stayed in the center, disarmed and stun-cuffed, but otherwise walking like expectant victims rather than humbled criminals. At the front, a squad trio kept their rifles raised as they approached bay C-17, listening for sounds beyond the bots whirring, the *Nautilus*'s continuous churn. No overhead announcements peppered the quiet, bringing an unsteady aura to the whole array.

Aurora could've been in a dream, a nightmare.

Instead, she felt her rifle's solid grip as she came up behind and then joined the front ranks approaching the bay door. Unlike the comm center, no windows graced the walls around the bays, a feature designed more for protection against accidental vacuum leaks than anything else.

Made for killer ambushes, though.

"Assume we're not on the winning side," Aurora said when she took her place at the front. "Anything could happen, and it's not likely to be nice."

"There should be more of us here," the squad's provisional leader agreed. "I'm not getting anything over our local band."

Not good news, that.

"Then here's what we do," Aurora replied. "Split your

crew. The back half take the prisoners, stash them in one of these closets and keep guard. The rest of us scout ahead."

"Split my force in half?" The leader held up a hand, halted the advance as the C-17 door, wide and closed and free from any living person, sat a few meters ahead. "Why would I do that?"

"Because if things turn dark, having hostages could be important," Aurora replied. "And the last thing you need is to watch prisoners in the middle of a firefight."

The man, a young one without enough scars to show much mission experience, threw a suspicious glower Aurora's way. She recognized the look, someone who'd found himself with a taste of battlefield power and wanting to keep it.

"You want to know why you should listen to me?" Aurora said. "Because I'm the one that's going to get you out of this alive. Just like I've done with my squad for years."

"I don't even know who you are."

"And I don't care," Aurora said. "Do it. Or I'll have Lamya replace you with someone smarter."

Diplomacy required time, required tact, and they didn't have much of the former, and Aurora never had any of the latter.

Lamya's little leader decided not to press Aurora's experience. He put her suggestions into practice, leaving five squaddies, himself included, surrounding the bay door while the others nudged the captured agents into a nearby supply room.

"Triggers ready," Aurora said, taking up her position at the door's right end, one squaddie behind her. Three on the other end. "Whatever we see in there, it's not likely to be friendly. Don't play nice."

Aurora caught what eyes she could. Not as polished, as hardened as Sever, but ready. These were still professionals, and Lamya's squad saw enough gritty action to prep them for the other side of this door. At her nod, the squad leader, her opposite, tapped his wristlet on C-17's scanner.

The door whisked down in a second, exposing the big transport and everything around it. The bay should've been clean, should've had its battery packs, potential provisions, gear and maintenance bots clustered around the sides. A clear blue-black metal floor should've greeted Aurora and the squad.

Should have. Didn't.

The materials splayed across the bay, stacked and strewn on each other in makeshift barriers. The transport, behind them, had its big ramps lowered and ready for boarding, the ship's yellow running lights mingling with the bay's bright white. Those lights flared past the barrier to light on bodies, so many bodies, mixing on the bay floor. Squaddies, yes, but the crimson black belonging to agents too. Laser scoring marred the floor, the bay walls and ceiling, and even the transport behind. Several bodies smoked still, the recent violence leaving its mark.

Aurora had to hold back a cough. The man behind her couldn't. The *Nautilus* kept its filters running hard, but they couldn't compete with burnt skin's raw, gut-twisting scent. The infernal char smell flooded the hallway, forcing Aurora to hold her breath as she peered around the doorway and hunted for enemies.

None showed. Not even behind the barricades, where Aurora would've expected any defiant force to be waiting. Maybe they'd made a run for the transport, but then why were the ramps down?

"Stay close, stay cautious," Aurora said. "Two up, two down."

Aurora and the squad leader peeled around the edge while the squaddies behind both took up positions at the doorway, rifles ready and covering. Aurora snapped a look hard right, hunting for anyone waiting just inside. An empty wall greeted her, though the wall itself had seen better days. Like everything else in the damn bay, it bore battle scars up and down its surface.

What didn't make sense was that this looked like an engagement. An actual battlefield, when it should've been a rounded up struggle between captured agents and squaddies. Aurora could see a few agents making a surprise attack in here, hoping to free their captive friends, but this spoke of a traditional conflict. And the bodies littered where they were? It looked like the squaddies had come into an entrenched ambush.

Keeping her rifle up and ready, Aurora turned back to the barricade. Snuck a glance at the squad leader, whose side proved similarly empty. Together, with synced nods, they advanced towards the barricade itself. The jumbled objects provided a motley line, maybe a little over a meter high at its tallest point. Behind it, the transport ramps gleamed empty, but the big ship's engines hummed a low whine.

Powering up and getting ready to leave. Not a good sign.

Choking in some air, blinking away stinging tears from the smell, Aurora approached the barricade. As she came close, her shoes scuffing along the floor as she stepped over the bodies, Aurora did a quick sidestep, and lunged for the barricade itself. Tried to throw off expectations.

Though her own died when she saw over the edge, saw what waited for them.

Agents, laying almost head to toe, with rifles and pistols held over their chests. Eyes open, looking at Aurora. She hadn't seen any because the bastards had been hugging the ground, and not in a way to get any good shots off. The way they were now, Aurora could gun half of them down before they—

The squad leader shouted, and not the triumphant gloat of catching an enemy compromised and ready to destroy. Aurora, finger slipping to the trigger as the agents started to move, took her eyes to the squad leader and saw him fly back from the barricade. With his second in the air, Aurora saw three bright flashes come from nowhere, blitzing out and striking the squad leader before he hit the ground, where the man didn't move.

There were times to fight and times to run. Aurora counted herself as brave, even foolhardy.

But now? With enemies coming up behind her and some invisible thing in the bay with them?

Aurora ran back towards the door, holding her rifle behind her, finger pressing the trigger and scattering bolts at the barricade. Not trying to hit anyone, anything.

Just buying herself another second to live.

TWENTY-SEVEN

Never Stop

SAI DIDN'T PULL the triggers expecting to live. Any bomber understood you don't stay near the explosion if you want to be there afterward. The *Prisa*'s prior owners, though, had invested a lot in their ship. Those plates surrounding the turret were thick, the glass coating the windshield had been reinforced.

When the turret triggered its overcharged shot, draining all the energy Sai could pull, the nozzles barely focused all that power into a bolt. Really, from Sai's view, it'd been more like a flood. A great wide burning power swath, waving from the *Prisa* and immolating the dagger fighter in much the same way a fly might vanish in a rifle's laser.

'Course, Sai had to infer all that from the shrapnel rain cascading around his little bungalow. The pet name, what he'd called his family's house, came in the dim aftermath, his ears buzzing, his nerves on fire, and his body reigniting burns received on Wexer that hadn't had time to heal. The *Prisa*'d taken damage, and that damage made the ship's left prong a cracked mess. Lockers and vents had burst, and some air recycler spattered and rattled.

All the lights died after Sai pulled the trigger, leaving him sitting in the turret's chair bathed in what starlight he could find. The intercoms did nothing, and the *Prisa* coasted on, Sai wondering if he might be the only person left alive. Not that he could do much with it.

The blast fried the turret controls, sent its heat cascading through the sticks and into Sai's space. The chair melted to his clothes, the grips sealed to Sai's hands. For long moments Sai sat there, wondering how he still lived, wondering when he ought to let go. Sai watched the *Nautilus* slide away, its bulk passing from his viewport, with no rescue coming.

So his bungalow, a small spot in a bigger ship, isolated and comfortable—once Sai grew used to the pain, not all that hard, seeing as a spot in Sever meant getting real familiar with hurting—began to seem a fitting coffin. Go out with a beautiful stellar view, safe in the knowledge that he'd fallen trying to save his squad member.

Die fighting, a vision rooted in the heroic tales his own parents had told his childhood self, cultivated by the warriors Sai had served with in DefenseCorp. Not, perhaps, with his katana, but Sai could take this finale.

Then the damn *Prisa* turned. Flipped on its head and accelerated, cutting the *Nautilus* and its distance. The big cruiser wasn't going to escape so easily, not from a ship no longer dead.

"Eponi," Sai said, his usual tenor a crusty gravel with a throat that'd come too close to inhaling fire. "You amazing . . ."

The words broke off in a coughing fit, a rise brought about by lungs, by a body compelled to action by a life's equation no longer resulting to zero. The bomb had gone off, but the demolitionist had a chance to survive.

But to survive, Sai would have to get out of this chair. Something ought to have been easy in zero gravity, easy in normal gravity and, hell, easy in the higher gravity reserved for big, dense planets proved itself a difficult proposition. For one, Sai's hands were still locked onto the turret's aiming stick, thanks to his gloves, now melted in place.

A tug with his fingers produced nothing more than a sticky sensation. No progress. Sai's palms did no better. There were animals that, when trapped, would gnaw off limbs to free themselves, and Sai looked down and wondered. He'd have to bite off both wrists, and both legs, a disgusting and suicidal idea.

Which left one option.

Leaning forward, Sai went for his left hand first. The gloves, meant to help keep a grip on something like the turret or a rifle's stock, slipped on tight and molded to his hands. They weren't designed to resist scratches, bites, and tugs. Like a dog, Sai used his teeth to snatch the thin fabric, black stuff that tasted like overcooked gelatin, and tear it off. One strand at a time until the only bits left were the pieces linking his fingers to the flight stick.

Though Sai's throat felt like it'd taken a long vacation to a desert, he managed to squelch up enough saliva to throw some spit on the stuck fingers. The liquid did enough, working to grease the melted strands, to eat at the ties to Sai's skin, so that, with another tug, Sai peeled off his left hand, leaving a few skin patches sticking to the glove.

Another burn to salve. Pretty soon Sai would just be that, all burns, instead of a body.

With one hand free, Sai plied his right one finger at a

time. While he worked at it, Sai continued to hear sounds echo through the *Prisa*. Eponi rumbling, putting things back together. Maybe even trying to get to him.

The *Nautilus*, out front, slipped further away.

Once he had his right hand free, with the gradual effort sparing those fingers and palm as much pain as Sai's left, the dire situation slid towards hope. The two of them were going to survive this. They'd find a way, even if the *Nautilus* left them behind.

Sai's legs proved the easiest. With both hands, and his pant's thicker material, Sai ripped his legs free, leaving himself wearing the first, and possibly only, pair of space shorts in existence. The *Prisa* kept things cool—heating things up in vacuum took energy, and Eponi surely wouldn't spare any for creature comforts—so goosebumps riddled Sai's exposed skin.

But damn if he wasn't free from the chair. Floating never felt so good.

It felt even better when Sai noticed a new blip flying away from the *Nautilus*. The small ship's lights flared their way, splitting into rainbows as they hit the shrapnel cracks in Sai's bungalow glass. Someone coming to pick them up.

Sai pulled himself around and kicked back down the crowded prong, brushing aside debris as he went for the connecting door. A circular portal ready to seal off the prong to keep out a vacuum leak, the *Prisa* had done the safe move and slammed its red-tinted doors down with the power surge. Without energy, and with minimal light, Sai looked at the thing and tried to figure out a good way to open it.

Easier to do that with two minds instead of one, so Sai pounded on the door. The hollow booms echoed around the ship, and after a minute, several more booms came back from the other side.

"Can't hear me through there, can you?" Sai asked, then felt stupid.

The door had been designed to prevent vacuum leak. No way it'd let voices through. Eponi's non-answer confirmed the assessment, so Sai knocked again.

This time Eponi didn't reply. Sai waited, then looked back down the prong to watch the oncoming ship draw closer. The silhouette looked familiar now, silver-gray streaking in towards them. A DefenseCorp drop shuttle. Whether those inside were friendlies, who knew.

A bright ping drew Sai's eyes back to the door. Little lights sprung up around it, lime green and cheery. Following the clear evidence, Sai tapped the open button and the door followed his command, whooshing open to reveal the *Prisa*'s central chamber and Eponi's head as she bounced up the stairs.

"Hey," Sai managed, before Eponi kicked her way at him and tackled the demolition man into a tight hug.

"We're alive," Eponi said, crushing her face into Sai's shoulder. "Can you believe that?"

"Not really," Sai replied, "I thought I'd be dead when I fired that shot."

"Me too," Eponi pulled back, eyes glittery, devious smile coming up. "Thought you'd gone and pulled a hero move."

"I tried."

"Yeah, you tried to leave me to die out here alone. Jerk."

Sai laughed at that, felt his lungs ache, and Eponi's look shifted to concern. She lifted up his left hand, frowned. Took in his shorts, frowned deeper.

"It wasn't easy getting out of there," Sai said. "Think I can get some salve?"

"I'll get the salve, you get some pants," Eponi replied.

"There's a shuttle coming, and nobody wants to see what you've got going on right now."

Sai found some new clothes in the crew quarters—the *Prisa*'s prior owners had plenty, and while Sai wouldn't say he had no guilt over taking all their possessions, the continual risks to their lives kept him from dwelling on it—and salved himself up, joining Eponi with a ready katana when the drop shuttle docked. The *Prisa* didn't have crap for working communications, so they had no idea whether their visitors were friends, enemies, or something in between.

With the katana and a pistol, Sai went down to the *Prisa*'s engine room. While Eponi would wait up top with her rifle for an initial greeting, Sai would hold for an ambush. Dart up from behind and cut off anyone coming from the shuttle. If things went real sour, Sai would use his pistol to shoot the *Prisa*'s battery until the thing overloaded and went boom, taking both ships.

The plan died when Rovo's greeting flew through the open hatch, taking with it Sai's resigned worries and prompting a gleeful shout from Eponi. They both met Rovo in the middle, catching the rookie as he limped into the *Prisa*.

"You flew the drop shuttle?" Eponi said, minutes later as they took their spots in the drop shuttle's cockpit, Eponi at the controls and Rovo sitting next to her.

"Strong word," Rovo replied. The rookie had the pallor that came with heavy wounds, and if Sai thought his own breathing sounded bad, Rovo's came like scratched sandpaper. "I told the shuttle to dock with you, and it did the rest. All I did was turn it on."

"Well, I'll thank you," Sai said. "Don't care how you made it here, just glad you did."

"Definitely." Eponi turned back to the console, started

tapping away. "I'm sealing the drop shuttle's clamps to the *Prisa*. We should be able to tow my baby back."

"Your baby?" Rovo asked.

"You heard me," Eponi replied. "What's the news on the *Nautilus*? Did we win?"

Rovo spilled into the story, dropping one detail after another that made it clear the squaddies, so far, had not won. That they were, in fact, stuck in a long fight with an adversary they couldn't count.

"I mean, they could be anyone." Rovo tried lifting his hands, twitched, and settled them back onto his arm rests. "The agents are everywhere, and they're not surrendering."

"Aren't the squaddies rounding them up?" Sai asked. "Bringing them to that bay?"

"Yeah, if you can round up someone you can't see, can't track."

"Then we'll have to be smarter," Sai said. "Eponi, can you raise Aurora? We need to get our next steps."

The call to the *Nautilus* comm center went short and snippy. Lamya jumped on the transmission to say Aurora had gone off on her own to bay C-17. Several other squads had been sent to the bay and hadn't been heard from. Now, Lamya said, they were sealing off that part of the ship.

"Something's gone wrong there, and we can't risk more troops until we understand what," Lamya said. "There's still too much of this ship we don't control to commit to one point."

Rovo had his eyes closed, looked like he needed to nap for a thousand years. Eponi chewed her lip. Sai felt the rippling sting along his back, his hands, his legs as the salve kept the pain from biting, but didn't numb it all. They didn't have armor, didn't have much for weapons, and weren't in prime condition.

But Aurora needed help.

"We'll look at C-17 and report back," Sai said. "Set up your perimeter and keep cleaning out the ship."

"Sai, I respect you, but I don't take orders from you," Lamya said. "If you want to save C-17, please do, but don't expect reinforcements. I will not risk my forces to save deserters."

"Copy that." Sai waved for Eponi to cut the transmission, and when she did, Sai snorted. "Can't believe she's pulling loyalties now."

"I can't believe you just said we'd run into enemy territory," Eponi shot back. "What're you thinking?"

"That it's what we do, Eponi."

Sai's statement didn't seem to sway the pilot's mind, but Eponi didn't fight the call and steered the drop shuttle towards bay C-17. Eponi did, though, mandate dropping the *Prisa* in an empty bay first. The gentle set down took several aggravating minutes, but Sai couldn't argue against preserving Sever's only ship. Eponi settled the *Prisa*, landing struts definitely not engaged, onto the bay's floor, wincing the whole way.

"Are you telling that ship sorry?" Rovo asked, not opening his eyes.

"I am sorry," Eponi replied, disconnecting the hook and boosting the shuttle spaceward. "It's my fault the *Prisa* took a hit."

"You flew well," Sai said. "We were outnumbered. It's your fault we survived, damage or no."

"Doesn't mean I don't owe her an apology."

With the *Prisa* ditched and relatively safe in its bay, Eponi swung the drop shuttle towards C-17.

"Nothing like attacking a ship way better than ours," Eponi said. "How do we wanna do this?"

Sai'd been pondering that exact thing during the *Prisa* drop, and while he didn't like his answer, it was the only one that made any sense.

"Give Rovo the controls," Sai said. "He's going to cover us while we hit the ground and find Aurora."

"So I'm barely a pilot, barely a gunner, and now I get to do both?" Rovo replied as the bay drew closer. "Hurrah."

"Step up," Sai said. "As soon as you get us covered, I want you to run. No sticking around, because that transport could toast this boat in a hot second. Eponi and I will find Aurora and evacuate, then we'll meet up in the next bay up."

"Gotta say, sounds like this is going to suck," Eponi muttered, but she stood up anyway after setting the drop shuttle on an entry vector for the bay.

"Does it ever not with this squad?" Rovo asked.

Eponi gave Rovo the pilot's chair as the drop shuttle went into the bay. As soon as the craft cleared the magnetized shielding, Rovo opened up the sides, giving Sai and Eponi a clear view of the massacre below. Squaddies and agents littered the ground, though others were moving around, loading up the transport.

"Looks like we lost," Sai said, looking at the black and crimson uniforms among those still standing, those now moving to target the shuttle. "Evacuate?"

"Now you wanna be smart?" Eponi said. "We have surprise, let's use it."

Outnumbered, outgunned, Sai and Eponi dropped from the shuttle. Sai had his katana in one hand, his pistol in the other, sending the first shots at the agents. The enemy reached for their rifles, pulled them up, and took bolts as Rovo lit up the drop shuttle's turrets. Swipe shooting might not work well against fighters, but in close combat? Against humans?

Sai landed amid a laser wash, dropping his pistol, raising his sword, and, feeling that adrenaline surge, went hunting.

Changing Stakes

By now, the experimental concourse felt familiar. Gregor, leaving the lift behind Vana, stared down its long length heading towards the *Nautilus* bow and left a lingering heartbeat on *Weapons Lab 3*. Yeah, he knew this place, and no, he didn't want to come back here ever again.

Vana seemed to feel the same way, despite bringing him here. The first words from her mouth when they left the lift were a curse, and she swept her hands back across her face, pushing her hair aside and leveling a steel look at Gregor.

"Let me do the talking," Vana said.

As to who Vana would be talking to, they swarmed the hallway. A full squad, not far beyond Vana and Gregor, making their way down and clearing rooms as they went. Some fifteen people, including soldiers and the scientists granting them access to the rooms. Lamya and the others making good on their job to sweep the ship.

Leaving the lift in a full power armor suit served to attract all the wrong attention, with alarmed calls marking Gregor's entry to the concourse, followed by swiveled rifles.

Vana threw her hands up, and Gregor spread the power armor's gauntlets as wide as the concourse allowed, showing he didn't hold any weapons.

The squaddies were just doing their jobs. No need to make things any harder.

"We're securing valuable material," Vana said when the squad leader separated herself enough to ask just what the hell Vana, dressed in her heavily armed version of the Quartermaster uniform, and a power-armored man were doing down here. "Up ahead, there's equipment we can't let fall into agent hands."

"Up ahead where?"

"*Weapons Lab 5*," Vana said. "I'd advise you and your squad to hang back. Let us handle this."

"You aren't the one giving orders in this situation," the squad leader replied. "We'll be right with you."

Vana hesitated, then shrugged, "Fine. I won't argue against the help."

And yet, Gregor felt pretty damn certain Vana didn't want the squaddies along. The squad leader sensed it too, and while her soldiers cleared aside to let them pass, Gregor's visor painted plenty with red potential threats. Those squaddie rifles aimed, however vaguely, in his direction.

"C'mon," Vana said as they passed by the squad. "Before they start asking the real questions."

"Like?"

"Like who you are. Who I am. Why they're going to die."

Vana kept walking, the squad shuffling off after them. Gregor's clanks overwhelmed the marching noise, but not the conversations sparking up in his wake. The suit picked up more than Gregor's ears would have, catching muttered questions about what armor like his was doing on the *Nautilus*.

"Why they're going to die?" Gregor asked.

"You ever hear the phrase, wrong place wrong time?"

"Sounds familiar."

"Apply it." Vana stopped in front of *Weapons Lab 5*. "Stay ready. If I'm right, this is where everything falls apart."

Vana relayed the same instruction to the squad, who fanned out behind them. The *Weapons Lab 5* entry spread out double-wide, designed for heavier work than the small chamber that'd held Gregor's power armor. When Vana tapped her wristlet, the door dutifully shunted aside, spilling into another gap room.

"You all wait out here," Vana called back to the squad. "Cover the exit."

The squad leader started a comeback, maybe a snarl saying, again, that Vana couldn't give her orders, but the agent turned her back on the troopers and walked in. Gregor followed, willing to ignore the tiff between the two sides. The conflict didn't involve smashing things, and Gregor had already done his diplomacy for the day with Lamya.

Besides, his visor pinged a warning about energy signatures ahead. Normally, a ping like that would mean rifles or other energy weapons were pointing Gregor's way. With a closed door blocking any sight, blocking most of any radiating power, there must be something particularly nasty going on in there.

"Careful," Gregor said as the first door shut behind them, separating the duo from their squaddie escort. "Something's active on the other side."

"I bet," Vana hesitated next to the inner scanner. "Gregor, I need to know something."

"What?"

"Your squad. What do you want?"

"I don't understand?"

"What's your goal?" Vana leaned on the wall next to the scanner. "Your commander, Aurora, talked like she had some major ideas in mind. Is that what you're after?"

There was a time for high minded discussions about life goals, philosophy, and so on. That time was not now. Gregor had a squad to get back to, a bridge to visit on his commander's orders.

"Open the door," Gregor said. "Let's finish this and go to the bridge."

"So you don't know what you're looking for."

"You heard me."

Vana shrugged, turned to the scanner, "Your call. I find it's easier to work with allies when I know their goals, but you do your thing."

"I will."

Gregor adjusted his stance, put himself square in the door's center and balanced on his feet, ready to burst forward. The armor didn't have any weapons beyond its big metal fists, and while that ought to be enough, Gregor would have to close to smashing distance to get any damage done.

The scanner clicked and the door slid open. Vana's lead up made it sound like *Weapons Lab 5* would be a horror chamber, like the rooms on Dynas where Felix's viral creations disintegrated in secret.

Instead, the place shone with the pristine perfection that comes from meticulous cleaning, the kind that came not from bots following an algorithm but patient humans with careers on the line. Glittering blacks and reds coated the room, with mustard-yellow circles placed beneath what looked like empty, hanging hooks.

Well, mostly empty.

Five hooks, spaced in sets of two, hung open, each one tied to an accompanying control console. The sixth, towards the room's middle back, held its prize. A snowflake white suit laced through with glassy metals, like power armor for a fashion party. No weapon attachments hung from its body, no big energy packs ready to turn kinetic force into booster jumps. The sort of suit an agent might design: pretty and useless in an actual battle.

Gregor's visor pinged it, and also caught two other signatures in the room, hugging the left and right walls. Despite the warnings, Gregor focused on the more immediate middle threat.

Renard, with a burnt uniform, battered face, and holding his left wrist, leaned on the hanging suit. He looked towards Vana with an expression that said he was trying to work up some haughty triumph but just couldn't get there. When he tried to talk, the man coughed, and some decidedly brighter red splashed onto the floor at his feet.

"Things not going quite as you planned, Renard?" Vana said, striding into the room.

"Careful," Gregor warned. "There are others in here."

"Your friend's right," Renard said, recovering enough to rasp out a sentence. "The plan may have needed some adjusting, Vana, because some people aren't smart enough to realize when they've lost, but we are still in control."

Vana, apparently not caring about Gregor's warning, went straight for Renard. She didn't raise the rifle, but strode in with all the confidence of someone who owned the room and everything in it. Gregor hung back, near the door, where nobody could get behind him. More worrisome were the visor's energy readings, which said there ought to be things on his left and right, but his eyes saw nothing near those walls.

No, not quite nothing. Gregor squinted, looking to his right, while Vana and Renard dipped into a quieter discussion. Along the black wall, a crimson line running right through its middle, the white light cast from the illuminating rows along the ceiling, bent here and there. As if being run through a filter, splashing at odd angles along the wall behind. The slightest shadows ran through the red.

So far as technology went, Gregor and Sever and DefenseCorp had played with stealth and light-bending tech before. The finicky things usually required all kinds of crazy power to keep up the illusion, and were awfully fragile. A single scratch or laser burn collapsed the show, rendering the suit's prime advantage useless early in a firefight.

Which was why they'd been dumped. If Vana had herself all worked up over a new stealth suit, then she'd missed out on the idea's history.

"Gregor," Vana said, turning from Renard and looking his way. "Mind coming in a little further?"

"Why?"

"Because Renard seems to think he's found a winning formula, and I want you to prove him wrong."

"I am not a toy," Gregor said.

"No," Renard responded, "not a toy, but invaluable proof. Vana tells me you are part of Sever squad, and I can't say I'm surprised to see yet another one of you sticking a knife into my side. Here, now, you have a chance to push it all the way through. Bring an end to my attempts."

Gregor didn't move. The energy signatures did. They both shifted closer, moving around the walls and towards his doorway spanning power armor stance.

"See, Vana?" Renard said. "Helix was only one part of our work. One branch on our tree. This, this here? This is the trunk, the roots, and the leaves."

Vana, rifle dangling, folded her arms and looked Gregor's way, "You talk an awful lot, Renard. I prefer show to tell."

"Then watch."

Gregor paid half attention to the words. Focusing on the energy pings, Gregor waited till they closed within a few meters, then shifted his weight to his right foot. The power armor obeyed, its bulk crackling to life as Gregor's own movement, his spiking heart rate, switched the armor into its active combat mode. Gregor might not have a rifle, might not have a hammer, but the mitts would do just fine.

With his right fist swinging in high and his left coming in low, Gregor's jumping attack caught the invisible enemy by surprise. Whomever sat inside the suit apparently thought they were safe, because Gregor's metal mitts struck home, bashing in and bending their target, the hit throwing the enemy back. Gregor couldn't see the impact, but he heard the squishy metal strike the room's right side wall, followed by a thud as his target fell to the floor.

Whirling, Gregor sent a kinetically charged kick back towards the second ping, creeping up from behind. This one played it smarter, dancing back away from the lethal metal foot. Gregor caught the light shifts as the suit stayed away. A mistake, letting Gregor settle back in. Now the invisible things had lost their numbers advantage.

And with the visor, that invisibility didn't do much anyway.

"I'm not impressed, Renard," Vana said.

"Don't fault the machine for the pilot's error," Renard countered.

"Then perhaps you need better pilots."

Gregor closed with the remaining invisible suit. The combat rush flowed through him, keeping his eyes tuned into that energy signature, his arms and legs feeling out his larger power armor, its limits and its abilities. The suit moved slower than Gregor's old one, its bigger plates weighing on Gregor's natural limbs, but the monster had been designed with fluid motion in mind, rapidly shifting momentum from one part to another, so that once Gregor started moving, he didn't stop easily.

His target didn't know Gregor's capabilities. The invisible specter darted back and forth as if he fought against more traditional power armor, with its stopping, starting, and standard combat functions. Instead, Gregor lumbered, wheeled, punched, and kicked in a grinding, massive sequence, every move feeding into the next almost without Gregor's assent. The armor nudging Gregor from one blow to another on its own.

This constant flow might've been the reason the suit sat in the experimental lab. To Gregor, dancing after the enemy, the experiment succeeded.

The invisible suit finally tried an attack, sliding in beneath a heavy Gregor punch and mistaking the lunging move as an opening. Instead, as Gregor felt, heard, some sort of blade glance off his suit's chest plate—another light-bending weapon?—Gregor brought his right arm in from the lunge, grappling and smashing the invisible enemy against him.

A lethal hug. The invisible armor, though, didn't snap and crack like normal power armor would. Instead, it bent around Gregor's crush, melting inward like a biological body might. The invisible one squirmed, and a distorted cry made its way out, before Gregor felt the movement freeze. He loosened his arm, dropped the thing to the ground.

And stared.

Stealth suits, once damaged, ought to be visible. Ought to be useless. This one still bent the light, still remained almost impossible to trace, save for its dwindling energy signature. If DefenseCorp had figured out how to keep a suit invisible while taking hits, then that—

"A waste," Vana said, and Gregor glanced her way.

Or to where Vana should have been. Instead, Renard had retreated to the room's rear wall, with a grim smile on his face. Vana and the remaining suit had vanished, and with it, a new energy signature appeared on the visor.

"Incompetent pilots wasting our resources," Vana said, her voice echoing with her as she moved around the room. "You should have told me you'd made it this far, Renard. It changes the stakes."

"I didn't even know you'd made it aboard our little vessel," Renard replied as Gregor tried to keep eyes on both. "But don't you see? This, and the girl, would change everything."

"What do the Casparians think?"

The Casparians?

"There aren't enough of them to care," Renard said, the rattled out another bloody cough. "If you would, Vana, I'm afraid we're already late."

"I suppose you're right." Vana's voice came from the room's far corner, near where Gregor had punched out the first one. "Gregor, I'm sorry to have led you all this way. I've had a change of heart, and now I cannot let you leave."

Betrayal. Gregor wished he'd never seen it, but loyalties tended to change fast with cash claiming the galaxy's core cause.

Besides, Vana was an agent, and Gregor would never get too hung up about trashing one of those.

"No hard feelings," Gregor replied, and barreled straight at Vana's energy signature.

He swept his arms wide, trying to cut off Vana's avenues. The invisible armor was thin enough that if Gregor caught a good hit, she'd be out of the game before the fight even started. Two steps brought Gregor across the room's middle, and when he hit the third, his visor cracked.

A blade, like a diamond arrowhead, speared straight through the visor's glass. Its point ended a few centimeters from Gregor's face. Gregor stumbled to a stop, brought in a a hand and yanked out the blade, pulling the visor's glass with it, leaving Gregor's face exposed.

Leaving him without any way to track those energy signatures.

"See, Renard?" Vana said, her voice coming from behind Gregor. "Proper piloting. Know the weaknesses and exploit them."

"Don't talk to me," Renard replied. "Kill the man and be done with it."

Gregor wheeled around, sending his arms in a wide swing. If Vana had been charging into Gregor's back, the punching would've caught her straight out. His fists only hit air, and when Gregor completed the reversal, the only thing he saw was Renard, standing there and looking ill.

Where'd she go?

Trying to find the bent light proved harder without the visor guiding Gregor's eyes. He blinked, rotated around, clomping in a circle and seeing nothing.

"Stop playing, Vana." Renard coughed.

The words changed the game. Gregor couldn't see Vana, but he damn sure could see Renard. Gregor jerked around and started a leap towards the agent leader. As the armor met Gregor's command and acted on it, a stinging burn came from Gregor's back. The big suit faltered as the power packs keeping Gregor's armor going blew out one by one, their conduits sliced apart.

Gregor didn't leap, didn't lunge for Renard.

He fell forward, hit the floor with a bang that echoed throughout the room and beyond. The suit's weight crushed on Gregor, who'd lost his breath in the fall and scrambled to get it back, to get enough air into his lungs to speak the keyword that'd blow off the armor.

"Very nice," Renard said, "and the coup de grace?"

"Again, apologies for being so rude," Vana said, her voice right next to Gregor's ear, something's sharp point touching his throat. "Sometimes, surprises happen."

Gregor couldn't even find the breath for a comeback. Frustrating.

The lab's door whisked open. The squad leader shouting towards Renard, claiming the man needed to stand down. That he was the target. The point pushing against Gregor's throat vanished, and he heard new, terrible noises seconds later.

Vana, going to bloody work.

TWENTY-NINE

Burnout

EPONI COULD COUNT the missions she'd done with Sever where they had fire support on one hand. With no fingers.

By the time Eponi hit the docking bay floor, in the huge transport's shadow, Rovo's drop shuttle turrets blitzed the air around her. Agents, having started to scramble when the drop shuttle came into the bay, sprinted towards the transport's boarding ramps, abandoning any return fire as their allies disintegrated around them.

The drop ship's turrets were designed to handle ship-to-ship combat, and their power did more than just fry their hapless targets. The lasers pounded into the unshielded bay floor, buckling tiles and bursting what lay beneath, prompting sparking gouts, steam flares, and a quick swap in the bay's lighting to a panicked orange.

DefenseCorp tied that color to vacuum breaches, and if Eponi had to guess, the *Nautilus* thought the bay's shields might fail. If that happened, Eponi's rifle fire wouldn't matter. Sai's katana and its victims—already several, going by the sword's red splatter—wouldn't matter. Even the big transport, with its boarding ramps open, would rip apart as outer space attacked.

"Time to go!" Eponi shouted, following in Sai's wake and picking off anyone Rovo's turrets missed. "Break for the door, or we're dead."

The docking bay door, at least, didn't sport much resistance. As the duo broke that way, the agents went the opposite, heading towards their transport.

"What if she's on their ship?" Sai said, ducking a clumsy swing by an agent trying to use his fists after Sai had chopped his rifle in two. As Sai crouched, Eponi snapped off a shot over his head, dropping the agent. "We'll miss—"

"We'd die on that ship, Sai." Eponi interrupted, almost tripping on another body. Rovo's turret barrage shifted, lacing behind Sai and Eponi now for cover. "Not a chance we take out that many, just the two of us."

Sai grunted an assent and kept moving. Their targets dwindled as they neared the door, the portal shunting open as they came close.

Aurora flew out. Not like a bird, but like a rock. Sever's captain struck the ground and rolled with the momentum, catching herself on a half-burned body. Aurora had a slicing cut on her face and down an arm, a broken pistol in one hand. Burnt holes pocked her vest, and in a snapshot, Eponi figured she was about to witness Aurora's untimely death.

Sai adjusted his course like a magnet finding its polar opposite, veering to his right and towards Aurora. Eponi looked towards the door, towards what could've flung Aurora like that, and saw nothing. Was about to say she saw nothing, when the bay's orange light vanished in a whole new, terrifying glow.

Pitched against the void, the massive lasers tossed from

ship to ship looked small. Splashing against the *Prisa*'s shields, they felt dangerous.

Fired from the transport's massive turrets, meant to support full-scale ground invasions, the bolts flared through Eponi's closed eyes, their heat boiled the air in the docking bay, and their energy crashed into Rovo's drop shuttle and the hull above and around it, cracking the shuttle's meager shielding and sending the craft into a fast, spiraling crash towards the bay's far wall. On its way down, the shuttle smashed into the transport's armored body, bending and breaking a turret or two before turning over, smoking, and sticking into the gap between the transport's very right end and the bay wall.

Eponi realized she'd hit the floor, skipping the states in between. Her rifle pressed against her chest, its pressure a reminder she was still, very much, in active combat. This wasn't a kart race, where a crash would leave you in a sort of peace, waiting for rescue.

"Watch out!" Aurora's warning pierced Eponi's ringing ears, bringing her back into the crackling, broken bay. "It's a new suit!"

New suit? Eponi pushed herself up, saw Sai standing in front of Aurora, katana at the ready. Ready for what, Eponi couldn't tell. Nothing seemed to stand between Sai and the docking bay door, and beyond it sat an empty, if blast-marked, concourse.

"What're you talking about?" Eponi said, seeing nothing. She chanced a look behind her, witnessing the transport's ramps climbing into the giant ship.

Which presented its own problem. If those engines came on while anyone stood in the docking bay, they'd all melt like ice on a hot day. And Rovo, if he still lived, would turn to ash.

Eponi broke into a run while Aurora shouted an

answer to the pilot's question. The Sever captain's words cut out quick when metal-on-metal clashes rang out. Eponi, dashing over body parts, didn't have to look to see what made that noise.

Sai and his katana had found an enemy. Good for him.

Ahead, the drop shuttle littered its parts to the ground. Burnt and broken plating made a shrapnel waterfall as the ship's structure fractured. Every piece fit into the sonic cracks left by Sai's fighting, echoing off the floor as Eponi cleared the bodies and broke into a full sprint.

Somewhere along the way, she'd lost the rifle. Somewhere along the way, she'd ceased giving a damn about the weapon.

"Rovo!" Eponi shouted as she made it up to the shuttle, staring towards the flickering engines as the ruined ship's ass made a bad first impression. "Tell me you're not dead yet?"

Up close, the shuttle's continued disintegration added blue and white crackles as its power sources flared their lives away. Burning everything suffused the air, and Eponi fought off the urge to cough, sneeze, and vomit all at once at the dusty fumes spreading from the wreck.

The shuttle's cockpit, where Rovo ought to be, hung several meters over Eponi's head, and she didn't have a great way to climb that far. On any normal planet, Eponi would've been stuck.

But the *Nautilus* wasn't a planet. It was a big rock with engines attached.

"I'm coming to get you, rookie!" Eponi shouted. "Don't do anything stupid!"

Before she jumped, Eponi cracked a look back along the bay, hoping to see Aurora and Sai coming after, ready to assist. Or, failing that, doing something to delay the big transport's takeoff. Instead, it looked like both Sai and

Aurora were doing some dance around each other. Sai's katana whirled and slashed, bounced off of something and rebounded, while Aurora ducked and swung, using the broken pistol as a weapon, aiming at the air.

"The hell are they doing?" Eponi muttered, then blinked her eyes back to the problem at hand.

Maybe Sai and Aurora had lost it. That could wait.

Eponi ran towards the bay's interior wall, a flat surface scored here and there with the remnants of engines past. Chromed silver steel wouldn't normally make for much of a foothold, but gravity's light touch helped Eponi adjust her jump enough to plant her right foot against the wall and kick off, back towards the drop shuttle and still getting higher.

Lower gravity made life feel magical.

Floating into a smoky, sparky haze ruined most of that magic.

Eponi crashed into the drop shuttle's open right side, the one facing the wall. Hull plates ruined by turret burns draped over the opening, and at least one sliced through Eponi's clothes, dragging on the cloth and probably drawing blood beneath. Eponi's eyes seared as she blinked through the ash, her feet coming to rest on the shuttle's haphazard remnants.

The craft had turned upside down in its crash, putting Eponi on a ceiling crossed over with handholds meant for landing troops. Now the damn loops served as small traps, dangling near her feet as Eponi went towards the cockpit. Keeping low kept the smoke going over her head, giving Eponi a chance to see a path forward, one lit by blown conduits and small fires still burning from the transport's assault.

"Talk to me, Rovo!" Eponi called as she started forward.

She'd be so, so annoyed if she came all this way for Rovo to be dead.

A drop shuttle's cockpit had all the amenities afforded a rusted out scrap pile. With the ships designed to be ditched at any moment, every expense was spared, except in the crash department. Protective padding, roll cages, and shocks built into the shuttles gave them the sturdy chance to let passengers and pilots survive a wild plunge to the surface. They did little to help with laser fire, so Eponi's first good look at the seats showed a molten, charred mess.

At least for all except the front pair, the ones farthest away from the disaster claiming the shuttle's back half. Deep blue-black smoke flowed up along the ruined seats, passing up and through the shuttle's shattered windshield into the bay. Like some half-dead prophet, Rovo hung in his chair, body parting the smoke. Eponi closed, avoiding the smoldering back seats and reaching for the clasps holding Rovo in.

"Can you hear me?" Eponi asked. Rovo's eyes looked closed, his head hung limp, and there was a brand new cut crossing the kid's forehead, but it looked shallow. Glass, maybe. "Time to go, Rovo."

The rookie said nothing. Didn't move.

Not a great sign.

"Guess we're doing this the messy way then."

Eponi reached for the clasps, felt them burn her fingers with residual heat, and she yanked her hands away. Winced as she realized what those hot straps must be doing to Rovo's body, trapped against them. The rookie didn't deserve this. Nobody did.

Well, maybe those agents.

Summoning up that kart racer courage, Eponi went for the straps again. Biting her lip, she ignored the burn, unlatched the clasps, which, loosed, crumbled away to pieces anyway. Rovo fell from the seat, a descent that should've had his head cracking to the drop shuttle's ceiling. Gravity played its reduced role again, though, and Eponi caught Rovo by the shoulders.

Before she could figure a way to get the rookie turned upright, the entire drop shuttle jolted. A new hum overrode every snapping, crackling sound around Eponi, as if the universe had decided to take up a low-grade monotone. Eponi started to curse, because she knew damn well what that hum meant.

They were out of time.

The drop shuttle tilted left, sending both Eponi and Rovo tumbling towards its broken side. Eponi's metal-sliced shoulder led the way, crashing into the shuttle's now downward-facing left side, with Rovo nestling into her. Another lurch, and the drop shuttle . . . dropped.

The descent wasn't all that far, they didn't fall all that fast, but the impact broke down what structure the shuttle had left. The side above her, its plates already riven by turret fire, by the crash, splintered, cracked. If Eponi didn't move, she and Rovo would be buried in burning metal.

Feet, hands, will. They all coupled with desperation to get Eponi moving towards that shattered windshield, pulling Rovo with her as she went over the broken glass and out onto the docking bay floor. Behind them, just missing Rovo's taller toes, the shuttle collapsed into a smoking charnel pit. One last alarm gave one last howl as the shuttle died, a fitting eulogy to a craft that'd performed its purpose.

Another ship living up to its ideals burst to life over Eponi's head. The massive transport had its maneuvering jets humming, lifting off the bay floor and getting ready for its departure. Unless Eponi and Rovo wanted a quick, fiery death, they had to move.

"You are gonna owe me so much for this," Eponi said, picking herself and Rovo up and breaking into an awkward run back towards those bay doors.

Only to see Sai dashing towards her, katana sheathed and arms pumping as he ran to meet them. Without saying a word—air was better used to keep running—Sai picked up Rovo's other shoulder and together, with one last torching kiss from the transporter's engines, they sprinted from the bay. Aurora, standing next to the door, slammed it shut as the ship turned up its acceleration.

Eponi laid Rovo down on the concourse floor, then flopped over next to him, blinking up at the red *Nautilus* lights. She took one breath. Two breaths. Tried to think of things that had nothing to do with fire, with ash, with the debris stuck in her hair and between her teeth.

"He's alive," Sai said, kneeling between Eponi and Rovo. "But he needs to get to the med bay fast."

"You're the healthiest of us," Aurora said, and Eponi sat up to see the captain had a few new bruises since the rescue. "Take him. Eponi and I can handle the bridge."

"Aurora, you're in no condition—"

"You heard me," Aurora said. "Go, now. When you're done, come back to the bays. I don't think Renard's on that ship."

Sai looked like he might press the argument a little longer, but the man always followed Aurora's orders, and now wasn't any different. With a huff, Sai lifted Rovo, still limp, still silent, onto his shoulders and took off down the concourse. Eponi watched them run until Aurora held her hand out.

Eponi eyed the offered, bloody fingers and palm, "You want me to grab that thing?"

"You're not looking so hot yourself," Aurora chuckled, somehow hoarse and wet at the same time.

"Been a long day," Eponi said, getting her aching muscles into action enough to stand. "What's on the bridge?"

"I want to see what you and Sai pulled off," Aurora replied. "And I need to know if Deepak's alive."

THIRTY

Partners

COMING BACK into consciousness upside down, the world bouncing along with someone else's footsteps, had Rovo pushing through his all-body aches and pains to flail around like a caught fish. His carrier stopped at the movement and swung Rovo up and over, planted the rookie on the cold, hard, comforting floor.

"Hey Rovo," Sai said, crouching with a cautious smile. "You back with us?"

"I don't know," Rovo replied, blinking at the crimson concourse light and tracing the litany of nerves making themselves known. "What happened?"

"The transport shot you down. Eponi saved your butt, and now I'm trying to get you to the med bay," Sai nodded down the corridor. "C'mon, we're almost to the lift."

"The med bay? Yeah, that'd be good," Rovo said. "Don't think the surgeon's going to be happy to see me again."

"Not your biggest problem."

Rovo held out an arm and Sai picked the rookie up. Rovo's legs weren't exactly strong, but he could walk, and together the two went towards the lift. The concourse had people in it now, squaddies that gave Sai and Rovo looks as they went past, running back towards the docking bays. Bots whirred along too, seeking out opportunities to repair, to find anyone in dire need of medical attention.

Sai had to keep waving those off.

"You could let them take me, you know," Rovo said. "Then you could help Aurora."

"Not happening," Sai said. "The agents launched in their transport, but Aurora thinks there might be some left onboard. You know where Kaia is, which means you're their most valuable target."

"Not just me," Rovo replied. "An agent sent out a message. They know what planet she's on."

Sai laughed, "Planet? That's all? Don't know if you've ever seen a planet, Rovo, but they're not that small."

The man had a point. Rovo only had to think back to Dynas—which felt like a million years ago—to know, even with a target's precise location, things could go way wrong before you ever reached the goal.

"She might leave, too," Rovo said.

"What?"

"Kaia. There's no saying her father wouldn't hop on another transport going farther away. Wexer wouldn't have many options, but Gillane Four?"

"More than a few."

Two squaddies stood outside the lift, holding rifles, and giving Sai suspicious looks. Rovo couldn't really fault them for it, as neither he nor Sai wore DefenseCorp uniforms, and the *Nautilus* had been put on watch for agents.

Sai and Rovo both put up their free arms, Rovo wincing with his motion, as a peaceful indicator. That didn't stop one squaddie from lifting his rifle while the other went forward to greet them.

"Want to use the lift?" the greeter said. "I'm going to need identification."

"Call Lamya," Rovo said. "She'll clear us. Rovo and Sai, Sever Squad."

The squaddie nodded, raised his wristlet, and the lift door opened behind them. The squaddie with his rifle raised wheeled towards the opening door and faltered. Rovo couldn't see what lay inside, but he could see the rifle squaddie lift up and fly across the concourse, a sudden motion that slammed the soldier into the far wall with bone-crunching force.

The tossed man's partner didn't fair much better, turning around and starting a shout before something picked him up and threw him over to his fallen friend. Sai pushed Rovo back, sending the rookie against the near wall. With his right hand, Sai drew the katana and faced off against . . .

A blur? A ghost?

Rovo blinked and tried to make sense of what he saw. Which was, mostly, nothing. The light flickered, twisted in parts, as if someone had put some crinkled plastic over his eyes, with the creases breaking the view. Sai looked a little more confident, squaring up in the concourse middle, katana out front and tracking a target.

Another person left the lift. Shambled, really, much like Rovo himself. The man had taken blows, or laser burns, and his uniform, a high-ranking one, bore blood stains on its crimson. His face had a false quality to it, a surgeon's mark, and Rovo placed it: the Wexer projection.

"You've fought one before," the man said, looking at Sai. "Where?"

"Rovo," Sai said, ignoring the question. "Know this guy?"

"Recognize the look," Rovo replied. "Uglier in person."

The man curled up a bruised lip, "Vana, let's move. Every second we waste is a risk."

Sai flicked the katana left, and something struck it, sparks flying and that classic metal-on-metal sound ringing through the concourse. Sai fed the block into a crossing slash, one Rovo figured earned Sai some distance more than anything else. The swing struck nothing, those flickers giving Sai space.

"His name's Renard," Sai said to Rovo, returning the katana to a ready stance. "You want to cap the leader of all this, he's your target."

"Don't think I'll be capping anyone soon."

Whomever Sai fought—Vana?—dove into another attacking flurry. Sai whipped the katana around, blocking what looked like two weapons. The blade's length, coupled with Sai's footwork, kept the man safe, and again Sai took the deflections and turned them into an attack.

Ditching the crossing slash, Sai stepped into a kick. The shot made a crunching noise, as if Sai had struck a particularly thick paper wad. Light clanks followed as Sai's opponent rocked back with the blow.

The laser flashed, burning from Renard's pistol. Sai, apparently reading the room better than Rovo, saw the sneak attack coming and ducked the fire. Rovo might've cheered, might've told Renard to do something pointed with his own anatomy, except those blurs moved into Sai's flinch and picked him up, neck first. Dropping his katana, Sai brought up his hands to wrap about what looked like flickering air. His face tightened as he struggled to breathe.

Rovo didn't have a weapon, didn't have the strength to get up and throw a punch.

But he could make an offer.

"Stop!" Rovo said, trying to shout but, instead, rasping out a decidedly weak demand. "Put him down, and I'll help you."

Whatever held Sai didn't respond, but Renard, turning his pistol on Rovo, took a step in the rookie's direction.

"What help could you offer us?" Renard said, and Rovo picked up enough genuine curiosity in the question to find some hope.

"You want Kaia, right?" Rovo said. "I can lead you to her. But only if Sai lives."

Sai's struggles slowed, his face developed a purple tinge.

"We already know where she is," Renard said. "You offer us nothing."

"You know a planet. I know how to find her on it."

"How?"

"Put him down, I'll tell you."

Renard studied Rovo, and the rookie felt like a book being read. The officer searched for plots, for points of interest, and peculiarities in the wounded man on the floor before him. As much as he could, Rovo tried to project honesty. He met Renard's eyes with an equal focus, trying to ignore that Sai had fallen still.

"Drop him," Renard said. "We have a different prize."

The thing holding Sai threw Rovo's friend across the concourse, landing him in a heap with the two downed soldiers. Rovo tried to sit up, tried to see if Sai moved at all, but before he could get a good look, he felt a hand grip his right arm and pull him to his feet.

"Can you walk?" A woman's voice in his ear, chilled with purpose.

"With help," Rovo said. "Slowly."

Apparently, that answer didn't qualify. Rovo's legs swept out and arms caught him, carrying the rookie like a rescued civilian. His carrier didn't wait for further instructions, marching on down the concourse with Renard shuffling behind, the wounded officer huffing as he worked to keep up.

This close, Rovo pieced together what he saw: a suit that could refract light, or could redistribute it to seem transparent, even if the edges left mars in the visual continuity. Like glass with hairline fractures.

But the invisible suit didn't register as Rovo's big concern.

"Did you kill him?" Rovo said to the woman carrying him, taking a guess as to where her head sat.

"No," the woman replied, keeping her voice low. "You spoke quick enough to spare his life. Be proud of that fact."

"I am," Rovo said, because he was. "Where are we going?"

"To another ship," the woman said as they approached the docking bays. "I'm going to stuff you inside, and you're going to cooperate, because if you don't, you'll get what your friend didn't."

"A friendly hello and some hot coffee?"

The woman stifled a laugh, "How does Aurora manage all of you?"

Rovo widened his eyes ever so slightly before catching himself. The woman knew Aurora? And didn't speak of her as some rival, or an enemy? Interesting. Something to play with, there.

"Aurora knows what she's doing," Rovo said as they reached the docking bays, albeit smaller ones on the edges reserved for private and specialty ships. "Do you?"

"We're taking chances on changing the galaxy," the woman spoke like a prophet. "I don't think you can ask for more."

"Don't think working with a goon like that guy is going to change the galaxy for the better."

"Sometimes, you don't get to choose your partners."

The woman waited while Renard caught up, while the man slapped his wristlet against the docking bay door. The portal slid open, revealing a svelte craft that resembled a leaf, or a tear drop. Its black, speckled panels showcased a design Rovo had read about many times: the speckles weren't just aesthetics, but instead adopted a physical pocking that played hell with traditional scanners. The irregular texture made the ship look like an asteroid to casual observers, giving it a chance to sneak in and out without much attention.

"Beautiful, isn't it?" Renard said, leading the way into the bay. "My very own custom order."

"Needs more guns," Rovo quipped.

"Just open the ramp, Renard," the woman said. "I don't care about your ship or how you acquired it."

The officer threw an ugly look towards Rovo, but not quite at him. The rookie figured a thousand insults coursed their way through Renard's mind and mouth in that moment, but reason—or the possible consequences of pissing off someone wearing invisible power armor—kept him quiet. Tapping on the wristlet, Renard prompted his ship to lower a very ordinary boarding ramp.

Just went to show you could look cool on the outside, be plain dull on the inside. After Calico Max and his crazy vested look coupled with a bog standard family unit on Wexer, Rovo was done giving people credit for their wild appearances.

Renard's ship had an interior that did nothing to change Rovo's philosophy. The man must've spent all the cash on the outside, because inside had a couple small cabins, a central area with food storage and a crimson table that folded down from the wall into a space not much larger than the quarters Rovo had to himself on the *Nautilus*. Renard hiked to the single-pilot cockpit while telling Rovo and the person carrying him to settle in.

"Setting you down now," the woman said as the boarding ramp closed behind her. "Don't do anything stupid."

"I'm half-dead," Rovo replied as she put him on the crash couch, a thin crimson—always crimson in here— thing lining the wall opposite the ramp. "Going to be full dead if I don't get some help before too long."

Rovo wasn't sure on that count, but the last numbing bits from his brief med bay dalliance had faded. If Renard and his invisible accomplice wanted to take Rovo hostage, they could at least make him comfortable.

"Renard," the woman called, "you have any medical supplies on this ship?"

"Check the storage, straight back," Renard sounded like he could use some help too, choking and coughing through the words. "Should be a case. I'm lifting off now."

Rovo leaned back into the couch as the blending light suit vanished away. The ship's engines hummed to lift, and Rovo felt that always-strange sensation as the craft floated up, rotated, and blasted out from the *Nautilus*.

A hostage.

But, like Sai, Rovo could live with that.

THIRTY-ONE

Messages

THIS TIME, Aurora waited for Deepak outside the briefing room. Sever's own turn for their assignment wouldn't come for a few hours, but the newly promoted admiral said he'd have a break around now, after dishing off another patrol contract to one of the *Nautilus*'s younger squads. Those soldiers, looking awful young, looking awful green, passed by Aurora with a few nervous looks at her rank and her hard eyes.

"Congratulations," JJ, Beacon's longtime commander, said as he trailed his squad. "Glad Sever's going to be in good hands."

"There's a spot open, you want to join," Aurora replied, throwing the old standby a threadbare smile. There was always a spot open.

Always.

"I prefer my enemies in front, where I can see'em," JJ said, clapping Aurora on the shoulder. "Besides, you already stole one of my best. Figure that's enough."

"Sai's a killer. Thanks for letting him go."

JJ's eyes flashed, "Sai's a father. Don't forget that."

The Beacon commander gave Aurora a final nod, then stalked off down the corridor after his people. Deepak took his place, measuring up Aurora with a straight look that carried precisely zero emotion.

"Well done, commander," Deepak said, starting the conversation the same way they'd ended their last: all formalities. "I was happy to see your name recommended for Sever's top spot."

"Were you?"

Aurora hadn't come here seeking a fight. In fact, she'd wanted the opposite. Some reconciliation, some way back from the odds they'd had. With her new position, Aurora couldn't afford to be on Deepak's bad side, couldn't afford to leave anything festering between them. Deepak would be choosing Sever's assignments as the *Nautilus* admiral, and anything less than the best for her squad wouldn't be acceptable.

"Walk with me," Deepak said, failing to hide a slight smile. "Turns out, being the boss means a busy schedule."

"You didn't answer my question." Aurora matched Deepak's steps as they headed towards the bridge.

"Was I happy to see you've made it to where you belong?" Deepak said. "Of course. Any admiral wants his crew where they'll perform best." He took a breath, and Aurora braced for the coming, non-official answer. "Besides, I'm sure the extra cash will make you happy."

There it was. Deepak had a way of coating harsh opinions in sugary, official trappings.

"I'm here because it's not just about me anymore," Aurora said, choosing not to engage on Deepak's terms. Slugging things out in a verbal mud fight could be fun, but Aurora had other responsibilities now. "My squad deserves their chances. We're ready to go."

"Noted," Deepak said as they hit the bridge, its big

doors opening for them. "Honestly, Aurora, business is going strong. I couldn't stash you and your squad away, even if I wanted to."

Exactly what Aurora wanted to hear. She'd get the missions, get the cash, and her newer members would get experience. Except, she couldn't quite get away from Deepak's last words.

"Would you want to?" Aurora said as they stood on the raised platform jutting into the bridge, a thousand people humming through their tasks as the *Nautilus* sped through space.

They both knew what Aurora meant with that question. The callback to a life that increasingly seemed ludicrous, couched in a fresh start and the gleeful hope that came with it. Nebula nights and mess hall days. Sneaking through back halls to each other's cabins. Love's flicker in dark space.

"I never want to put my squads in harms way," Deepak said, measured and matter-of-fact. The slightest hesitation after. "Is there anything else I can do for you, commander?"

Aurora watched for a hint without giving any of her own. Deepak kept his official face on, no pearls to find in those eyes.

"No, that's all."

"Then congratulations, and I'll see you at the briefing."

AS A RULE, Aurora didn't spend much time on her history. With Sever Squad, with DefenseCorp, spending too much time on the past—and too much time might be a minute or less—could cost you the future. And yet, rushing down the concourse with all the speed two beat-up, ash-blown people could manage gave Aurora space to run it back with Deepak, with all the years burned in these space-faring halls. Different soldiers crowded them now, standing at checkpoints looking for any leftover agents, but the shiny metal look, the clank of boot on floor, those stayed the same.

Aurora took a wristlet from a junior squaddie, one who didn't have the stomach yet to say no to someone with Aurora's now very visible bad-assery. Sever's commander didn't have any rank with DefenseCorp anymore, didn't have a uniform on, but the scared and stunned looks floating her way proved just as effective. Backing them up with her straight-eyed stare and words that brooked no refusing, Aurora took her determination to see the bridge and turned it into a weapon.

That skill, too, had come about through these corridors. Aurora had been a trigger-happy security guard when she first arrived, but the discipline and its cash rewards chiseled her raw edges into sharp, strong habits. They—

"We didn't shoot it," Eponi said, interrupting Aurora's focused advance. "The bridge, right?"

"What?"

"I didn't really think about it, that you wouldn't know." Eponi, while keeping up with Aurora's light jog, brushed more ash from her hair with her hands. "But you said you wanted to check out the bridge. I'm telling you, whatever happened there, not my fault."

Aurora blinked, focused on her steps, "We couldn't raise the bridge from the comm center, so something went wrong."

"Well, yeah," Eponi said. "They started shooting at each other, then the fighters came after us and we booked it."

"They?"

"I guess the agents? Deepak gave the order to round them up, and I don't think the ones on the bridge took it very well."

"Good."

Given Deepak's stunned look when Aurora took out the pistol, showed some force in the meetings this morning, the ones that seemed about a thousand years ago, the admiral needed to get his hands dirty more often. The man still led a combat force.

The bridge entry backed up Eponi's version of events. The wide door sat half closed, the occasional spark still popping the gliding slits. Blood and blast stains marked the walls and floor in front, and two soldiers, both bearing bandages and looking exhausted, swung rifles up to meet Aurora and Eponi as they closed.

"Friendlies," Aurora said, pulling up and raising her hands. No sense going this far to get shot by a trigger-happy squaddie. "I'm trying to find out if Deepak's all right?"

One soldier barked for their identification, a command that came as more of a yip, a desperate attempt to get some order back into a frazzled day. Aurora didn't have any identification to offer, and she started to spin up some excuse when Eponi launched instead.

"Identification?" Eponi said. "Do you have eyes, man? Do you not see that I have no weapons on me, she's wearing a busted pistol, and we look like we just took a spin cycle through a crap machine? Who's in charge here, because it better not be you."

The squaddie's mouth opened and shut like a gulping fish, and then, not finding any suitable comeback, the man told his teammate to keep his rifle up and vanished inside the bridge.

"Well said," Aurora noted.

"I feel like trash and I look worse," Eponi said. "The faster you get to talk with the admiral, the sooner I can get to a shower."

Whatever kept you motivated.

The soldier returned without anymore casualties, verbal or physical, and said Deepak waited inside. Aurora led the way, catching Eponi giving the soldier a hard eye roll on the way past. There were many reasons the pilot had found her way to Sever Squad, not least because standard-issue discipline didn't fit with Eponi's worldview.

Today, Aurora could live with that.

The bridge bore little resemblance to Aurora's earlier, unpleasant experience. Where before workstations had stretched down and away from the entrance like a networked, mechanical hillside, now broken and burnt shreds remained. The pristine walls, swooping in a big curve along the bridge's back, bore hideous black pocks, while the grand viewing shield . . . wasn't. All the fire, smoke, and damage had coated the glass in mottled gray-white, making the bridge feel less like the stellar apex of a great ship and more a rotting egg.

"It's going to take some work," Deepak admitted as they walked in. The admiral, leaning on his standing-height consoles, offered up a haggard grin. "Which is why I was so happy to hear you also destroyed my back-up bridge."

"Blame the agents." Aurora came all the way up to the admiral and gave him a once-over. "How many shots did you take?"

"Three. One in the leg, one in the shoulder," Deepak sighed, looked down, "and, somehow, one on my foot. I think the shooter fired as he fell." Returning to Aurora's face, Deepak didn't quite suppress a chuckle. "Looks like I'm not the only one taking heat today."

"We're alive, that's what matters," Aurora said.

She wanted to ask the admiral how he really felt, wanted to ask why he was standing here at all and not getting to the med bay. Those bandages on his wounds couldn't be doing much to help. But asking those questions wouldn't get Sever where it needed to go.

"You need to get fighters out, after the transport that just launched," Aurora said, nodding past Deepak to a console showing near-field scans, which had the transport showing as a big blot in the otherwise empty deep space. "The agents are on there, and they have a weapon we don't want to let get away."

Deepak didn't move, "We? Aurora, I gave you your lockdown. I told my soldiers to round up the agents, a move which may guarantee my removal from this post. That *will* guarantee I'll have to check my room every night for hidden traps before I sleep, lest some agent deliver vengeance. I did this for you—"

"Cut it," Aurora snapped. "You didn't do this for me. You did it because you knew anything else would be suicide. The agents don't give a damn about your troopers. I do, because I used to be one."

Deepak nodded, "I saw your message. Very good, with all the right words. Not that it will matter."

"Because?"

"Because by the time your missive reaches the right people, the agents will have ensured their loyalty, or replaced them with ones receptive to their demands. That's what I was trying to tell you before. There is no winning here."

"Then why?"

Deepak closed his eyes, shook his head, "Because I'm an idiot who cannot let go, that's why."

Cannot forget? Aurora tried to parse that, follow

through Deepak's words from start to finish. Started, and stopped when an officer shouted up from below, one stationed at one of the few remaining workstations still running.

A ship had left the *Nautilus*. A small one, registered to Renard.

"Stop that ship," Aurora replied, brushing past Deepak and looking towards the officer. "Shoot it down, if you can."

"Admiral?" The officer did the proper thing and ignored Aurora. Hurtful, but right. "What should we do?"

"You heard the commander," Deepak said, sounding ever more tired. "Renard's a traitor and a danger to everyone here. Bring it down."

Aurora thought Renard had been on the transport, had already departed the *Nautilus* for another hideaway. The big ship had already fled beyond the reach of the *Nautilus* turrets, and Aurora would be asking Deepak why he hadn't fired on it. Renard, though, would be an easy target for the *Nautilus* teeth.

"They're hailing us, sir," called the same officer, whose flustered state amplified with every declaration, like a top winding up. "It's Renard himself."

"Then send it, man, and calm down," Deepak replied. "He cannot hurt us from his little ship."

Aurora couldn't be confident in that, but she let Deepak have his station. Standing behind him as the admiral turned to see the incoming hail light up the console, Aurora saw not Renard's grainy head, as expected, but a different one.

"Rovo?" Eponi said, as confused as Aurora felt. "The hell's he doing with Renard?"

The rookie didn't look well, and his eyes were closed.

Head lolling to the side, Rovo sported bruises, cuts, and all the evidence of a day gone far worse than planned.

"Deepak!" Renard's voice cut in, and the officer stuck his face into the frame, a leering glare. "See my precious cargo? One of your friend's squad members, I believe. A young one. Shoot me down, and he goes too."

Renard hadn't stopped, his ship still cruising away. In seconds, he'd fly beyond the *Nautilus*'s reach. Deepak had to make a decision, and Aurora knew she could pull the trigger for him. Rovo was a Sever Squad member. She could tell Deepak to fire, and he would.

"A deserter, and a civilian," Deepak offered Aurora a solemn look, his finger navigating to the mute button, cutting off Renard's continued jibes. "A single casualty falls within the limits. We should fire."

The words weren't loud enough to trigger a response, weren't directed at the others on the bridge, or back at Renard.

Aurora didn't flinch.

"No," Aurora answered. "Don't shoot."

"ALWAYS KNEW you had a heart in there somewhere," Eponi said as they ran down the concourse, behind a soldier ready to scan them through to the target. "All that talk about cash and command and here—"

"Eponi, shut it," Aurora said as they hit far enough to enter the *Nautilus* bays.

On the upper level, the slots stayed fixed for official ships. DefenseCorp bigwigs and important visitors. Except for a trio meant as fast-access fighters, sharp craft designated as a last ditch escort for officers forced to flee.

Deepak suggested the idea, offering them up as an option if Aurora wanted to try and save Rovo. Aurora had dished off a thanks and left. Deepak would survive, would no doubt mention this little moment later.

Maybe Deepak had been trying for the same thing, shoving Sever into all those safe slots. Rovo, though, had been taken hostage. Not his fault, not his choice. Rovo didn't deserve to die for that.

"First one's good," Eponi said, and the soldier scanned them through, right to a shimmery yellow ship crammed with turrets, shields, and two giant engines stuffed into its half-moon shape.

For a rescue, the ship would serve.

The Left Behind

PUNCHED, shot, even stabbed during an early DefenseCorp assignment roaming the streets of a planet in a rebellion, but never choked. Not with a hand holding him up off the ground, squeezing Sai's life away one second at a time. His legs went numb first, as black spots danced over his eyes. His hands, at first trying to get the grip off his throat, went limp, like a power switch turning off.

The blood pounded through his head, trapped and circling and dying.

And through those black spots, Sai saw the tearing glimmers, the false bending tied to the strange suit he'd fought back near the transport and now here. Through the schisms, Sai saw Renard, the officer at the heart of all this, talking to Rovo. The spoken words went into Sai's ears, where they vanished into the panicked, pulsing cacophony wracking his desperate self.

The throw registered only as relief.

Sai took a long time to move after he'd been tossed aside. Beneath him were the two ruined soldiers, dead by virtue of their own misfortune. Any other station but that lift, at that hour, and they'd have glided through this whole day without a problem. Now Sai used their cooling, hardening bodies as a nightmare bed.

He should've forced himself up. Should've forced himself to grab that katana and sprint after Rovo. Thrown everything he had at those two bastards.

Except Sai couldn't move.

You die a thousand deaths in a career like this. See yourself at life's end time and time again until you acquire a certain mocking attitude. That shot, this mission, those bombs should've been the ones to cast Sai into the great beyond, but they didn't, and they never had. Even Anaskya's virus, tearing through his body, or the patrol craft on Wexer, or the hero laser blast on the *Prisa*.

In the last few months, Sai had knocked on death's door plenty and come away without an answer.

But none, not one, of those moments had made him feel so damn weak.

"You want to go?" she asked him, on that rainbow rain day beneath the glassy, manufactured sky. "Leave all this?"

This, as it was most other mornings, consisted of a frenzied dash to get his son and daughter ready for school. To get his wife into a place where she could resume the always-on responsibilities due an engineer. Finally, to get himself into a uniform, to the apportioned place in the vast city where Sai could stand, sit, or walk for hours and pray nothing that day would take him from the next.

Today, though, went slower. His children, as they had throughout the years, needed less and less. They made their breakfast, they packed their bags, they left with a wave to their waiting friends. His wife blurred from the bed to the board room, leaving Sai pulling together a meal with nothing but the birds. Today had been like yesterday, like the one before that and the one—

"When did you know," Sai asked, "that this is what you wanted to do?"

The kids weren't home yet, wouldn't be for a while. The porch, with fearless birds ducking inside the covering to avoid the rain, served as neutral territory. The soft lab-spun cedar made for a beautiful table, a gift Sai had given his wife, on a month's salary that she made in a day. The hanging flowers her stamp on things. Equal partners in an equal space for an equal conversation.

"When I saw the impact," his wife replied.

"You're more charitable than me," Sai said, his eyes drifting to the katana. It sat near the doorway back into the house. He'd been practicing in the yard when his wife came home early, after he'd called. "They look up to you, you know."

"You too." She always had that way, always knew how to turn a compliment for one into a success for all. "You're brave. Strong."

"Static," Sai said. He couldn't be that today, though. The offer had come through, an opening for someone with his skillset. "I don't want them to watch me get old. To watch me do this every day."

Six months later, after passing through more tests and training than Sai had ever done, the mercenary minds at DefenseCorp passed him along to the *Nautilus*. He'd left home with open tears, hard hugs, and a promise to come back when Sai felt like he'd earned his rest. In the meantime, the extra cash would pay for schools, would pay for his wife's parents to come live with her. All benefits.

Those last looks would be the terrible cost.

"SAI," the heavy voice said, "wake up, my friend."

Sai saw the concourse, felt the bodies beneath his

hands. He must've passed out again. His throat still hurt, that dull ache ringing when Gregor held a small water cup to Sai's mouth and forced the liquid down.

"There's medicine in there," Gregor said. "You'll feel better."

At some point, maybe. Gregor's tonic didn't work instantly, but Sai pushed himself into a sit anyway, legs sticking out like a child. Gregor loomed over him, near the lift, while other squaddies tended to the bodies behind Sai.

"They have Rovo," Sai said, the urgency coming back. "We have to—"

"Gone," Gregor replied. "The cowards fled. Aurora and Eponi are chasing now."

"Where? Can we catch them?"

Gregor shook his head, leaned down and helped Sai up. The man gave Sai an odd look as he did so, no doubt tracking the shredded burns from the *Prisa*, the bruising along Sai's neck.

"What happened to you?" Gregor said.

"A lot," Sai replied, glancing back at the fallen squaddies with a sigh. "They didn't make it?"

Gregor chased Sai's look, matched his sigh too, "Does not look like it. Who?"

"Someone in a new suit, I think." Sai picked up his katana, gripped it tight. "Fought two of them today. Invisible bastards."

"Ah. Me too," Gregor said. "Dangerous."

"Renard came here too."

"Not surprising. I followed them." Gregor shifted Sai towards the lift. "Do you need the med bay?"

"Wouldn't be a bad plan, I think." Sai ran a mental count of his aches, his pains, before settling on Gregor's disappointed look. "'Cept I get the feeling you've got another idea?"

"Renard left behind evidence. We should destroy it."

"What?"

"Follow me."

Following, here, meant trailing Gregor down near the mess hall, on the *Nautilus*'s bottom floor. Past the doors leading to the ship's large labs, and finally to one near the concourse's end. Squaddies posted up here too, putting broken bodies on stretchers to send up to the med bay.

"The same thing you saw above. Vana," Gregor said while they watched, "is very dangerous. More than Renard. But I am not certain whose side she is really on."

"Looks like it's not our side." Sai gestured to the bodies as the two Sever members stepped past them and into the lab beyond.

The squaddies didn't challenge Sever, maybe because they knew Gregor, or maybe because they had enough problems right now that didn't need adding to. Either way, *Weapons Lab 5* sported one big broken power armor, some empty hooks, and marks in the walls and floor telling a tough story.

"She could have killed me," Gregor said. "It would have taken only a second, but she did not."

"You look pretty tough to kill, Gregor. Maybe she didn't think she had the time."

"The blade was at my throat. I couldn't move."

Sai shrugged, watched as Gregor went further into the lab. The man took a right turn, headed for the room's corner. As Gregor bent down, Sai saw the flickers, the light bending. Without a second's hesitation, pushing through the aches, Sai had his katana back in his hands. No way he'd get caught off guard by one of those suits again.

"It's okay," Gregor said. "This one is smashed."

With his katana ready, Sai crept closer, watched as Gregor felt around the glitchy air and found the suit's release. Like some bad movie effect, the suit's visor retracted, revealing a man's face, with a bloody broken nose and glassy eyes. Still breathing, though.

"You left him, alive?" Sai asked, lowering the katana towards the target.

"Legs broken," Gregor said. "Didn't want the others to find him."

The man coughed when Gregor gave him a light slap on the cheek. His eyes flipped open, bloodshot and hurting.

"Name?" Gregor asked.

The man replied with a curse, directed Gregor's way with a sore loser's spitting vigor. Sai had the katana's point at the man's chin before the words finished firing out.

"Try again," Sai said.

"Conyers," the man said, eyes on the blade. "Not that it matters. Gonna kill me anyway, I'm thinking."

"But not yet," Gregor said, then the big man nodded away from Conyers, towards the room's empty space. "Is the other your Casparian friend?"

"Only two agents left Renard could find," Conyers affirmed, his attitude draining in sharp gasps as his wounds caught up to him. "We took him from the med bay down here."

"He is gone," Gregor said. "Now, you can talk."

Except Conyers couldn't. As Gregor spoke, the agent's eyes rolled back and the man passed out again.

"You're too scary," Sai said.

"Perhaps." Gregor stood. "Or perhaps it is time we go to the med bay."

"Now there's a plan I can get behind."

Sai and Gregor each took a suited body. Thankfully, the invisible things were light enough that Sai only felt piercing twinges every few steps. The walk back came with a gradual shift in the *Nautilus* itself. Lights changed back to their usual white. Orders calling for repair crews rang over the intercoms. The med bay itself hummed, crowded with squaddies, captive agents, and, now, one member of Sever squad.

On the bed, when the nursing bot asked Sai if he needed anything else, the man had one request.

Pull the videos from his inbox. The ones from his family. Sai expected them to be sealed, but the nurse bot complied. Sent along a little screen, and as the medications hit his nerves, Sai saw the smiling faces of a family he'd left behind for far too long.

THIRTY-THREE

Break Point

WHILE THE FIGHTER didn't have anything on the *Prisa*'s strength, the thing packed speed into its twin engines. As soon as Aurora said go, Eponi had the fighter popping up and bursting away from the *Nautilus*.

The seat sat snug around Eponi, closing in on her shoulders, back, and neck to help with stability through endless barrel rolls and snap dodges, either in atmosphere or dark space. The flight stick, a solo number jutting up between Eponi's knees, played tight, causing Eponi to over-turn her target twice before settling into a strong approach.

Difficulty came too in finding Renard's ship at all. The damn craft fuzzed out on the fighter's screens, like a whisper in a large room. Eponi would've had a hard time finding the ship at all except she knew where the man was heading, and the big transport had as much stealth as Gregor on a bender. Tracking back from the boat let Eponi's scanners find just enough anomaly to get her pointed in the right direction.

Eponi punched the engines, and soon enough, Renard's stealth couldn't cover for close proximity.

Orange-hued graphics splashed onto the bubble-style windshield, haloing Renard's ship and surrounding it with translucent numbers counting down to firing range, estimating velocity, and, with a slight ghost white arrow, guessing at Renard's direction. Not that Eponi needed that help: the big transport shone in the distance, an obvious escape route.

"Figuring it out?" Eponi said, the pilot sending her words back to Aurora, whose own hands wrapped around the main turret's gunnery sticks.

"It's a turret. I'm fine."

"Even with the hits?"

Eponi knew she wasn't feeling all that fine. The rush to get to Rovo helped push through the lingering shock from the daring-do rescue attempt and the *Prisa*'s near starbursting, but Aurora looked like she'd taken it far worse.

"I'm fine."

Nothing followed. The ice came through the comm. Eponi didn't question it.

"Approaching mark," Eponi said, the little fighter doing its job and closing with Renard. "If they don't start shooting, you should have a clear angle for the engines. If we get fire—"

"I won't miss."

Okay. If the iron in Aurora's voice had a say in things, Renard was done.

The fighter breezed into laser range with a clear chime. Eponi watched for a turret, for any counter attack, but none came. Either Renard thought Sever wouldn't risk attacking with Rovo on board, or he'd spent all the cash on hiding and none on surviving.

Eponi slid the approach angle down. She'd come in sharp, swooping behind and then underneath the ship.

Aurora would have a broad window to line up and take enough shots to pierce shields and burn out the engines, and while the fighter didn't have any way to take Rovo on board, Deepak had another drop shuttle ready to go.

Easy.

So easy, that Eponi answered the incoming hail without any concern. Normally, you don't interrupt an attack run with idle conversation, but Renard's total lack of evasive maneuvering and Eponi's confidence in Aurora's trigger fingers, meant she could take Deepak's call and tell him to get that shuttle ready.

"You'll hold your fire if you want your friend to live," Renard's voice crackled through, crashing Eponi's sanguine approach. "If your fighter sends a single laser my way, your man dies."

"You kill him," Aurora said. "You lose your chance to find Kaia."

"Wrong," Renard replied. "I merely delay it. We have her planet, we know her father. We will find her."

Eponi watched the distance dwindle. They'd be entering target range in seconds.

"So we let you go?" Aurora said. "With Rovo? Not happening."

"A hostage is still alive, commander. A corpse is just that."

Eponi muted the call while slowing the fighter down.

"Gonna have to make a choice here, Aurora," Eponi said. "I can sit behind Renard, but he's getting close to that transport, and I don't want to play tag with those big guns if I don't have to."

"Can you think of any other option?"

"Right now? You and me, we're in a tiny capsule without much flexibility," Eponi said. "Maybe we could jostle Renard's ship enough to knock him over, but without a boarding party, we're tied."

"If he gets to that transport, we'll never see Rovo again."

Aurora's voice had that dead finality to it. The tone Eponi had heard the captain use a few times before, when circumstances sent another squad member around their final lap. Aurora might be deploying it as a safety valve for her own psyche, calling the race before it ended to save herself the pain.

Eponi had done that herself. She'd also made reckless attempts to get back in it, push for victory against terrible odds.

The last time she'd done that, it'd ended Eponi's career.

"Call us off," Eponi said, "and let's turn back. They won't kill Rovo. Not right away at least. We can try again."

"Try again? When?"

"We follow. Pick the place, time, and get our rookie back."

Eponi eased the fighter in behind Renard's ship, floating behind the larger craft's engines. With a tap, she brought in the transport's signature over the windshield, a new number set telling Eponi how long they had till the transport could start taking pot shots.

"I'm assuming the silence means you're mulling over your options," Renard said. "If it matters, I wanted you all dead. Your damn squad ruined Dynas, and I thought you deserved payback. But now you've given me what I really needed, and in exchange? I might not kill you all."

Aurora's cursing carried through the cockpits. Enough for both of them.

"You hurt him," Aurora said, "You do anything to my

squad again, and I'll make sure you never see another dawn."

"A threat?" Renard laughed, a wheezy thing. "Please. I've heard far worse. If things go well, I'll see to it that your rookie is left with enough cash to buy transport home, wherever that happens to be. Now, please take your fighter away, or I'll be forced to make a mess."

THIRTY-FOUR

Wishes and Wants

ROVO RECOGNIZED THE ROOM. A DefenseCorp standard special: no frills, all function. And this room's function was recuperation. Rest en route to a destination. Rovo laid on a thin cot, with a black screen on his left pulling numbers for his vitals: heart rate, respiration, temp, all yanked by his contact with the bed.

The room sported a thin chair and a small hanging screen in a corner for entertainment or, as Gregor called it, sanity preservation. A single soft white door, with no handle or scanner to open, sealed Rovo inside the pocket-sized chamber. Even if Rovo had a wristlet, he couldn't get out unless someone watching let him.

Because, even on transports, soldiers could snap. Trauma, anger, panic. All those things necessitated spaces where a squaddie would be kept from harming himself or anyone else.

Not that Rovo had to worry: his own body still felt so sore, beat up, and unwilling to cooperate with aggressive action that he stayed on that cot and stared at the feature-less gray ceiling overhead. He remembered, through scattered flashes, what'd happened on Renard's ship. The man had spoken with Aurora, it seemed. With Deepak maybe. Threatened Rovo's life.

Well, that wasn't too surprising.

If you're going to take a hostage, you might as well use them.

The door hissed open, and Rovo expected Renard. Instead, he saw an older woman. One he recognized. One who'd been with Aurora when she came waltzing into the comm center to start that firefight.

The agent.

"I've been waiting for you to wake up," the woman said, sitting in the chair and crossing her legs, like some therapist about to deliver life-changing advice. "Took you awhile."

"Been a rough day."

"For many," the woman replied. "Which is why I'm here. We took you along because we're hoping you can make all this pain worth it."

Rovo rolled up onto his side, his sore chest protesting the move, but he wanted to get a straight look at the woman.

"By giving Renard what he wants."

"We'll get there," the woman said, delivering a patient look like the one Rovo's mom used to deliver when he wound himself up too much. "How about we start with names? I'm Vana."

Not much harm in introductions.

"Rovo."

Vana inclined her head, "Nice to meet you, Rovo. Do you know where you are?"

"On a transport," Rovo said, "and let me guess, it's going to Gillane Four?"

"Are all you Sever Squad members this smart?"

"We're impatient."

"I see that," Vana said, not once slipping away from that pleasant smile. "Then let me dispense with the pretenses. We're going to Gillane Four to get the girl, because she has what we need."

"You're talking like it's some object she's carrying, instead of her blood."

Vana dismissed the words, moving on, "You saw the suits. I didn't believe Renard could pull it off, but he has. Casparian cells woven in with standard reflective material. Keeps it healthy and resilient, like a protective paint coating. Except it's fragile."

"Didn't seem so fragile to me," Rovo said.

Vana seemed fine explaining the show, and Rovo figured he wouldn't stand in her way. The more information he had, the better. Sever would be coming after him, and when Aurora caught up, Rovo would love to share what he found.

"It can hold a punch or a laser blast well enough," Vana said. "Casparians, however, are sensitive things. They can't take extreme temperatures. Renard believes the suits will fail outside of controlled climates. But blend in the working resistance from that scientist's virus, and now?"

"Congratulations, you have everything an agent could want."

"Everything DefenseCorp could want," Vana countered. "The galaxy is a dangerous place, Rovo. Despite our position, DefenseCorp has to protect its interests. We cannot rest. A suit like this would put our power at the top. And there's room up there."

Ah. There it was.

"You understand," Vana said. "I can see that. Help us find the girl, and you'll help yourself. These suits will change our entire organization, and in change, there's opportunity. With Renard and I backing you, you'll have more power, more cash than you could ever need."

Rovo struggled to keep from blinking, from laughing. He'd joined DefenseCorp for adventure, not cash, but maybe Vana couldn't figure that. Couldn't figure why anyone would do this for something other than money and power.

And that realization gave Rovo an opening. A chance.

"I'll help you," Rovo said. "So long as she won't get hurt. Kaia."

"Not more than a normal doctor's visit," Vana assured. "A little poke, a little sample, and that's all we need."

"Then when we land, I'll find her for you."

Vana stood, "You'll find her for you. Welcome to our team, Rovo. Rest up and recover. I'm afraid your old friends may not see things the same way. and you may well have to persuade them."

Rovo watched Vana leave, walking up to the door and glancing towards a silver nub in a corner. Watched the door shut tight, sealing the rookie inside.

No, Sever wouldn't see things the same way. Rovo would make damn sure of that.

THIRTY-FIVE

The Choice

THE DISTANT NEBULA bloom rose through the *Nautilus* viewing deck. Personnel from all branches stood and sat at thin tables, sharing cheap wines and scrappy finger food. The prettiest place on the *Nautilus* still danced to Defense-Corp's profit-pushing fiddle, but the dry crackers and the fruit juice couldn't do anything to diminish the view.

"We've set the course," Deepak said. "We'll be behind you, of course, but your back-up will arrive eventually."

Aurora nodded, smiled a bit at her bandages in the viewing deck's deep purple lighting, meant to draw focus to outer space's varied wonders.

"What made you change your mind?" Aurora asked. "Before, you were willing to give Renard whatever he wanted."

"I still would if I thought it would keep my command safe," Deepak replied. "Your squad, however, ruined that opportunity."

"Oh no. You're being forced to do the right thing. How terrible."

Deepak threw a sharp look Aurora's way, "I lost troops

today. A lot. DefenseCorp will compensate their families, but the pain they'll feel when they learn their son's, daughter's, or parent's fate won't be covered up with cash."

"Better to die protecting a free galaxy than live under whatever Renard's planning."

Deepak didn't reply to that. For several minutes they both watched the stars, surrounding conversations bubbling quiet around them. Aurora's mind bent towards Rovo, zooming towards Gillane Four. She believed Renard when the man said he wouldn't kill the rookie: agents had a way of wringing all the use they could out of someone before dumping them dead in an alley.

Eponi had posted herself at the *Prisa*, supervising repairs. Deepak had promised Sever new stocks of power armor and weapons, something Gregor had put himself to managing. Sai still occupied a med bay bed, burning the hours while the salves did their work. All told, they would be ready to depart the *Nautilus* in a few days, speeding off in the *Prisa* after Renard, after Rovo.

"I'm sending messages to all the other admirals I know," Deepak said, breaking the silence. "Backing up the words you already sent. It will carry weight, maybe enough to turn them against Renard and the agents." The next line seemed to struggle from his mouth, as if he couldn't quite believe he spoke it. "I don't know that DefenseCorp will survive this."

"Maybe it shouldn't," Aurora said. "Maybe we shouldn't live in a galaxy where one organization has this much power. Where a few people can decide the fate of trillions."

"Isn't that what your squad is doing right now, Aurora? A few people, deciding the fate of trillions?"

Aurora counted the aches, the scratches, and the burns playing their painful notes across her nerves. She ran through Dynas, Wexer, and the *Nautilus* corridors that'd brought her right here. Sever's five had broken open a secret plan, had turned DefenseCorp against itself, a corporate civil war that could . . .

She wasn't much for speculation.

"I guess you have to choose," Aurora said. "Renard's ideas, or mine."

Deepak nodded slow, "Think I've already made that choice."

Outside, the rose nebulae seemed to flare against the dark. A star sending out its final goodbye to an endless universe, or just a trick of the light?

Aurora picked up her glass, clinked it against Deepak's, "Then let's go get the bastard."

SEVER SQUAD'S *adventures continue in GRIM TIDE—Read on for an excerpt!*

An Excerpt from GRIM TIDE

SEVER SQUAD BOOK FIVE

The sparkling water buzzed his lips with something beyond the lemon flavor, perhaps the tingle responsible for the water's name: *Jolt*. Not quite as strong as Aurora's coffee on the ship, but for a lunchtime boost, it would do.

Gregor and Aurora held sway over a rounded outdoor table, watching the DefenseCorp offices on the walking avenue's other side. Aurora munched on her sandwich, while Gregor's crumbs blew away in the breeze. Gillane Four had enough birds, likely brought over from other worlds, that'd clean up the scraps. Somewhere nearby, a busker plied his trade, the rough melody bouncing off the buildings in a pleasant echo.

"This is dull," Gregor said. "We have been here an hour."

"Stakeouts are dull. That's the point."

Aurora's plan had changed from a slam-bang demand for Renard's location to a more targeted pursuit. They'd wait for some solo person to exit the office, then jump the poor sap and get the information they needed without risking a problem with bigger numbers.

Thus far, there'd been a few scattered souls heading in and out of the office, but nobody sporting the crimson uniform showing they actually delivered data for Defense-Corp. Aurora and Gregor needed a source, not a random civilian, and—

"There," Aurora said. "That's one."

Sever's captain shoved the remaining sandwich in her mouth as Gregor turned, spotted the newest exodus from the offices. A plum lady with that deep red uniform and harried hair pounded the pavement. Away from the office, and away from the two Sever squad members.

"Let's go." Gregor stood, lurching up with a little too much excitement and catching his chair before it clattered over onto the light-blasted, creamy stones.

The two fell into pursuit, a chase Gregor felt far more comfortable with. He'd gone after targets time and again, a much more satisfying task than sitting and waiting. He missed the heaviness on his back where his hammer used to sit, waiting to be unlimbered for mass destruction. Instead, while Aurora hid a pistol beneath a jacket, Gregor kept his own pocket shooter in an ankle holster, hidden by flaring, billowy pants. Not exactly fashionable, but Gregor met every raised eyebrow with a steady stare, and soon enough any would-be critics blinked away.

You didn't need to use muscle to take advantage of having it.

The target ambled on towards a crowded intersection, a circular square dominated by yet another water-related statue calling attention to Salinity's founder, her family, or some other person Gregor had neither the interest or time to know. Thus far, the target had kept herself around too many people to make for an easy snatch-and-grab.

"She's turning," Aurora said. "Be ready."

"Always ready."

"Of course you are."

The captain called it right, though. The woman angled away from the square and towards a quieter path heading towards a residential collection. The stacked condos up here looked too nice for what Gregor remembered of his DefenseCorp salary, but perhaps she held a higher rank than the uniform would suggest, or Salinity paid the DC staff here hefty bribes to keep things quiet.

No world wanted to be known as a festering crime pit, while DefenseCorp had every interest in publicizing its well-done peace-keeping efforts. Balances tended to be struck between controlling interests, with cash going into the DC coffers and statistics dying out. A mutually beneficial relationship, and one Gregor had always taken without much comment: so long as he had the opportunities to crush the criminals, who cared where the cash went?

The thinning crowd around the target forced Gregor and Aurora's hand. Before, they'd been able to maintain some distance and count on the disparate species, outfits, and their combined noise to keep Sever hidden. Now, with a person here and there, the tailing would be obvious if the target ever turned around.

"Go," Aurora said, soft. "Try to pull her to the side."

The solid block style Salinity put into their buildings negated alleyways and offshoots, the typical spots Gregor might use for take-n-threaten work. Instead, he'd have to play things mild. Try not to make a scene.

Letting Aurora fall behind, Gregor lengthened his stride, closing with the target. The woman had her wristlet up now, appearing to swipe away. Good timing. Reading a message, watching a video, both and either would serve to keep her eyes and attention off the hand about to land on her shoulder.

"Come quietly," Gregor said, feeling the target stiffen

as his hand planted. "No one needs to get hurt. I only have a question."

Gregor steered the woman with his planted hand, taking her to the right and under an overhang for a leasing office that looked, thankfully, closed for the lunchtime hour. Deep glass windows showcased stands covered with projected pictures of glitzy property for purchase, and Gregor used the display to put himself and the target facing that glass.

Just looking at dreams they could never afford, that's all.

"What do you want?" The target said, a tremor belying the tenor tone in her voice. Not used to getting made a hostage, then. "I don't have much cash."

"Not cash. Information." Gregor watched the world through their reflections on the glass. Nobody paying attention. Aurora had herself spotted up opposite Gregor, shape visible. With her hand signals, she'd give Gregor a heads-up if something went sour. "The agents. Where are they?"

Again, the target twitched, the jerk carrying up through Gregor's still-planted hand. Surprise?

"What agents?"

"DefenseCorp. Your counterparts. Where are their offices?"

"I don't know? Do they have any here?"

There were lies and there were liars. Anyone could attempt the former, spill out some words and hope they were believed. The latter performed a skill, manipulated reality for their audience. This poor DefenseCorp staffer fell into the former camp, and her voice, her stature, her lack of conviction betrayed her in the same way a pretender betrays themselves the moment they throw their first punch.

Gregor tightened his grip. Dug the fingers in enough to convey the meaning, "You heard me. Answer."

A sharp breath this time. In the reflection, the target's gray eyes slanted away, pulled towards the ground. Another tell, another breakaway moment to come up with an excuse.

"A little girl's life is in danger." Gregor headed off the attempt before it started. "Help us save her, or live with a four year-old's death."

"Tragedy happens every day," the target said, but her voice lost what little gravity it had. Weakness grasping for a hold. "It's not my fault."

"It is. Give us the location, and we will save her."

The woman's eyes closed. She'd fought the fight, done the minimum DefenseCorp expected of its personnel. Resist, then relent. DefenseCorp would rather not have its low-level employees murdered. Besides, the giant company could extract any vengeance it pleased on the perpetrators. No need for the woman to sacrifice more than she had.

"Okay," the woman said. "It's not far. I can show you, and then you'll let me go?"

"Yes."

The simple answer spurred a walk. The woman led them back away from the residential district, through the intersection, and towards another commercial sector. Aurora stayed well back as Gregor walked alongside the target, keeping herself apart.

The target pointed Gregor towards a glossy-looking store billing itself as an outlet for used gadgets, gear, and whatever else the proprietors happened to find on outer space salvage missions. A cover that might actually serve as a solid side business for DefenseCorp, as they had to get plenty of junk from bashing up pirates and rogue ships polluting the stars.

"In there," the target said. "Ask for the owner. That'll tell them what you're really there for."

This time, no twitch. No tremor. A truth-teller's level voice.

"Thank you," Gregor said.

He didn't need to add anything else.

The big man left the woman standing in the street, heading straight for the salvage shop. The woman wouldn't get far. Aurora would keep tabs on her and, if Gregor's request for this owner came back blank, the Sever captain would reconvene the hostage situation.

Inside the salvage shop, Gregor took a second to find his bearings. Glass lockboxes littered every surface, scanners tuned to open up if a staffer's wristlet approached. In the meantime, the highlighted goods sparkled at their various possibilities. Some boxes held weapons, others spacecraft parts, while still more held what signs claimed to be unique relics from worlds far across the galaxy. Crystals, metals, glowing shards stuffed with energy, these all shared space with random trinkets too, from children's toys to an adult shirt woven entirely from green sand beads.

Two employees coupled with a checkout bot to man the store. One looked to be fiddling with a newly arrived junk dump, picking through it behind the store's wrap-around glass counter and putting things in one pile or another depending on, Gregor assumed, their presumed value. The bot hung near the entrance, waiting for someone to place an object on its purchase pad. Its happy monotone welcomed Gregor to the store, while the big man also noticed a nerve-nuking stun shooter the bot pointed right at the door.

Theft prevention taken to serious lengths.

"Help you?" the second employee said, coming around in a peach t-shirt and soft white pleated pants and a look that went from bored to curious as he took in Gregor's sheer size.

"I'd like to speak to the owner," Gregor said.

"Uh, the owner?"

"You heard me."

The employee swung his peach face to his partner, still picking from the pile. No rescue there. Gulping, the man went back to Gregor and offered up an ill smile.

"Okay, just give me a sec, all right?"

"Fine."

Peaches-and-cream turned tail and ducked back through an employee's only door, leaving Gregor to wander the aisles for a long few minutes. He kept one eye on Parts-picker, who seemed to give not one single care about the large man roving his store. Gregor's other eye found a neat long-handled steel staff, heavy duty walking support or, in a pinch, capable of holding a door shut against vacuum leaks.

Gregor found the price, winced at the mark-up Salinity's planet-wide cost of living threw onto the item's worth. Still . . .

"Hey," Gregor said towards Parts-picker. "I'd like to buy this."

Parts-picker followed Gregor's nod towards the staff.

"Sure thing," the man said. "Be right there."

Gregor turned back to the staff, trying to figure out how best he'd wield it to deliver a good smacking or three. The seconds swam by, until things shifted into the uncomfortable, and Gregor turned back towards the parts pile. Instead of the idle picker, Gregor saw both staffers standing behind the counter, pistols raised and dead set.

"Time to talk, dude," said the Parts-picker. "You're not one of ours. What're you after?"

Steady hands, no nerves in those words. These two had

to be agents, or close to it. Gregor couldn't count on a sudden move to throw off their aim.

"Renard," Gregor said. "He's here. I have business with him."

"Thanks," said the Parts-picker. "That's what we needed to know."

Their fingers went to the triggers, and the storefront's window shattered.

Gregor took the distraction and moved, using the chaos to get behind the high-stacked lockboxes. Lasers flashed as the agents fixed their broken nerves and shot at him, at Aurora. The trash bin Aurora had used to smash the glass rolled along the floor, coming to rest near Gregor's feet. The Sever captain, meanwhile, returned potshot fire at the two agents.

Shouts, screams came from the broader street as the fight went public. Security would be coming quick. No time for games.

Gregor reached forward, picked up a lockbox holding some special wristlet model, turned and whipped the container back towards the agents. Aurora's lasers had them ducking and weaving, but a chunky box took more effort to dodge. Gregor's toss clipped Parts-picker in the shoulder, bounced him into his own crap pile.

Aurora sprayed covering fire in the ping-ping-ping pistol rhythm while Gregor spun the opposite way, taking three long steps through the store, ending with a crashing charge into the counter. Glass shards bit into Gregor's thick sweater, a few marking scratches, but the big man's momentum carried him through to the other side.

Peaches-n-cream swiveled, bringing his pistol level with Gregor, and took an Aurora shot to the skull for his troubles. The man dropped, and Gregor used the space to tackle the just-rising Parts-picker to the ground. Wrestling away the pistol, Gregor turned the hot barrel on its owner, delivering a whisper with the warning.

"Give it up, or die like your friend," Gregor said.

"Giving it up, giving it up," Parts-picker said. "Don't shoot me, man."

Gregor had another hostage, but going by the sirens outside, he didn't have much time either. Aurora crunched her way into the store, hair frizzed out by the firefight's rolling demands. That white jacket had some new stains, and a single burning black hole that, thankfully, didn't have a match on the captain's body.

The door bot issued a hearty welcome her way. Ever on the ball, that one.

Pulling Parts-picker to his feet, Gregor surveyed the ruined shop, the blast marks scouring the walls, the glass-coated floor. A small fire burned where a stray bolt struck something with power.

Now, now it felt like a Sever mission.

Sever Squad's adventures continue in GRIM TIDE—available now!

Acknowledgments

This novel is the product of my family and friends refusing to let a dream die. My wife Nicole, for letting me write in the early mornings and making sure I don't starve. My brothers and parents for their continual comments, support, and enthusiasm.

Evan Aaseng, for being a constant sounding board and reeling me back in whenever my ideas went too far.

And, of course, you, the reader, for giving me a reason to write.

About the Author

A.R. Knight spins stories in a frosty house in Madison, WI, primarily owned by a pair of cats. After getting sucked into the working grind in the economic crash of the 2008, he found himself spending boring meetings soaring through space and going on grand adventures.

Eventually, spending time with podcasting, screenplays, short stories and other novels, he found a story he could fall into and a cast of characters both entertaining and full of heart.

Sever Squad has more adventures to come, along with new plots, settings, and stories in the future. From there, A.R. Knight plans on jumping through to other worlds and finding new stories to tell in the limitless borders of our imagination.

Thanks, as always, for reading!

For more information:
www.adamrknight.com

To Andy